ERRANT BLOOD

A NOVEL

by

C.F. PETERSON

Scotland Street Press
EDINBURGH

For Olivia

Prologue

When the blue bird arrived in the third year of Joshua Malafu's exile in the land of dreams, it was the first real thing he had seen in nine hundred days. He had no choice but to fold the piece of cardboard around his five wallets, stand up from the pavement, dust down his trousers, and follow.

The bird, which was a tattoo on the forearm of a short, fat, strong looking man wearing a t-shirt and flip-flops, swung, like a heartbeat, balancing the movement of the baguette in a paper packet at the end of the other arm. The real bird swung through the unreal world, like an *nkoso* back home, a real *nkoso* moving from branch to branch through the forest. Already at this time in the morning, at this cold time of year, there were beads of sweat on the forearm, glistening through the wings of the bird. And as Joshua followed through the unreal streets, past the unreal shops and through the ghosts of people, the arm and the fat body and the man's big square head followed the bird into the real world as Joshua remembered him. He remembered the face, the hand and the arm coming out of the darkness as lightning flashed. He remembered the world twisting and spinning and the bird glistening with rain, not sweat, and the mouth open, snarling in a strange tongue, and the gun in the hand. And behind the man, white eyes in the lightning, other faces; real faces.

He followed the man along the beach front, past the amusement rides, past the moored boats bobbing on the waves which danced in the light of an unreal sun without warmth. He followed the bird and the arm and the man away from the beach and into a quiet, old street, where cars were parked and bougainvillea adorned the walls of villas that had been here since before the tower blocks and hotels, from the time when the town was just a fishing village on a beach. The man entered a villa by an iron gate, climbed a stairway and entered an apartment; number seven. Joshua waited beneath a lamppost. When the man had been inside for the best part of an hour, Joshua sat on the pavement and laid out his piece of cardboard and five wallets, his entire stock. It was an unlikely spot for a hawker, this silent street that smelt of cat piss and the sea, but he would rather go hungry than let the bird and the man escape. He waited.

He waited until the sun fell beyond the hills and the sea to the west, until cars had entered the street and moved and moved and stopped; until people had come home from their work and ignored the dirty immigrant crouched in a gateway selling cheap wallets and until he no longer noticed his hunger and thirst. He would speak to him. He would ask. The man would be reasonable, now. There would be no gun, no shouting, no sickening sea, no rain, no lightning. That night had passed, long ago. The man would speak to him as another man, not an animal, not cargo. But Joshua stayed sitting on the pavement, because he was afraid that if he spoke, somehow, by the strange magic that this world worked by, the man would not be behind door number seven. He would have vanished. Or the blue bird would take flight from the arm and become part of the dream again. Joshua could not bring himself to move.

When it was dark and beginning to grow cold the man came out onto the balcony of the apartment holding a glass and a cigarette. Joshua watched him look down on the black beggar crouched in a pool of street-light. Of course he sees the beggar, but at the same time he sees nothing. Black, immigrant, beggar, nothing. He does not recognise. The man smoked his cigarette. Then he recognised. Joshua felt it as surely as a hand reaching across the darkness that separated them. You are nothing, less than nothing, and yet he sees you and seeing you does something to him, deep inside. He sees your yellow eyeballs gleaming in the light from the lamp. He sees your tired, dusty clothes and the shoes that are too big for your feet. He sees the way you sit, too tired to hold yourself upright, knees under your chin, propped against the lamppost. He sees the dirty African, the cockroach, the half-beast from the jungle. But he sees another thing too. It is betrayed in the way he narrows his bleary eyes and the way he spits and drinks and flicks the cigarette butt into the garden below. It is betrayed in the urgency with which he turns to go back inside, shutting you out. But you are inside him now. He has seen you. This is no longer a dream. He has seen Malafu, Joshua, Cargo. He has seen Singa. Joshua waited. In three years on the streets of Fuengirola, Benalmadena, Torremolinos, all along the coast from Marbella to Malaga, he had had enough time to learn the efficacy of waiting. He tried to remember the man's name, but it was lost.

Towards midnight the man came out again and lit a cigarette. He was drunk now, trying to obliterate the dirty African. He smoked, spat, drank and looked. Joshua waited. The man finished his cigarette and went back inside. Joshua thought about crossing the street and climbing the stairs to the balcony but the man came back out again in a hurry, the door knocking against the wall as he opened it. He ran down the stairs, through the garden and out of the iron gate. He was carrying a cup in his hand and Joshua flinched as it moved towards him. The salt fell around him, a thousand tiny beats on the pavement. It hit his face and knees. '*Vete!*' cried the man, '*En el nombre de Cristo Jesús! Vete!*' He is casting you out, in the name of Christ. He expects you to vanish in a puff of smoke. He is afraid. He stood panting, breath pushing against the night air and the light from the lamp. He brandished a crucifix and then threw it. It bounced off the wall behind Joshua's head and landed on the pavement. Joshua did not move. Somewhere within himself he felt the strangest stirring, all the more strange for being familiar. For three years he had not felt an inkling of a laugh. The feeling brought back memories of dense green forest, light and faces. The man leant forward, placing his hands on his knees, and took deep breaths. He moved urgently to the lamp-post and vomited white vomit. Then he straightened up and wiped his mouth with the tattooed arm. He approached the being that was not a ghost, leant down and slapped a hand against Johua's leg and pulled at the arm that covered the lower half of his face. The man's expression was hollow, as if looking into the barrel of a gun. Still, he does not speak. His mind is not working. Then he reached into a trouser pocket, took out a crumpled pile of notes, and tossed them onto the cardboard. Look, he is going away! He thinks he has solved you! Stop him. Say the words.

'*Dónde Singa?*' said Joshua in a loud clear voice and the man stopped on the other side of the street, one foot on the pavement. At first he did not turn. '*Dónde Singa?*' said the African, louder and harder. The man turned and spoke in Spanish.

'*Dónde Singa?*' he said, 'Where is your Singa? How should I know? The boat has been gone since three years!'

'*Dónde ? Dónde barco? Dónde Eloissey*'

'Dead! All dead! Like you!' he waved his hand down the street and turned his back, '*Vete!*' Joshua did not move. As the man climbed the stairs to the balcony he called out again.

'Where is the boat?' It sounded more like an insult than a question. The man paused for a moment on the stairs but continued to number seven and slammed the door. '*Dónde Barco?*' shouted Joshua with all his strength. Then he stood up and shouted again and again at the door, 'Where is the boat? Where is she? Where is *Eloissey*?' But another door opened further up the street and a light went on in the villa behind him and he stopped shouting and sat back down, feeling weak and nauseous. He had shouted for the first time in three years, and he had almost laughed. He smiled as he drew his knees up and lay his head in the crook of his arm. For a long time his breath came in short gasps. He was alive again. Alive, and about to faint from hunger and thirst. He was awake, no longer dreaming the long dream of begging and hawking up and down the Costa, from town to town, through the overflowing tide of ghost people in the summer and the ghost towns of winter. But the dream world was beckoning him back. He had a premonition of physical pain, the price he would have to pay if he was to stay alive. As his eyelids were about to fall he got up, crossed the street and climbed the stairs to door number seven.

From inside came the blare of a television; clapping and laughter. Joshua knocked and waited, knocked and waited, and then tried the handle. The door opened to reveal an untidy living room, the details dancing in television light. Beer cans and a half-eaten meal on a low table; an overflowing ashtray; clothes piled on couch and chairs. The man came into the room from the one behind. Joshua watched the fat fists clench and unclench.

'*Dónde barco?*' he whispered from a dry mouth. The man threw himself across the room with both hands outstretched, catching Joshua in the chest, knocking him back against the wall, upsetting a table and smashing a vase. He thought about fighting back, but it would have been pointless. Although drunk, the man was agile and fast, and much stronger. Joshua had never been strong, and the years of near starvation had pared his muscles to the last essentials. The man could see this and chose to slap rather than punch. He slapped the beggar to the ground and placed a knee on his chest and slapped his face until the lips and nose bled. Then he pulled the limp figure upright and threw it across the room. Joshua lay where he fell on the floor, expecting more. But the man sat on a couch and lit a cigarette, watching him.

'*Dónde ?*' said Joshua. The man picked up an empty beer can and threw it at his head.

'*Dónde Eloissey?*' said Joshua. The man threw a full beer can. Joshua lay his head on the carpet and watched him smoke. When he had finished the cigarette he took out a phone and touched the screen.

'It didn't work. He's in my apartment. What now? I don't have a pistol, and even if I did, what do I do with the body? He wants to know where the boat went.' He listened. 'You serious? What if *does* get there?' He listened again, began to smile, then shrugged and put down the phone.

'Listen shit-stain. Do you know where Scotland is?'

CHAPTER ONE

Finlay Mack was a fireman and had seen some terrible things. The fire crew was based at Aberfashie on the road to Inverness and they were called to car accidents mainly, especially in the summer. A house fire was rare, and Finlay had never put out one that was fatal. But he had seen the body of a child of ten that had been thrown through the windscreen of one car and on to the windscreen of another, leaving an imprint of cracks and blood, and then on into the ditch where the blood had stained the leaves of nettles. The body, he had thought at the time, had been discarded by the child, like a pile of clothing. Another time he had comforted the mother of a child with a broken neck, her eyes stunned into dullness, staring into the abyss which forms within the entrails of the dead; the forgotten, fathomless maelstrom at the centre of life. Finlay Mack had reached over the bowed head of a corpse to switch off the cartoons on a blood spattered iPad. But these were accidents. These were the cruelties of an unknowing, unseeing universe. These were dark things moving in the dark and catching the unlucky; the corners of a metaphysical table in an unlit room. But what he saw when he saw the victim of the fire in

Glencul, the small body on the crude wooden platform, was of another order. What he saw in the black encrusted lump, steaming with the water from the hose, was cruelty. He saw it and he looked away. He carried on spraying with the fan hose but turned his head, so that the body was a shadow in the corner of his eye. He looked away at the flashing engine, at the others in their suits and yellow helmets standing on the lawn, and when he saw their faces he looked above the rooftops of the houses to the hills where a pure snow lay upon the silent words spoken by the mounds of heather and rock. Cruelty was a thing worse than death. Cruelty revealed the gentleness of death. And cruelty had pierced him like a poisoned blade, leaving a dark stain within, that seemed to live, to turn and to breathe a foul breath. The child had smelt of roast pork, like a Sunday dinner, or a barbecue. The child had smelt of a hot afternoon after working hard in the garden, the girls laughing and his wife smiling as he downed the first beer and a roast was being sliced on the table.

He had gone home and attempted to wash the smell from his body and mind. He had sat at the table and his wife had expected him to eat. After dinner he had not been able to stay in the house and watch television because the smell of the finished meal, the smell of the couch and even the scent of his own daughters had reminded him of the smell of the corpse. He had gone for a walk by the raging Ash and had stood in the dark, listening to the water racing between the banks, watching the waves and whirlpools etched by the moonlight, and had willed the river to cleanse him from the image of the body and the smell. He had tried to think about Joel Kennedy, his friend and fishing buddy of old, but in his mind the figure of Joel Kennedy in his torn jumper and beanie hat was tiny and insignificant, so easily washed away by the waters, compared to what Joel Kennedy had done.

In the days following the death the details filtered into the castle on the edge of the village, like a stain creeping across the carpet of leaf mould beneath the beech trees, like a stench from a broken sewer. The capillaries were Kirsty, or the gardener, Mike, or the postwoman, carrying pieces of the sorry news with them; unwanted, hideous scraps of information, gossip and supposition. On the third day Eamon did not want to hear anymore. Sitting in one of the wingback armchairs in the upstairs living room, he stopped himself from reading the newspaper report and tried to shut out the death with corrupt politicians and environmental catastrophe, but it was there now; it had happened. It was there in the rooms of Duncul, among the trees and in the village, a shadow upon all their lives that would probably never go away.

'Mike says that he probably died from the smoke before the flames got to him. Probably choked, first,' said Kirsty. She was sweeping in the corner of the room, using one of those long handled dustpans; standing, sweeping up what? She was just hanging around in the corner, that's what. Why was she sweeping in here, of all things, now? She just wanted to talk about the death. Old women are fascinated by death, especially the death of a child.

'How does Mike know?' said Eamon, staring at the paper, a frown on a high forehead above a long, thin nose, beneath thinning, blonde hair.

'His brother Finlay is in the fire brigade. He was the first to see the body.' Kirsty's voice was thin and frail, not just an old woman's voice, but as if the death was choking her. What was she doing? Sweeping what? Eamon sighed, put down the paper and tried to look at his cleaner with sympathy.

'Where's the mother?'

'She's back from Inverness,' said Kirsty. Eamon got up from the chair and paced in front of the window that looked out over the wood towards the village. 'There's a police lady with her.' The damn woman was still sweeping the same corner of the same rug. He felt like ordering her to make a cup of tea, just to get her out of the room, but it didn't work like that. Kirsty Macrae would make tea at three o'clock, and not before, and Eamon had never ordered her to do anything in his entire life. She spoke in codes; women always spoke in codes. 'There's a police lady with her,' meant 'There is nobody with her,' which meant, 'Somebody *should* be with her,' which meant, '*You* should be with her.'

'Where's Joel?' he said, feeling the name sticking in his mouth. Kirsty give a faint shrug.

'The police have him.' The mention of Joel Kennedy seemed to turn the rain clogged sky outside a darker shade of grey and thicken the shadows at the back of the room.

'I suppose I'd better go and see her,' said Eamon, turning from the window to his cleaner, but she was already leaving. Eamon paced some more, wanted to smoke but resisted, then left by the south tower, picking up a waxed jacket at the bottom of the stairs. He walked without hurry, letting the rain wet his hair and face.

He had not been outside for a week but did not welcome the fresh air. He wanted to be inside, alone, preferably asleep. A month after the death of his father and a week after Kate had left him he had given up the flat in London and returned north without any enthusiasm or sense of nostalgia. Somehow, somewhere, someone that was never definitely himself had made a decision that he should return.

It had been raining as he had arrived, as it had been on the day of his father's funeral and as it would do for the next two months. The castle was as it had always been; cold, austere, suffocating with an excess of history and memories. He had been overcome with a sense of futility and foreboding and had retreated to the library, a small room with a high, north-facing window. He had put up a camp bed, kept the fire lit and tried to lose himself in books and boxed-sets. He ate upstairs in his father's study and did his best to shun visitors. But they had come; the minister, the Catholic priest from Aberfashie, his factor, his father's remaining friends from neighbouring estates, and strangers; the kind of people who upon seeing a Highland castle cannot prevent themselves from exerting a right to visit. In the last week he had had the pleasure of a man 'in financial services' who had felt compelled to walk around the house barking comments upon paintings and furniture. Then a long haired photographer and his nervous wife who bowed with gratitude when Eamon allowed them to take pictures from the grounds; and then an American novelist who was living in a caravan outside the village, who instantaneously considered Eamon a lifelong friend. Eamon was civil to everyone, and cursed himself for it, but he neglected to charge his phone so that the only phones were the landlines which he could not hear from the library, and he spent most of each day in bed, trying to retain convulsive dreams until his body could no longer stand the inactivity and his feet and mind began twitching. He did not consider his behaviour anything to do with grief. He had been relieved when his father had died.

And beyond the cannon-proof walls the rain fell relentlessly on the castle of Duncul, the village of Glencul, the forests and surrounding hills, Loch Cul to the east, the river Ash to the south, which thundered in spate and flooded the fields of the farms downstream to the west. The rain forced its way between slates and into cracks in the walls, enlarging the damp patches in attic rooms. The rain and the cold and the darkness; malevolent, and conniving, inveigled their way into every aspect of everyone's lives, advancing from the ground, from the sky, from the hills, from the trees; as if the land breathed a contagion of dampness that crept into hands, heads, feet, limbs, lungs and minds. In the village the pensioners turned up the central heating, drying themselves to husks and absorbing television. The men who had to work outside wore luminous waterproof suits and took every chance to huddle in cabs and portacabins, hunched over sausage rolls and coffee. Those who worked in Inverness, forty miles away, scuttled back and forth in heat-blasted cars, little hot submarines twisting their way through underwater forests.

Joel Kennedy with a fishing rod was the image that held Eamon's mind as he walked towards the village. Joel had loved fishing. Even after he had left school he had always been keen to go up the Ash or down to the loch, or up to one of the hill lochs on Ben Fuar. When everyone else had moved on to the fascinations of girls and cars, vodka and weed, Joel had kept on fishing, in spite of the fact that he had only ever had one of those beginner rods with the automatic reels and had never had a box of extravagant lures like some of the other boys, only one or two cheap meps. Lucky meps that he would never lose. Eamon remembered him diving into a pool in the Ash to retrieve one of his hooks from a submerged branch. That was what he remembered of Joel Kennedy, before he, Eamon, had gone off to boarding school for the last two years and then on to university, and then to Sandhurst and Afghanistan and The City. But he had seen Joel in the holidays, still fishing, still wearing the same beanie, a thin lithe figure, full of energy and always grinning, and then Sandhurst and Afghanistan and The City and he didn't remember seeing him then, for those years. Eamon didn't think of the mother and the child that had been killed as he walked because he had not met either of them, and didn't even know the child's name. He thought perhaps Kirsty knew and wished that he'd asked her.

The woman's house was on the council estate. 'Estate' was too grand a word. It was a cul-de-sac of some thirty houses built in a field twenty years previously. He remembered that his father had objected to selling the council the land and that there had been a lot of cursing in Duncul and brandishing of lawyer's letters. 'They want to build a gulag and fill it full of bloody tinks!' had become for a season his father's favourite line, repeated to anyone who would listen, spluttered out between mouthfuls of whisky. His rage had been increased by impotence, and perhaps self-reproach too. His own father, Eamon's grandfather, had practically run the old county council. It was taken for granted that he would never have allowed such a thing to happen. But perhaps, Eamon considered, perhaps Pappy would have been quite happy to see the council build much needed housing in the village. Perhaps Pappy would have encouraged them to build more and given them the land for nothing. But Eamon's father had not been able to see this. As far as he was concerned everything the council ever did, from running schools to laying a footpath, was a waste of money and would end in disaster. Eamon could remember, far in the past, the fights his mother had put up to keep Eamon in the local school. 'He'll be a homosexual communist by the time he's sixteen!' his father had bawled. He had only got his way and packed his son off to Chulzit 'The last decent school in the country!' once his adversary was dead and buried. 'It will be the best thing that has ever happened to you boy! Guts! That's what you'll get from Chulzit! Guts!' Eamon had been put on the train not a month after his mother's funeral.

His father had been right about one thing though; the resemblance to a gulag. Especially the lights, which were a striking eyesore. As far as Eamon was aware the local council had never put them anywhere else. Instead of many street lights at the level of first floor windows there was one giant lamppost perhaps a hundred feet high, right in the middle of the houses, with four powerful floodlights illuminating everything.

The lights could be seen from Duncul, hovering like a space-ship above the little grey houses. The only uglier places he had ever seen were army estates. It was a hideous little pocket, a blight upon an otherwise picturesque village, nestled in the midst of oak woods that his great-great-grandfather had planted. Then, a few years back, the council had thought to augment the aesthetic pleasure provided by the giant lighting pole by attaching a chunky CCTV camera fifty feet up from the base. Yes, father had been right about 'gulag', but not about 'tinks' as he referred to travellers. Travellers had their own little gulag somewhere near Dingwall. The people that moved in to Tarr Bow, named after the small river that ran through the village to the Ash, were all sorts, from all sorts of backgrounds, and many were families that had lived in the village for generations. Not the dead child though, nor his mother. They were from lake Kivu in north-east Congo apparently, and Eamon was going with his condolences, in the knowledge that his childhood friend had killed the child; had poured a can of petrol over the shed in the back garden of one of the little houses, and had set fire to it, with one, two, three flicks of a lighter, while the child, a three or four year-old boy, lay strapped to a table inside the shed. Eamon was going to see the mother without knowing her name nor that of the little boy. They were strangers, refugees; a single mother and child, escaped from God knows what living hell; living and dying, in Glencul, in his village.

The house was like a child's drawing of a house, but without the sun and blue sky above and flowers in the garden; a grey, featureless block, an unhappy child's drawing of a house. There was a black Ford Fiesta and an off-road bike parked on the road in front. Behind, where he assumed the garden shed had stood, there was a large white tent surrounded by a ring of burnt lawn and around the whole garden there was a yellow tape endlessly printed with 'police police police'.

The woman that answered the door was not from Lake Kivu. She had straight grey hair down to her shoulders and a thin, grey face. She was dressed in the clothes of an office worker, a knee length grey skirt and a black cardigan, so Eamon assumed that she was the 'police lady' that Kirsty had mentioned. He introduced himself to the woman as 'Eamon Ansgar, from the castle', and as he said it, remembered that this was the way that his father had introduced himself, as 'Asgard Ansgar, from the castle,' or 'Asgard Ansgar, Duncul,' giving where he was from as the signifier of his position; as if to say, 'in case you are not aware, from a castle,' and implying, 'in these parts, *the* castle.' Simply declaring, before anything, 'Asgard Ansgar. By the way, I own the place.' Eamon wondered at himself. When he had been a teenager he had been embarrassed by this, and up to now he had never introduced himself thus. Why now? He was asserting an authority that he had always considered to be nothing more than bullshit. The woman let him in without saying anything.

The mother of the child was sitting at a table in the corner of the small living room. The curtains were drawn and most of the light came from a dim lamp. The woman's hands lay before her, clasped together over some papers. She was facing the wall, but turned as Eamon came into the room. She had a tangle of thick, black hair, unbrushed since sleep, and her face was contorted in an agony of grief that verged on a kind of terror. Her forehead was knotted in a frown that Eamon noticed never unfolded while he was there, and her eyes were sunken, bleary and bloodshot. She tried to smile at him, but the effort seemed too much for the lips which only quivered as he approached. Coming into the room he had thought briefly about what he should say, but then, coming close to her grief he remembered his own, and felt the veil that was drawn over it lift, as if he was back in the room with his mother's coffin, and he remembered that there was nothing to say. The only adequate response to death was silence. She reached out and he felt her hand, cold, dry and rough-skinned, and without speaking she invited him to sit. He sat on the edge of the sofa next to the policewoman and noticed the other person in the room, who he had not seen when he came in because he was sitting on a chair almost behind the door. He was a thick-set man, wearing black military style trousers and a black bomber jacket. His balding head was shaved close. When Eamon looked at him the man smiled a thin-lipped brief smile, strangely out of place in this room of sorrow. Eamon wondered if he too was with the police, but the smile was irritating and he chose not to look at him again.

'I'm Eamon,' he said to the mother. 'I live here in the castle. I'm sorry, I do not know your son's name.'

'Magakwa,' said the woman, again attempting the failing smile.

'Magakwa,' repeated Eamon.

'It means, Blessed One,' she said, and the terrible irony of this sent a fresh shock of agony through her, so that her whole body shivered.

'What is your name?'

'Isabel,' she said, with a soft 's'. She did not presume to offer a surname. Issabel, of no particular clan, Issabel, claiming no place for herself in the world. Issabel, of nothing and with nothing.

'If you need anything… the funeral. I can help with the funeral,' said Eamon.

'It's all been taken care of by the council,' said the policewoman at his elbow. She had a harsh, crackly voice and a lowland accent.

'With anything else. Your family. Where is your family?' said Eamon.

'It's all been taken care of Mr Ansgar,' said the policewoman.

'Well, if you think of anything,' he said to Isabel. He sat for a long time in silence. The man behind the door drummed his fingers on the arm of his chair. Feeling that perhaps he was intruding on some necessary official business Eamon got up to go and the man in the bomber jacket rose to open the door for him, but Isabel offered her hand again and he went over to her, and as he took it she pulled him towards her, surprising him with her strength. She held both his hands in both of hers, and for a moment looked frantically into his eyes. He thought she was about to say something but she simply held his hands tight. She had the strength of a man. He was about to pull away when he felt a hard shape pushed into the palm of his hand. She folded his fingers around it. 'Thank you,' she said and pushed his hands from her, a movement like a command. Eamon obeyed, and left the room, nodding goodbye to the policewoman and the man at the door. He put the object in the pocket of his jacket and walked quickly out of the estate with the look on the woman's face fixed in his mind, the image like an instruction, 'take this and go!'

He walked without looking back, only slowing his pace when he was in the village proper and turning to take the road to Duncul. He realised as he walked what it meant; 'Eamon Ansgar, Duncul. Asgard Ansgar, from the castle.' What it meant was that was all he had to offer to that woman, to anyone. That was all he had become; landlord, owner, Laird.

He felt the hard, round shape in his pocket. It was flat and smooth and heavy; it was a stone, of a size he could conceal in the palm of his hand, threaded with a string; something to be worn. But he did not take it out. He did not want to. The woman with her hard hands and her grief had pushed it into his hand with a force beyond the physical. The urgency and secrecy had pierced and penetrated him. She had not wanted the woman and the man in the room to know. Why not? His first thought was that there was craziness here; grief making her mad. He had done his duty. He had visited her and offered his condolences and anything else he could do. He did not want to move any further into her suffering. He did not want to take the stone out nor take it home. He walked on past the gate to Duncul and made for the river and the Ash Bridge.

On the bridge he took it out. It was a black stone on a piece of cord, the cord woven from green and red threads and the stone marked in a crude way, scratched with a nail or a knife, with figures. These were like letters but not fully, and they were figures that he recognised. The recognition hit him with an almost physical effect. They were *his* markings, the markings of the Stone of Duncul. His *own* markings; his, his father's once, but now only his; his personal property and mystery. The Stone of Duncul was a Pictish or Viking or prehistoric stone that was built into the walls of the dungeon beneath the castle. He was about to turn back to the house in the gulag, to question the woman, when he saw the doorman or policeman or whatever he was, in black bomber jacket, helmetless, riding slowly towards him on the motorbike that had been parked outside the house. The engine, only ticking over, made a low continuous growl. The doorman gave a thin smile of recognition. Eamon knew exactly what he wanted. He held up the stone by its string and quizzed him with his eyebrows. The doorman revved the engine and cruised to a stop next to him.

'But it's not yours,' said Eamon, folding his fist over the stone. The doorman snatched with both hands. He was fast, and he caught Eamon's fist. Eamon pulled back but felt an extraordinary pain as the man did something with his thumb, twisted the wrist and opened the fingers to take the stone. He gunned the bike and stamped it into gear. Eamon reached out with his free hand and caught a fold in the bomber jacket. It was ripped from his hand but the man lost his balance and as the engine whined the front wheel went up and the bike sped from beneath him. He fell hard onto the base of his spine on the wooden planks of the bridge as the bike crashed into the handrail and slithered to a stop. Almost as if he had bounced, the man got to his feet and faced Eamon. He put the stone in a jacket pocket and zipped it. Then he raised his fists and kicked straight into Eamon's face.

Eamon felt the running shoe scrape up his jaw and tug at his ear. He was wearing leather soled brogues and the deck of the bridge was wet. He was wearing a baggy waxed jacket. He was not dressed for a fight. He raised his hands, ducked, and felt a punch glide off his forehead. The doorman was in the mood to give him a beating, and the mechanical, methodical way in which he was going about it betrayed a lot of training in this sort of thing. He kicked Eamon hard in the stomach, but Eamon saw it coming and tensed against the blow. He could see no choice but to fight back and launched himself forward, too close to be kicked, and hooked with his left, then right, and close enough, thrust his forehead down upon the man's nose. He caught him, and the man uttered a surprised grunt and stepped back, touching the blood that flowed. Eamon came at him with some rusty jabs and a straight right, but he couldn't move fast on the wet floor, moved off balance, and the man grabbed the lapels of the waxed jacket, twisted his hips and threw Eamon hard towards the deck. Eamon felt the breath go out of him and pain flood through his back. The doorman stood over him but let him get up. He was smiling a little. He had the advantage of weight and strength and he knew it. As soon as Eamon was on his feet again the man moved and caught him in the sternum with the out turned heels of his hands. Eamon was knocked back against the iron railing of the bridge. The doorman kicked straight for the stomach again and this time Eamon had no time to tense. The pain was sickening, so bad he felt it in his head, and he doubled up, thinking about what happened next. Curling into a ball and taking a kicking was what happened next, until the doorman got tired of it. He did not expect the hand thrust into his groin and the other on his throat and he did not expect the feeling of lightness as the man lifted, and thrust. 'Probably not a policeman,' was his last thought before he hit the water.

The river embraced him with a thousand icy hands and dragged him down. By the time he surfaced he was a hundred yards downstream of the bridge and moving fast. He looked up. The man was watching from the railing, a grin beneath his bloody nose. At first Eamon made an effort to swim, but the waxed jacket ballooned and tangled around his chest. He let the river take him.

CHAPTER TWO

'You did what?' said Clarice Wright, her pinched grey face pinched again into a frown. Isabel sat, mute, in the corner of the room.

'I got stone,' said Grigor Semyonovitch, holding the stone out in the palm of one hand while he held tissues to his nose with the other. 'You asked me get stone. I get stone.'

'You threw him in the river?'

'It was fight. It got little bit crazy.'

'Jesus! Do you know who that is?'

'He's a guy. He took stone. You tell me get stone.'

'Fuck. Shit." Clarice tapped her phone and paced. 'You've got a problem,' she said when it was answered. 'Only the Russian psycho has gone and thrown Eamon Ansgar in the river. Christ knows. Latvian, whatever. He took a stane from her. Nothing. Just something she gave him, this weird stane that the child wears; used to wear. She was trying to tell him something. I dinnae ken! I told psycho to get it back. He did. Eamon Ansgar. The laird. They guy who owns this whole fucking place! The guy who owns the dam!' She listened, nodded, then tapped the

screen. 'He says get on your bike and get back over the hill, now. Right,'
she said, turning to Isabel, 'you're been transferred tonight.'

'Where are we going?'

'Don't worry, somewhere nice darlin'. Pack a bag.' There was a long
silence before Isabel spoke again.

'There is nowhere nice for me now. My son is dead.'

'Now now darlin', dinnae be like that, you're still young, you'll have
another one.'

About a mile downstream from the bridge the river had burst its banks
and was flowing through a wood of alder and birch and into the fields at
the bottom of Burnum Farm. Eamon was able to kick out of the current
towards the trees and then pull himself from branch to branch until he
found the ground beneath his feet. As he began to wade he heard the
staccato of the bike engine and saw the bike moving along the road that
led south from the bridge, and disappear into the oak wood beyond. The
sound of the engine continued, revving high, and then began to fade.
He was confused for a moment by the sound of another, louder, engine
close by. On the side of the field that was not submerged a young woman
was riding a quad-bike towards a herd of black cattle.

Although he was shivering from the cold, Eamon stood still and
watched her. Her hair was red and cut in a bob. She wore jeans and
wellies and was taking a bale of silage to the cattle. Though he had not
seen her in ten years he recognised Rona McColl. For a moment he
thought about waving and asking for help, but stopped himself. Instead
he watched her as the cows surrounded the quad, milling about and
tossing their heads, and she rolled the bale off the back of the trailer and
began slicing open the cover. Then he moved off, creeping through the
woods and the water to where the bank of the river emerged again. He
walked back upstream towards the bridge. He checked his phone but it
was blank, and as he walked his shivering became violent. But he walked
back across the bridge, into the village, to the gulag. The car had gone.
He knocked on the door and looked through the window. The house was
empty. He went back to Duncul and got into a hot shower, waiting for
the shivering to subside. When he got out he wrapped himself in two

dressing gowns and called the nearest police station, in Aberfuar. There was an answer machine telling him to dial triple nine in an emergency or Inverness headquarters for other matters. He dialled the Inverness number and was answered by a young female voice.

'Police Scotland Inverness.'

'I'm looking for the police officer who was here today in Glencul. It's to do with the murder of the child,' he said. He was surprised at how irritable he sounded. He was asked for his name and gave it.

'One moment Mr Ansgar.'' There was a click, another ringing, then another voice; a low, soft, West Highland accent.

'Detective John Maclean here Mr Ansgar, how can I help?'

'I'd like to speak to the woman police officer that was here this morning. She was with the mother of the child that was killed in the fire in Glencul.'

'Can I ask what is your connection to Mrs Mtetu?'

'I'm a neighbour. I was there this morning, and there was a police officer with Mrs Mtetu, a woman, and a man, who I don't believe was a police officer. I'd like to speak to the female officer if I may.' There was a long pause. He was on hold. Then the voice came on again.

'Did she give a name?'

'No.'

'Did she tell you she was a police officer?'

'No, not exactly. But I assumed,' said Eamon, feeling foolish.

'It would have been Social Services. Do you know Mrs Mtetu well Mr Ansgar?'

'No, not at all. Are you saying there were no police here this morning?'

'It'll have been the Social Services.'

'How can I get in touch with them?'

'The council has a website. Were you a witness to the incident there on Monday?'

'No. Where is Isabel Mtetu now?'

'She's with Social Services. Do you know Joel Kennedy?'

'Yes. I did, but not recently.'

'I see.' The man waited for Eamon to speak.

'I haven't seen him for about five years, at least,' said Eamon. There was a moment then, he was later to reflect, when he could have told John Maclean about the man on the bridge. And, he was later to reflect, that could have prevented blood being spilled. It could have saved lives. Is a man obliged to tell the police that he has been beaten in a fist-fight? And was it only embarrassment that kept him from doing so? Only embarrasment and a low tolerance for tedium; the long process of reporting, of having every moment taken down in the clumsy handwriting of a uniformed officer, and having to justify why he had pulled the man from the bike, and why he had hit back, and yes a certain uneasiness with the police; a mistrust born of four years dealing with corrupt military versions in the coalition camps of Afghanistan. Embarrassment, mistrust, a low tolerance for boredom; none of these were noble motives. Later he was to reflect that not telling the police everything then had been a terrible mistake.

'Will there be anything else Mr Ansgar?'

'No. It doesn't matter. Thank you for your time.' He hung up before the man could reply and looked up the number for Social Services. A young female voice again;

'Social Services Highland.'

'Hello, I would like to speak with Isabel Mtetu.'

'Who?'

'She's the mother of the child who was killed here in Glencul on Monday. The police tell me she's with Social Services.' He was asked his name and switched to a recording of classical violin. Another voice came on; older, less friendly. Eamon repeated his request.

'Are you a relative of Mrs Mtetu's, Mr Ansgar?'

'No, a neighbour.'

'Can I ask what this is in connection with Mr Ansgar?'

'It's a private matter,' said Eamon. The woman did not reply. He could hear her breathing, then the violin again. After a minute she spoke.

'I'm afraid it's not possible right now.'

'Can you give me the name of the woman that was with her this morning?'

'I'm afraid I can't give you that information Mr Ansgar.'

'Look, I'm a concerned neighbour. Can you at least tell me, is she with you?'

'Who Mr Ansgar?'

'Isabel Mtetu, is she with you? With Social Services?'There was another long pause. He thought he could hear whispering.

'I'm afraid I'm not authorised to give you that information Mr Ansgar.'

'Jesus!'

'Would you please refrain from being abusive Mr Ansgar.'

'I'm not being abusive! I'm merely trying to get in touch with Isabel Mtetu!'

'Mr Ansgar, I'm informing you that in accordance with Social Services Highland's guidance on abusive callers, I'm terminating this call.' There was a click, then a low buzzing. He redialled the number but it rang for a long time without anyone answering. He put the phone down, closed his eyes and took some deep breaths.

When she had finished feeding the cattle and taking a load of fence posts up to the top park, Rona McColl took the quad back to the implement shed and unhitched the trailer. She lifted the seat of the machine and knelt to look at the carburettor. The engine had been misfiring all morning and experience told her it was either a worn HT lead or water in the fuel. She shut off the fuel and drained the carb, but laid down her spanner when she heard a muffled calling of her name from the house.

She went straight to the sink in the kitchen to wash her hands. A woman with white hair, a pale, lined face and a mouth drooping at the corners, was sitting in a wheelchair by the stove. Rona had been able to tell by the tone of the call that her mother was in one of those dark, immutable, inscrutable moods, that could easily be provoked into outright rage. So for a while the only sound was the trickle of water into the sink, until Rona could think of something that might cheer her up. She dried her hands. 'I saw Eamon Ansgar,' she said. Harriet McColl stared at the wall. Rona put the kettle on the stove and took some onions from the fridge.

'Oh,' said her mother. There was a long silence, which was broken by the rap of the knife on the chopping board. 'How did you manage that?'

Her voice was refined and precise.

'He was in the woods, by the river. He looked like he'd been in the river,' said Rona, chopping. Again there was a long pause before her mother replied.

'Well, he must have had his reasons. Did you talk?'

'No. I was busy with the cattle.' Her mother sighed deeply.

'How enthralling.'

'Lasagne or Bolognese?'

'I'm not hungry,' said her mother. In the silence that followed the kettle began to boil and she raised her hand towards it with a slow, quivering movement that paused before reaching it, while her mouth opened slightly in an expression that conveyed suffering nobly borne. Rona crossed to the kettle and made the tea.

CHAPTER THREE

The theft of the *Rage III* went smoothly. At 2 p.m. the captain and all ten of the crew went ashore in the launch with Brighton. They went laughing and joking, out of their white uniforms, dressed in jeans and open-necked shirts beneath weatherproof jackets, in anticipation of a fabulous party. They were going to dinner in a Michelin starred restaurant. Then, young, moneyed, good-looking, they were going to be let loose on Lisbon. In spite of it being December, they were going to have a good time. They were going to get hammered, high and laid. They were going to celebrate Samson Vanneck's eighty-second birthday and he was being unusually generous. While he was waiting for Brighton's return Samson jogged around the deck.

From bow to stern she was fifty metres long. The previous year, in New York, he had run a half-marathon. After each circumlution he stopped to do a set of press-ups, a set of sit-ups and a set of lunges. After ten rounds he slowed to a walk, resting his hands on his hips. The sun was high over the sea to the south-west. It was a winter sun with no heat in it, but it caused the sea to shine. There was a gentle wind, and the sea undulated sensuously beneath the boat. He felt, he told himself, ignoring the twitching pain in his knees and wrists, not more than twenty years old. It was a beautiful day, the fifteen-thousandth and three-hundredth beautiful day since Dr Samson Vanneck PhD had synthesised 2,6-diethyl-4-methyl-7-hydroxyspartanone. Forty-two years of beautiful days.

At 3 p.m. Brighton, a handsome man in his thirties, wearing a white peaked cap and a nautical jumper, returned with the launch. The two men did not speak. Brighton went to the bridge, and Samson went downstairs to the owner's suite.

The bedroom was dark and warm and the stale air carried the scent of flowers. He pressed a button that opened one of the blinds and sunlight lit up the bed. She was sitting up, propped by a pile of pillows, her head falling to one side and her eyes closed. Her face was powdery white. He knew she had started to apply makeup but had grown tired and given up. Her long white hair was tied back, but wisps had escaped and were falling about her face. Her thin lips, relaxed, expressed fear and sadness. There was a breakfast tray on the bed before her. Of course, they were all gone, there had been no-one to remove it, but still he cursed. He took it and placed it on the floor. Then he sat on the floral pattern of the bedspread and smiled. That was her choice, a floral pattern, clashing with the monochrome charcoal and ivory and walnut panelling and chrome detailing of superyacht design. Vanneck felt as he had felt the day he had met her fifty-two years ago; that mixture of trepidation, concern, awe and desire. Her fragility, perhaps the wellspring of his devotion, had always terrified him and for many years he had questioned whether a feeling of protectiveness, an irresistible and permanent urge, was a sound basis for a marriage. He had wondered for the first decade whether it was right for a man to feel what almost amounted to pity for his wife. But later, after he had become wealthy and no longer worried about whether or not he had the means to care for her, when he no longer doubted his own strength, it had ceased to worry him, and as his wealth had grown so had the solidity of his love. He had never encountered another woman who had inspired anything like the feelings he had for her. He had never been casual with his affections, even as a teenager, and he had been fortunate to discover his *métier* while still at school; a subject to which he had been able to give himself entirely. In that sense she was not his first love, but the paradox was that chemistry, drawing so much out of him, allowed him to love purely, as few men do. Chemistry acted like one of the solutes which are so fundamental to the art, drawing off all that was unwanted in a man; all the lusts, the jealousies, the fractiousness, the spites that threaten a marriage. He had been able to give her the best of himself, he thought. He had been able to make her happy; half a century of happiness, unmarred by regrets, untrammelled by the trauma of child bearing and rearing which neither of them had wanted. He had been able to give her everything that money could buy; peace, comfort, solace, beautiful places and things, inspiration for her poetry, houses to decorate, parties, friends, charities, health, but now, death was taking all of that. He could feel its presence in the room, somewhere in the shadows and the smell of wilting flowers, somewhere among the pots of potions and scents on the dressing table, and somewhere beyond, over the open sea, which always, in its depths and in its winds, in its myriad hues of green and grey and blue, in the spray whipped from wave tops, carries the scent of death. Death, he knew, inhabited her, as she lay there dozing on the pillows, like a simulacrum of her; dead her, lying imposed upon her body. And his hope, his desire to banish death, was like a simulacrum that inhabited himself, or rather he inhabited it. He inhabited his hope, like a man climbing into an image of himself, or a special suit designed to enable the wearer to go into space or into the darkness of the abyss or into the fire of a volcano. Sometimes, often, he was not sure if the suit fitted, or if it would function, but he wore it doggedly now, day in and day out. He held her hand. It was soft, frail and cool. The hand of an old woman. Only eighty years old, he told himself, only eighty, and what is that? A drop, a drip, an inkling of a moment of time. She opened her eyes.

'I'll stay here,' she said, smiling. 'You go without me.'

'Don't worry about that.' He got up to go to a cabinet set into the wall and returned with a glass of water and a straw which he held to her mouth.

'I was having such a wonderful dream.'

'Tell me.'

'We were in Yosemite. Do you remember? By that waterfall, and we were naked, sitting in the long grass. I could feel it tickling my thighs. I could feel the mist from the waterfall on my face and breasts, and I could smell it, that smell of waterfalls, that brings the air to life. I could see a butterfly flying up through the mist, and the sunlight was catching on its wings. I felt such a feeling of peace and contentment, an overwhelming feeling, as if all my worries and fears had dissolved, like a membrane between me and the world, and I was looking at the world as I did when I was new-born or a little child. Such a beautiful world Sam, and you don't have to do anything. The imperative is gone. We were there, together.'

He climbed onto the bed with her and put his head on the pillow next to hers. He wanted to rest with her, but the imperative was strong within him. He began to wonder about possibilities, began to think about what Bartlett, the captain, would be thinking, and began willing the five-hundred euro a bottle cognac that Bartlett preferred down his throat, willing the acquiescence, willing laughter and some slender blonde on the man's knee. He began thinking about satnavs and radars and tides, winds and the power of the engines, and about the mind of Brighton, the promised expertise. Brighton who was used to sailing cats in the Caribbean. Brighton who had said it was a walk in the park. Brighton who he had listened to perhaps too much already. He could not keep his eyes closed and had to leave her with a kiss, and go up onto the deck and the bright air.

Vanneck and Brighton waited until the sun was going down over the Atlantic and the fifty-million-dollar boat had turned against the tide towards the western horizon. Then Brighton pushed some buttons and moved some switches that raised the anchors, then pushed some others that kicked the three-thousand-horsepower engine up to top speed, and they felt the boat propel them out into the open sea.

'How long before they notice?' said Vanneck as they stood on the bridge watching the roseate glow.

'Probably not until tomorrow afternoon. You're throwing an expensive party.'

'Then what?'

'Then they'll contact the harbourmaster, and he'll call us on the sat phone.'

'And then?'
'Then we tell him to piss off, it's your boat.'

CHAPTER FOUR

When Eamon opened his eyes the last muted grey was being drained from the sky beyond the window and only the embers in the grate lit the study. He put on sticks and logs and breathed into the fire. Then he took a bunch of keys from a desk drawer and walked into the shadows in the corner of the room furthest from the window. He pulled at a book in the bookshelf and the bookshelf swung away from the wall, becoming a door into a spiral staircase. The steps of the south tower were worn from centuries of use. Bare bulbs hung on a cable from the low ceiling and he had to bow his head to avoid them. In his descent he moved repeatedly from light into darkness. He passed a low, arched, iron studded door on each floor, and carried on past the door that led outside on the ground floor marked by hats, jackets, boots and sticks. The stair twisted on round, twice, three times more, and ended in half-light at a door that was lower than the others. Eamon turned the key and flicked a switch.

A fluorescent tube illuminated a vast vaulted room with narrow windows high above. There were piles of tea chests and a tangle of old bicycles, a bookshelf of mouldy books, mildewed armchairs, an ancient heatless boiler; a workbench, tools on a rack and a winch suspended from a hook in the distant ceiling. The room was cold and smelt of dust and damp. He took a torch from the workbench and pushed past a pile of couch cushions and a hat stand into a corner where there was another door only as high as his chest. A padlocked chain tied iron rings on the door to the wall. Eamon tried several of the keys on the ring before the padlock unclicked. 'Superstition,' he said as he pulled the chain out. There were several steps down again, into another tall, narrow room, which further narrowed as the walls rose, like the inside of a steeple. These walls were hewn from the solid rock, and there was a damp smell; the smell of a cave. He swung the torch beam.

The stone was set into the rock face, above an altar-like slab set on two large boulders. The markings were similar but not identical to those on the stone Isabel had given him. They were things that were not quite letters; V's and upside down V's, parallel lines, crosses, and circles, cup marks he had heard them called, set around a circle in the middle. Could it be a bizarre coincidence? But then, why had she given him her stone? Did she know about this one? No-one ever came down here. Ever. He remembered his father, very drunk, insisting to Kirsty that the room be kept locked at all times. 'Barbarism!' he had called it, 'Barbarism and witchcraft!' About once in a decade an academic would arrive and ask to look at the stone. Eamon stood staring for a long time. It did have a mesmeric effect, perhaps simply to do with its age. More than two-thousand years BC, he remembered hearing. How did they know? But he knew that the Ansgars had been here for eight hundred years, and the stone and the cave had been here before the castle. His father had become convinced that human sacrifice had once been practised here, and that there were bloodstains on the altar. Eamon found himself using the torch to look closely. It occurred to him that Isabel had copied the design from the internet, so he re-locked the room and climbed the staircase back to the study.

There were no hits. There were hits for Duncul of course, plenty of photographs of the castle, but nothing of the stone. He scrolled down until the pictures began to repeat. He searched for Pictish stones. There were plenty of these, all the famous ones with the common motifs, and interpretations of these, but there was nothing on the Stone of Duncul. When he scrolled further he found motifs that were similar, but also of obscure origin and meaning. These were found only on fragments of stones, in the Orkney and Shetland Islands. But it didn't make sense that an African, from Congo, should have copied them. What would they mean to Isabel? Again he considered the possibility of pure coincidence. Perhaps the tribe or culture that Isabel came from had simply developed a similar script or system of symbols? He went up onto the roof to smoke and to look out at the lights of the village, when a single headlight and a quad bike with a loose exhaust sliced through the darkness up the drive. It could only be Rona McColl. She must have seen him in the flooded field. She moved out of sight below him to the front door and pulled the big bell that hung there, the one that nobody used anymore. He cursed and put out the cigarette. How long ago had that happened? Rona McColl. Ten years?

He had never noticed her before her father's funeral. He had died from a heart attack, suddenly, while feeding his cattle. Eamon had noticed her then, this beautiful girl, who like him had lost a parent at sixteen. He remembered wanting to talk to her, to console her, but not being able to say a single word. He had sipped a drink and watched from the other side of the room, while she sat on the edge of a couch staring at the standing mourners, scratching an ankle, smiling politely at a consoling aunt who came to sit next to her. After that he had seen her going to school in Fort William, waving and smiling to him from the school bus, and he had smiled back but had begun to understand that what had tied his tongue was simply desire. And there had been something not right about desiring her. She was too vulnerable, and simply too young. The six years between them had seemed like an unbridgeable chasm then. And then there had been the night of the dance in Aberfashie, when he had been back for a weekend with friends from Sandhurst. That night he had got drunk and stopped caring that she was too young, and he had regretted it ever since. Rona McColl, what did she want?

He went down to open the door, lighting another cigarette as soon as he stepped out under the porch. She still wore jeans and a fleece and wellingtons and was carrying a plastic bag with something heavy in it.

She was even more beautiful than he remembered.

'What were you doing? In the bottom field?' she said with a frown, without introduction, as if they were in the habit of speaking every day.

'Walking.'

'You were wading up to your waist in the river. Are you ok?'

'I'm fine.'

'Mother sends a lasagne,' she said, holding up the bag.

'Thanks.' He took the bag. 'How is she?'

'Fine. Still terrorising the neighbourhood.' Eamon gave a weak smile. 'I'd better go in,' he said.

'Are you alone?' He did not want to invite her in. He did and he didn't. 'Aren't you going to invite me in? It's only polite.' He smiled but at the same time felt a familiar disdain for her, for her happy, bright, beautiful face. He had felt this before, for other women, and had acted on the impulse before, and had resolved more than once not to.

'Perhaps some other time,' he said, putting the cigarette out.

'If you don't invite me in now, I'll be so insulted that I'll never come back,' she said, holding his gaze with a steady smile. He paused before replying and for a long time afterwards he was to remember this moment, the moment when he had made a choice for her that he could never be sure was born out of anything akin to love.

'Can you keep secrets?' he said, with what he thought was a patronising smile, and he saw on her young face a flicker of something that he had not anticipated, that he remembered from the face of a child at a funeral a decade ago, a seriousness and a courage. 'She did not care,' he thought later, and for a long time afterwards. 'She did not care what I thought of myself.'

'Yes,' she said, and stepped over the threshold.

He did not feel like eating but she insisted on heating the lasagne and opening a bottle of wine, and he found himself following her lead and laying the table in the study. He put out cloth and silver and candles but then, as they ate, it again occurred to him that he should tell her to go home to mother, and he became reticent. Then he tried to ask her about her mother and the farm, and at the same time, as the wine had its effect, he felt himself longing for a world of simplicity and contentment that was explained by her face and the candlelit table; a world that would be made sense of by a girl like her. It was a kind of miracle that she drew him out, away from sullenness and sentiment, and he told her everything.

'Where the hell was he going, up the hill on that bike?' he said.

'If you carry on with that footpath it'll lead you over the hill to Glenfashie. There's nothing there. I suppose if you go east, you'll get to the new dam. If you go west you'll get to Loch Houn, eventually.'

Later, standing before the stone in the cold basement he thought he could feel the warmth of her arm across the inches that separated them. She was silent for a while, staring at the stone, and he could hear her gentle breathing.

'Does nobody know what it means?'

'No. A long time ago an odd man came and said it was something to do with aliens. My father chased him off the property.'

'If you touch it perhaps the walls will move.'

'And the castle turn into a spaceship? I've tried that.'

'Aren't these runes, like in *Lord of the Rings*?'

'No. Runes are understood, and these ain't runes. Pictograms perhaps, but nobody has been able to decipher them. My dad said somethings are not meant to be understood. It might be code for a method of human sacrifice for all we know. "Paganism, that's what it is!" he said. What I want to know is how the mother of that poor child came to have a copy of this and why she gave it to me. What was she trying to tell me? Why was that thug so desperate to get it back? What do you know about Joel Kennedy?'

'Not much,' she shrugged. 'Drugs. Used to see him now and again in the village, can of lager in his hand, in the rain, without a jacket. He was friendly. Not sleazy. Like a kind of fairy. Impish. Then lately, he became sad-looking.'

'What about his parents? Kathleen Kennedy and Lachie. Are they still here?'

'Still on the croft.'

'It's going to be hell for them, now, with the trial, and the newspapers.'

'Eamon,' she said, and in the half-light he turned to see the look of shock on her face.

'What?'

'I thought you knew. His parents were told today. Joel Kennedy killed himself in his cell last night. He cut his wrists.'

Eamon absorbed the news in silence. Tears welled up and retreated from his eyes, making the symbols on the torch-lit stone swim and blend with each other. He closed his eyes and the image of Joel with beanie and fishing rod appeared. Death was like being kicked, or being operated on; like having something extracted.

'Let's get out of here,' he said. 'I'll go to see the Kennedy's tomorrow.' They climbed the stairs.

'I'll come with you,' she said when they were upstairs again. He offered to drive her home but she insisted on taking her quad, in spite of the rain. The engine roared and the headlight scythed through the darkness.

CHAPTER FIVE

At first light Eamon walked to Isabel's house in Tarr Bow. The house
was empty and dark. He peered through the window into the room
where he had sat the day before. Nothing had changed. It was almost
cell-like; nothing on the walls, just a desk, a couch and the chair where
the doorman had sat. He knocked on the neighbour's door. Peggy
Drummond answered; a thin, tough looking old woman. She grinned,
held her arms crossed and blew cigarette smoke through false teeth.
Eamon asked her if she had seen the two women leave the day before.
'Aye,' said Peggy, but volunteered nothing more.

   'Do you know where they went?'

   'No.'

   'Did you see the big man that was with them?'

   'Aye,'

   'Do you know who he was?'

   'Something to do with Social Services. Social Services are here all the
time.'

   'How long had the mother and child been living here?' The woman thought and smoked.

'Since the summer. You should know.'

'Should I?'

'Aye, you should.' She gave a knowing grin. Eamon was about to ask her what she meant when the howl of a child emerged from behind her in the house. She flicked her cigarette butt into a puddle and went inside. He did not call her back. Peggy Drummond had never made much sense to anybody, as far as he could remember, and the visit to Stevie Van was on his mind.

Stevie Van, because he lived in a van. At least, it had started out as a van, then another, then a caravan, then another; all joined together and surrounded by a collection of derelict cars, and all collected in what had once been a quarry on the north side of the village, up a short track, partially hidden by a stand of ash and bird-cherry. Smoke was rising from a chimney. Eamon remembered that Stevie was always in. His knock on the caravan door was answered by a short man wearing a heavy hand knitted jumper. He had thick, red stubble and red hair streaked with grey that looked like it had just emerged from a hat. His face was dry and tired-looking and a decade older than Eamon's. An unlit rollup hung from the bottom lip. He uttered a low grunt.

'Stevie,' said Eamon.

'Lord Ansgar, what an honour,' said Stevie in a guttural lowland accent.

'I'm not a lord, Stevie.'

'Whatever. Haven't seen you around for what? Ten years? You have trouble finding the place?'

'Can I come in?'

'I don't know. What would you say if I was standing on your doorstep?' he paused, stony-faced, waiting for an answer. 'Fuck it. You're letting the cold in. Shut it behind you.' Eamon followed him in and was struck by the smell; weed smoke, wood smoke, cooking fat, and the particular damp of a caravan in winter. A caravan in winter occupied by a single man. Stevie Van's caravan. Eamon remembered that once upon a time it had exerted a certain fascination. Something to do with living outside of constraints; something to do with music and weed. Stevie sat in a decrepit armchair, put his feet up on another, and took out a tin of tobacco. Eamon sat on a plastic chair. A stove made out of a gas cylinder blazed in a corner. On the wall above Stevie's head hung a sheep's skull painted with red, green and blue swirls. There were two enormous speakers in the corners of the room and a shelf stuffed with hundreds of LPs. There was a tiny television and another shelf of books. There was a certain kind of tidiness, the kind that men affect in a combat zone, without the discipline of the barracks. The cups and plates were washed and on the drying rack. The carpet had been hoovered, but it was all done with neither rigour nor any attempt at refinement. For décor there was the sheep's head, a poster of Bob Marley, and a poster that advertised, with retro psychedelic font, 'Midsummer Minds! Equinox in Glencul!' and some names of bands.

'You've missed some good parties,' said Stevie, lighting his cigarette, 'while you've been away fighting terror. Any luck, by the way?'

'With what?'

'Killing terror. Not an easy task, killing an abstract noun. Especially when women and children keep getting in the way.' Eamon took out a cigarette but did not light it. 'No, I know,' said Stevie, 'not your thing. You didn't like being at the pointy end. What did you go for? Signals? Logistics?'

'That sort of thing.' Eamon wondered how Stevie Van knew anything about his last ten years.

'You prefer to be the guy that makes sure the guy that kills people has enough bullets.' Stevie looked at him, deadpan, waiting for a reaction. 'Daddy must have been proud. Anyway, 'nough of the chit-chat. What can I do you for? Or don't tell me, you've grown out of it.'

'You could say that.'

'Not like you can't afford it. Unlike some people. Now that Daddy's passed from us.' He drew heavily on his cigarette.

'What happened to Joel Kennedy?' said Eamon. Stevie looked at him with an irritated frown.

'How the fuck should I know?'

'You knew him. You sold him drugs.'

'So what? You think that because somebody smokes weed they kill babies?'

'He didn't just smoke weed. You know that.'

'Is this some sort of blame thing? If it is, you can fuck off.' Eamon lit his cigarette.

'Weed, e's, coke, speed? What else do you sell? To everyone. To kids still in school.'

'Are you damaged?'

'You've got a daughter haven't you?' Eamon tried to remember her name. 'What is she now, fifteen? Do you give her a wrap of speed at the weekend?'

'Selma lives with her mother, in Berlin. And the answer is maybe, if she asked for it. If it was good stuff.' Eamon blew smoke into the silence.

'I was looking at some papers this morning. Title deeds. I don't suppose you know who owns this little haven that you've got going here?' Stevie put his cigarrette out in a mug.

'You can fuck off now,' he said, with a steady gaze. Eamon put out his cigarette in the same mug and got up. Stevie spoke as he reached the door. 'You know, if you think about it, I've been here for longer than you.' Eamon turned to look at the face. It was hard as stone. 'You're a cunt Ansgar, a cunt from a long line of cunts.' Eamon stepped out, leaving the door open.

During the night the sea had succumbed to a deep swell that *Rage III* rode easily, but the rain was falling hard and the lashings of water were accompanied by a low, mournful moan from a rising wind.

'What the hell Flieber?' said Vanneck, speaking into the handset of the satellite phone. 'Why are you only telling me now? One of the boys *died*? How?' There was a delay on the phone, the second it took for a signal to go into space and back, and the voice on the other end was muted and flattened. Vanneck looked at Brighton. Brighton was looking ahead, as if there was something to see beyond the glass. Even in profile Vanneck could tell that he had that 'I told you so' look on his face; patronising and calm.

'A mistake,' said the voice on the phone, 'Someone made a mistake. Sam you cut me off! I'm working with both hands tied behind my back! For three fucking years! You should be grateful they're not all dead!'

'So what are we dealing with? You've got a *body* on your hands? Jesus!'

'It's a little more complicated than that.'

'What? What could be more complicated?'

'You just need to get here as soon as possible. Like yesterday. Where are you now?' Vanneck turned to the impassive Brighton.

'Where are we?'

'Off the coast of Portugal, heading west,' said Brighton.

'Coast of Portugal, heading west,' said Vanneck into the phone.

'How long till you get here?' said the voice.

'We said a week, ten days,' said Vanneck, trying to regain his calm. What was more infuriating even than the death of the child was the feeling that he was caught between these two rivals, both little more than children, and somehow, by some perversity of fate, he was depending on them.

'What are you in? A rowing boat? Can't you go any faster?'

'He wants to know if we can get there sooner,' said Vanneck to Brighton. Brighton shook his head.

'Not if we stick to the plan.'

'What if we go through the Irish sea? Isn't that quicker?'

'The plan is we keep out in the Atlantic. This is a distinctive boat. We don't risk being seen if we can help it, and besides, in this weather it's safer.'

'A week, ten days. We can't go faster,' said Vanneck into the phone.

'And I need money. Cash. People have to be paid,' said Flieber.

'How am I supposed to get you cash? I'm in a boat in the middle of the ocean!'

'Can't you pay someone to pay me? Send a courier?'

'I'm a scientist Flieber, I'm not a gangster. I don't know how to do that kind of thing.'

CHAPTER SIX

Grigor Semyonovitch squatted with his back against the base of an old larch on the edge of the forest, thinking about his performance on the bridge. He was only half pleased. His nose was still swollen and red but he did not mind that, he was used to it. What annoyed him was that he had wanted to do a flying kick to the face, but at the last second had hesitated because he had thought the deck too slippery. But when he had been walking to pick up his bike, after he had seen the man in the green jacket borne away at the speed of a fast run by the churning, white-streaked river, he had checked the deck for slipperiness and it had not been too bad. He could have made the flying kick, and it would have been spectacular. He could have broken the guy's neck. Instead he had pushed him in the chest, like a kid fighting in a playground, like a drunk outside a nightclub, and he was disappointed in himself.

He had been waiting for an hour under the larch. It was beginning to rain again, and he was becoming irritated. Flieber had told him to go with the truck driver into the forest and wait by the big tree next to the road. For how long? He tried to phone Clarice, but there was no

signal. He was practising some kicks against the tree trunk when he saw
a little blue Peugeot approach. He quickly sat down again and stared
into the trees; he had been told not to attract attention. The blonde guy,
Sigurson, was in the car. Fucking Sigurson. He had hated Sigursun since
the moment he had met him, a week ago, but he was finding it hard to
pin down exactly why. It was something to do with the way he dressed, as
if he was about to go skiing or climbing in the snow, always wearing lined
trousers and puffed up jackets and climbing boots and some bright hat.
Today the hat was orange and too small, sticking up from the big blonde
head. A complete lack of style, that was part of it, and the clothes were
always new, always changing, so that they seemed not to belong to him.
Sigurson was like a dummy in a shop window. It was also something to
do with the long blonde hair, the hair of a beautiful girl, shiny and cared
for and falling down his back in a ponytail. And something to do with
the paleness of the skin, so white the blue of the veins on the back of
his hands was clearly visible. It was something to do with the big hooked
nose. But mainly it was to do with the smile, the constant wide thin-
lipped grin, as if there was a hidden joke behind everything, some secret
pleasure that he was enjoying that he couldn't tell you about. And then
in the moments when he wasn't smiling, when he wasn't looking at you
with piercing blue eyes, the expression on the face was too serious, as if
contemplating some awful or profound truth. Sigurson called from the
car and Grigor jumped up and ran to it.

'Whassup?' said Grigor

'Whassup is we've got a job to do,' said Sigurson. The accent was
hard to place. Sometimes American, or Australian, sometimes Scottish
or Scandinavian. A Scot trying not to be Scottish perhaps, trying out new
voices.

'I supposed to go south yesterday.'

'Change of plan. Got to dig up a box.'

They drove north for a while. Grigor stared through the rain flecked
window at the darkness beneath the pines. That was the deal. Ask no
questions; now go fetch a stone from a guy, now do nothing, now go dig
up a box in the woods. Take your money, keep quiet.

'Why they give us this shitty little car?' he said. They were both big men but Sigurson was taller by a hand and the ski hat was touching the roof. 'Why they not give us pickup? Pickup is better for this job I think.' Sigurson was driving slowly but they were feeling every stone in the road. He did not reply.

'Why it always raining in this country? Rain rain rain. In my country it is cold in winter, freezing, but not this shit rain every day. It not good for health.'

'If you don't like it why don't you go back to your country?' Sigurson turned with a big grin.

'In my country there is no money. I have to come here for money.'

'How come?'

'How come what?'

'How come there is no money in your country? What's wrong with it?'

'The gangsters steal everything,' said Grigor with a weak smile. The car bumped, the rain fell. Grigor stared at the pines. 'Is pity. I was looking forward to go South. Get out of rain. This shit rain.'

'A little bit longer,' said Sigurson, staring ahead and grinning.

'What you mean? You know where I go next?' Sigurson nodded towards the satnav on the dashboard. Soon he stopped the car. He put on a bright yellow waterproof jacket and took two spades from the boot. Grigor followed him up a firebreak and then along a narrow path into the pines. Sigurson used his phone to find a small clearing with a floor of short grass.

'What is in box?' said Grigor. Sigurson took out a measuring tape, walked to one side of the clearing and beckoned Grigor.

'I didn't ask,' he said. Grigor came over and Sigurson told him to hold the end of the tape against the base of a pine, then he walked out into the middle of the clearing, pulling the tape. He stopped and made a mark with his foot in the ground. 'Let go!' he called, and the tape zipped back into its case. They measured again, at a right angle to the first measurement. Sigurson marked the ground next to the first mark, and cut out a square of turf. 'You dig first,' he said. 'We'll take turns.' Grigor shrugged. He needed the exercise.

'How deep?'

'A metre. If we don't find it by a metre we'll widen it.' Sigurson leant against a boulder and took out an e-cigarette. He watched Grigor dig. He dug fast through the soft peat and was soon a metre deep.

'Nothing.' He had not even broken sweat.

'Go that way a little. Dig the same square.'

'You know those things are bad for health. They put holes in your lungs.' Sigurson puffed and smiled. 'I know what is in box. Is guns. In this country you have to bury guns. In my country guns is not such problem.' He continued to dig.

'Why did you throw that guy off the bridge?' said Sigurson. Grigor answered without looking up, with a shrug.

'I don't know. I was improvising. The river was asking for him.' He looked up. 'I thought it was a good scene, you know, like in a movie.'

'You think you're in a movie?'

'No. I never get a chance to fight. When I get chance I like to make it good.' He climbed out of the hole. 'One metre, nothing. You want I dig another?'

'Yep. Dig another, at the end of that one. It's got to be there. Metal box, you'll know when you hit it.'

'Look, I was told "get stone" so I got stone. Nobody said "don't hurt the guy". You know what I did in Latvia, before I came here? I was kick box champion, whole Latvia. You know what that means?'

'No, what does it mean?'

'Nothing. It means Fanny Adams Fuck all. It means I train for ten years, nothing but training, spend all my money on training and eating right food, train train train, fight fight fight, and I beat shit out of every guy in Latvia who wants to fight me, and you know what I got? I got belt made of plastic and five thousand euro. Five thousand euro! I pay credit cards, and next day, after win, I go back to work in nightclub, on door. I am best fighter in Latvia. But I make more money in Scotland digging holes in woods.'

'Did you know who that guy was?'

'Sure, the guy lives in old castle near village.'

'Did you know he owns the dam?'

'No. So what?'

'Do you know how much trouble you would have caused if you had killed him? Do you know how many people would have been at his funeral? You see the hole you've just dug Grigor? He owns that hole. He owns these forests, he owns the river you threw him in, he owns the village.' Grigor frowned.

'So, he's our boss?' Sigurson shook his head. 'So why did he take stone? Why she give him stone?' Sigurson closed his eyes and sighed. Grigor hit a root with the spade, and hit it again and again.

'Problem?'

'Root. Spade is blunt.' As Grigor looked up Sigurson was coming towards him with a long, thin knife, a fishing knife with a curved blade that glinted in the weak light.

'You hold it,' he said. 'I'll cut. Turn around, kneel down there. I'll get it from here.' Grigor knelt in the trench. The damp earth was tight around his shoulders. He put out his hands to grasp the root and for a moment he was reminded of kneeling in a church back home in Latvia, a long time ago, making a confession.

'I praying,' he said with half a smile.

'Good,' said Sigurson. He raised the knife above Grigor's neck. Grigor pulled and tugged at the slippery root. Then he looked up to see that Sigurson had closed his eyes and was smiling again, at some inner vision, holding the blade at shoulder height, about to bring it down.

'What you waiting for? Cut!' Sigurson did not move. 'Cut it. What wrong with you?' Sigurson opened his eyes and looked into Grigor's.

'You know what,' he said, lowering the knife, 'Leave it. It's not here.'

'It not here? You sure?'

'Not today. Get in the car.'

That afternoon Eamon took his father's old Renault and picked up Rona at Burnum farm. He told her about his visit to Stevie.

'Are you really going to kick him out?'

'I'm going to speak to the man who knows about these things.'

'He's been there for thirty years. I was thinking, how did he get to put up his caravan in the first place? I mean, that was your land and from what I remember...'

'Dad had a thing about tinks, and new-age travellers, and junkies and riff-raff and dole-scroungers. I know.'

'And your dad knew what he owned.'

'Every stick.'

'Unlike you.'

The Kennedys had had one of the crofts on the outskirts of Glencul for as long as Eamon could remember. He was not sure if the single story white harled house surrounded by a neat garden belonged to the estate. If it was a croft house though, it would be passed to the next Kennedy generation. That would have been Joel. Now it would go to his sister Marie. Was it worse than having a child murdered? To have a child or a brother as a murderer?

Kathleen Kennedy, a frail looking woman with short white hair, opened the door. Eamon had been dreading making this visit, this intrusion upon their strange grief. He had not been able to imagine how he would be met, and the expression of anger on the woman's thin face was a shock to him. Anger and a hollowed out, hungry look, as if a rage had run its course, leaving her exhausted. She paused for a moment as Eamon greeted her, without replying, looking as if she would like to close the door in his face. But generations of deference to the House of Duncul provided a solution to her dilemma. Still, she did not smile, and turned her back on them, leaving the door open, and she was unable to keep a harsh edge from her voice as she called to her husband as she passed along the corridor that led to the kitchen.

'Lachie! Duncul is here!' Lachlan Kennedy, a big man with remnants of hair surrounding a bald head and a face that Eamon remembered as cheerful, welcomed them into a living room that was neat and comfortably furnished, but dark and cold with an empty grate and drawn curtains. Lachie had the uncomfortable look of a man who has dressed hurriedly. He bade his guests sit. A clock ticked loudly from the mantelpiece.

'I'm sorry,' said Eamon, into the silence. He looked at the mantelpiece and the photographs of Joel and Marie. The two of them in school uniform. Marie with her two daughters. Joel in a mortarboard and gown.

'Joel was a friend of mine, when we were at school.' He couldn't think of what else to say. 'I didn't know he went to college.'

'Nursing. Three years. Then he dropped it,' said Lachie.

'I can help with the funeral,' said Eamon.

'He'll not be buried here,' said Lachie, looking at the floor.

'And why not?' said Kathleen, appearing in the door with a tray of tea and biscuits.

'Kathleen...' said Lachie. She put the tray down.

'That woman was evil. She did something to him. That black bitch!'

'Kathleen...' said Lachie.

'What do you mean?' said Eamon.

'Spells. Black Magic.'

'There's no such thing, Kathleen,' said Lachie.

'What he did, he would never have done that, never, not Joel. Joel would not have hurt a fly,' her voice rose as she spoke, hardening and breaking. Tears filled her eyes. Rona rose and held her. 'Never mind a child. Never mind a child! That woman! Nobody knows where she's from! Nobody knows anything about her! Nobody! Nothing! Only Joel. Only Joel spoke to her.'

'They were friends?' said Eamon. Kathleen, recovering herself, sat down and poured the tea.

'He visited her. People in the Tarr were saying things. That black bitch. She had a hold on him. He wasn't right after she came. He'll be buried here.' She defied her husband with her eyes.

'And how did he die in jail?' said Lachie, as if catching the theme of injustice from his wife, staring at Eamon as if he should know. 'Are they not supposed to be watching? Razor blades in jail? How does he get razor blades?'

'I don't know,' said Eamon.

'That's not right! Did they let him do it?' Eamon let the question hang in the dim room. They drank tea.

'Wherever you want to bury him,' he said, 'I'll help. He was my friend.'

'He had a job,' said Kathleen. 'Fencing. Joel was trying to get off the drugs and Stevie Van was feeding them to him. I know it! Everyone knows it. He doesn't belong here!' Eamon nodded and looked at the floor.

Later that afternoon, after he had dropped Rona at Burnum, Eamon drove the twenty miles to Grey Acres, where he had an appointment to meet the Glencul factor, Edgar Dupuy. As always when he made this journey he noted the changes in the landscape as he moved eastward, the size of the fields increasing; more houses, bigger houses. He was moving out of the West, the impoverished land of peat and heather and the Gael where the farms were small and few, into deeper, richer soil. It was almost another country, he had always thought. Grey Acres was a large former farmhouse at the end of a long drive lined with poplars. He parked next to a shiny black Range Rover.

'It's good to see you!' said Edgar, coming out of the porch. He was a young with a fresh face and black wavy hair, dressed in a tweed jacket and checked shirt. He shook Eamon's hand with two of his own and showed him down a flagstoned hall to a bright kitchen where an Aga hummed with heat. 'How about a drink? Special sherry? Can't get this one in Sainsbury's.' Eamon declined but his host poured one into an elegant glass for himself. 'By the look on your face this is business rather than pleasure. Let's go into the office.' He led the way into a small room furnished with a large walnut desk, many drawered cabinets, landscape prints, and a view of a long lawn sheltered by a yew hedge.

'I know I've never taken much of an interest,' said Eamon, sitting in an armchair. 'But of course I ought to, now that Dad's gone.'

'Well, your Dad and my Dad were a pretty good team. They left the place in reasonable shape. They pretty much saved it with the dam.'

'I suppose I ought to go and take a look at this dam.'

'You certainly should. It's splendid, and a lovely walk, if the weather was a bit better.' Eamon drummed his fingers on the arm of the chair.

'And rents? What about rents?' said Eamon. He was surprised to see Edgar frown at this question, almost imperceptibly, only as if a shadow had fallen on his face.

'Well the dam is rent, really, from the electricity company. But you mean cottages, farms, that sort of thing?' He talked quickly, finished his sherry in a gulp, and shuffled some papers on the desk. 'Rents don't bring in much. That's why your father sold a few things, Tarvin lodge, for example. And then he practically gave Burnum Farm to the McColls when McColl died. 'Gainst my dad's advice I have to say. Even so, they struggle to pay the mortgage so I hear, which may be an opportunity to get it back. Something to bear in mind. The thing is rents don't pay, once you've taken into account all the maintenance and the fact that you can't change the tenants because they've been there for generations. There are about twenty crofts for example which bring in precisely nothing.'

'How many tenants do we have?'

'Oh, top of my head, thirty, not including Mohammed, who rents all the hill ground, for a pittance I have to say. Again, God knows why.'

'Is Stevie Van one of them?' Eamon saw the shadow leave the face. Edgar brightened and relaxed.

'Ah, Stevie Van. No. He's never paid rent.'

'Never?'

'Never.'

'And we definitely own the quarry?'

'Eamon, apart from a few parcels here and there, houses and so on, you own the whole glen. As far as the eye can see.'

'So technically, he's a squatter?'

'You could put it like that.'

'And why haven't you done anything about it?'

'Well, my Dad perhaps ought to shoulder the blame rather than me.'

'Yes, of course. So, why didn't he?'

'That, Eamon, is a very good question. He never mentioned it to me.' Eamon watched Edgar's face. There was an eagerness there, a freshness, almost an innocence, but there was the shadow too. Sometimes the eyes were open, wide, ingenuous, and then they would narrow to dark slits and the brow would come down.

'I'd like to know for sure what his position is.'

'Well. I can look into it. I can check.'

'Now?'

'Well we're not exactly computerised here. It's all papers, papers, hundreds of years of papers. Trust me, this is only the tip of the iceberg,' he gestured at the cabinets behind him. They both got up. 'You must come to dinner one of these days. Ginny would love to see you and you must meet the girls. Tell us about what you've been up to all these years.'

What I've been up to all these years, thought Eamon, as he walked across the gravel to his car and Edgar stood behind him in the doorway, is catching out people who are lying.

CHAPTER SEVEN

At the beginning of their second night at sea, when they had turned north and were beyond all light from the land and the harbourmaster had given up calling them on the satellite phone; when they were alone with the waves and the spray and the darkness beyond their own lights, and the boat had begun twisting beneath them like a thing come alive; when they were alone against a steep chop that came at them from the north west, lifting the bows and slapping them painfully against the next and the next and the next, causing ripples of shock to echo to the stern; when the rain had become cold, hard and malevolent, as if they were being cursed by something hideous from the darkness ahead, Vanneck, sitting in the soft leather of the captain's armchair, felt trepidation like a crack in the hull of the mind, and fearful thoughts like seawater seeping in. Brighton, sitting in the chair a few feet away, affected unconcern. Vanneck would have liked to have been able to blame Brighton. Even now, when Brighton was his right hand man, without whom he would not have have been able to do any of this, he did not like him. He did not trust that clean-shaven, strong-jawed, bright-eyed face of his; he couldn't stand the affectation of the nautical cap and the well made clothes. Brighton was not a scientist. He had completed his doctorate, but it was only a means to an end. There was nothing of the nerd in Brighton, no pathological meticulousness, no devotion to scrutiny of the obscure. Brighton had a devotion to fact, true, but only the facts of money and power. Brighton was the son he had never had nor wanted, waiting avidly for his death so as to take over the empire, and then Brighton would expand, aquire and manage. He would raise billions on the stockmarket, turning *Lilco* into a pill manufacturer, churning out money for shareholders. Brighton would probably destroy everything Samson Vanneck had built and go against everything he had ever believed in. He would sell the soul of *Lilco*, but then, Vanneck had to remind himself, what they were doing now, finally, was exactly what *Lilco* had been created to pursue. It did not matter what Brighton would do in the future; he was essential now.

'Stop worrying, Sam,' said Brighton, 'This is nothing. She's built to take far worse.' Vanneck hated to hear the abbreviation of his name when it came from the young man's mouth, in that nowhere accent of his, but it was his own fault. He had always encouraged the use of his first name abbreviated and familiarised by his students and employees. He had always aimed for an open, at ease atmosphere at *Lilco*, long before it had been the fashion; no ties, no real hierarchy, a collegiate atmosphere; rewards for innovation, hard work and imagination and not for toadying and box-ticking. He had learned, over four decades, how a certain type took advantage of not being told what to do and didn't produce any results, and he was used to getting rid of those sort of people. How had Brighton managed to make himself so indespensable without being one of us? Without being one of the brotherhood of scientists? Brighton had no right to call him Sam, and yet he did, a hundred times a day, and Sam couldn't stop him. Sam tried to stop thinking about it. He went downstairs, steadying himself on chrome handrails and against carbon-fibre walls.

She had been heavily sedated as soon as the weather had begun, and was sleeping in her floral nest, the stamen surrounded by petals. He went into the salon and helped himself to a green tea. He had ordered that there be no alcohol on board, but now, for the first time in years, he craved a drink; a neat malt, no ice. He sat on a couch, and felt the strangeness of the boat, with her dark walls and hidden lights and acres of leather and walnut and chrome; a strange thing amid the strange darkness beyond the windows. He was in the belly of the beast she had become; enveloped, swallowed and oppressed by the luxury. Suddenly he realised that he hated the boat, as much as he had once loved her.

The *Rage III* had been an eightieth birthday present for Lillian. He had even considered changing the name to something more feminine, even Lillian or Lily, but in the end he had maintained the tradition of their smaller yachts, *Rage I* and *II*, because now at this age and with Lillian's frailty and illnesses, the name had even greater meaning. *'Do not go gently into that good night, but rage, rage, against the dying of the light'*. It meant everything now, that rage, and this journey was the summation of the courage to give everything to it, to succumb to it, to sacrifice for it. She had had to be the third *Rage*, and Lillian had understood.

For a decade Lillian had been unwilling and unable to fly, and although she had been to every kind of therapy money could buy, her phobia had only increased. They could have chartered yachts but they were like floating hotels, and she had never been comfortable in hotels. *Rage III* was a floating palace, a home from home. It was significant that it was their own; the ultimate reward for their success, and she had loved it from the moment it had sailed into the harbour at Montezuma, on time to the second, as the smoke was still drifting from the cake. He had been nervous that it would disappoint and then nervous that even this, fifty-million dollars worth of the latest technology, would not convince her to sail across the Atlantic, to go home after a decade of exile, and he had watched her eyes as he proposed the journey to her, waiting for the merest iota of resistance. But she had smiled with unquenchable warmth and immediately consented. In that moment she had re-awoken the old gladness, the adventurousness of their youth, and had rekindled the wavering flame of hope that he carried like a candle sheltered by a cupped hand. He marvelled in retrospect at that moment on the terrace of their house at Montezuma, amid the palms and flame vines, looking out over the glittering bay, surrounded by their friends from four continents and a hundred of the fraternity of *Lilco*; all those young eager, intelligent faces, all that hope and love and courage. It was strange how a smile, a moment of assent, can change the world, like the moment she had said yes to marrying him, like the moment he had held up a test tube to the light in a laboratory at the University of Michigan forty years ago, and realised he was going to be a billionaire. Red and it would have been nothing, another failure in a failing life, another nudge down the long rough slope towards mediocrity in a mediocre institution; blue and it was the gateway to another universe; to light, fame, wealth, beauty, power.

With that assent, a 'yes' to a trip to Europe, merely a holiday visiting the cities they had hitchhiked to in their twenties on love and fresh air, she had enabled him to grasp hold of that hope, that desire, that courage, that rage. It was the same courage that had made him rich; the same hope and fear and rage that had won him, at the beginning of middle age, the sole ownership of those mysterious infinitesimal movements of atoms in that blue test tube; electrons and protons on the fringes of the imagination; in themselves, almost nothing, insignificant, the mere cusp of an idea, that meant everything. It was the same courage that had built Montezuma, almost a city, out of nothing, nowhere, on the coast of Belize. It was the same courage that had fought a hundred battles with governments around the world; the courage that had scoffed at laws and ethics committees in ten capitals; the courage that had built *Lilco* into something far more than a corporation; a city-state almost, a university in the true sense and an entity that had altered the course of human history. The courage that yes, had failed, he knew now; that had been shipwrecked on the shore of an obscure sea-loch in an obscure glen in his native Scotland. Scotland; perhaps he should never have had anything to do with that dark, damp half-existing country. Scotland that had given him nothing. Perhaps the mistake is to believe in bad luck, he told himself. He should never have believed in bad luck. Perhaps he should have persevered three years ago and ignored the disaster and listened to Flieber. If he had done that, where would he be now? In three years, what wonders they could have achieved. If he had listened to Flieber, and not Brighton. Flieber after all, for all his faults, was a genuine scientist. Flieber was the real thing; the diminutive Flieber had balls. Brighton, Flieber, Brighton. He had chosen Brighton. Brighton had been right, Brighton was always right. For the sake of *Lilco*, for Montezuma, for his legacy, for Lillian. He had even dared to say that, for Lillian! And where had that led? Where was Lillian now? Dying, yes dying, behind him in the bed, and he was dying too, yes, face it, and ten of his friends, clients, investors were dying because he had listened to Brighton. Maybe, somehow, this was what Brighton had wanted all along, maybe he had engineered all this. Well he could have what he wanted. He could have it all. If he could get them to Loch Houn, and get them out of there, back to Montezuma, he could have whatever the hell he wanted.

When he found himself alone again in Duncul, Eamon thought about inviting Rona for dinner, but when she answered his call he hesitated. The night she had come, he had been exhausted. It had probably been a mistake. Instead he told her about Edgar.

'Lying about what?' said Rona, her voice tightened by the phone.

'I don't know. Something. Something to do with Stevie Van, I think.'

'His father, and his grandfather were factors, weren't they?'

'And?'

'Well, isn't there some sort of loyalty there?'

'Perhaps. But it's not unheard of for factors to cheat estate owners. I mean it's an easy enough thing to do. My father was unusual, he took an interest. Most are like me, they just swan around the place oblivious to the nuts and bolts, where the money comes from and where it goes.'

'You were at school with Edgar, weren't you?'

'He was a junior. Insolent little shit as far as I remember.'

'Could be it be something to do with drugs? With Stevie?' she said.

'Maybe. I couldn't work out if he was reluctant or not when I asked him to find out about Stevie's quarry. There was just something generally shifty about him, the way he was watching me, as if he was trying work out what I knew.' There was a long pause. He was about to break it by asking her to come over when she said she had to go. He sat in silence in the dark, cold room for a long time, looking into the empty grate. 'Leave her alone you arsehole,' he muttered as he began laying the fire, but before lighting it he noticed that it had stopped raining and he went out.

At first he did not know where he was going. He felt the urge to walk, and the stars were out for the first time in weeks. He walked through the village, past the gulag and found himself half way along the track to the quarry before he realised where he was going and turned back, through the village again. He crossed over the Ash Bridge and went on, perhaps a mile, until he came to a long, low building beside the road that at first looked like a farm steading, but which an ill-lit sign declared to be *'The Misty Glen, Public House.'* The only car was a delapidated white Transit parked in the yard. Eamon could not remember the last time he had visited, but he had, a long time ago. He had a vague, inebriated memory of the place. He half expected it to be closed but there were dim lights in the dirty windows and through a half-glass door he could see a figure moving. He was about to push open the door but saw Stevie and hesitated.

He had a clear view of the bar. A short man with long grey hair wearing a black cowboy hat and a black leather waistcoat, and a woman with long grey hair tied in a ponytail, were standing behind the bar at the far end from the door. Stevie was leaning on the bar and talking to the man with the hat. There there were two other men in high-vis jackets sitting at a table, sipping pints. The woman was old and fat but dressed in leggings and a hooded top, like a teenager. She was listening but staring at the floor. Then she must have seen something out of the corner of her eye because she looked up directly at Eamon. Eamon opened the door and stepped into the room with a smile. Everyone looked at him. There was music playing, but not very loud, some sort of heavy rock. No-one spoke.

'Evening,' said Eamon as he approached the bar. The woman came over to him wearing a scowl. He asked for a beer.

'What kind?' said the woman, she had a Northern English accent.

'Heavy.'

'Only got lager.'

'Well I'll have one of those,' said Eamon. He glanced up at Stevie and nodded. Stevie stared. The woman poured from the only tap at the bar. Eamon paid and sipped. It tasted odd.

'Out for a walk?' said the woman.

'Just passing,' said Eamon, looking around the bar. The only decoration was an electric guitar hanging on a wall, and a framed t-shirt with the legend 'Judas Priest'. A pool table squatted in the shadows beyond the two men in yellow jackets who had returned to their pints and an inaudible conversation. 'Nice place you've got here,' said Eamon.

'We like it,' said the woman. She returned to the other end of the bar and continued staring at the floor. Stevie finished his conversation with the man in the hat and walked past Eamon to the door without even a nod. Eamon carried on sipping. The beer was not good. He made it through half of the pint before saying goodnight.

The sky had clouded over and he could hardly see the road in front of him. He walked as quickly as he could back towards the village. He was almost at the Ash Bridge in a particularly dark part of the road beneath the elm trees when he heard a voice out of the darkness.

'You following me?' said Stevie Van. Eamon spun around in surprise.

'Where are you?'

'You following me?'

'Don't be ridiculous. Where are you?'

'In your head,' said Stevie, laughing. Eamon made out the shape of him, standing beside one of the trees. 'It's all in your head.'

'Fuck off Stevie.'

'Wouldn't you like that.'

'Did you hear about Joel?' There was a long silence. Eamon peered at the still, dark shape.

'I suppose that's my fault as well?'

'No it couldn't possibly be, could it,' said Eamon, already regretting his own cruelty. Stevie had been friends with Joel, just as he had. He heard a sigh.

'What do you want, Eamon?'

'I'll be coming to see you again, in a few days, if you're not in I know where to find you.' There was no reply. He looked for the shape beneath the trees, but it was gone, there was only darkness, cold, and a light rain beginning to fall.

Back at Duncul he lit the fire in the study. He intended to go to bed but did not feel tired. He listened to the Highland News on the radio.

'Police are treating the death of a child on the November 1st this year in a fire in Glencul as suspicious.' Idiots, they even got the date wrong, December 1ˢᵗ, not November. He turned off the radio.

In the early morning he went up to the roof to smoke and stood listening to the rain fall, the water trickling in the gutters and the rush of the Ash in the woods behind. Staring out at the gate and the first streetlight of the village at the end of the drive, he saw a car pause. A little grey Fiat. It remained there for a few minutes with its engine running, then drove on. He immediately thought of calling Rona, but waited until the weak sun was glowing behind the clouds to the south.

'Someone's watching me,' he said. He told her about the car.

'It could be a tourist, looking at the castle.'

'There's no tourists at this time of year. Look, can you go to the gulag today, and ask some questions? It's better if it's you. Just see if anyone knows who that car belongs to, if it has been around before. And speak to Mrs Drummond. She said something funny to me the other day, "You should know," she said, about how long the woman and child had been staying in the house.'

'What are you going to do?'

'I'm going for a walk, we can meet up here before dark, if you like.'

'Ok,' she said. How did she do that? It had been ten years ago, but how did she forget what he had done?

He met Kirsty in the hall. She was plugging in a hoover. 'I want you to keep the front door and the tower door locked,' he said. He changed into walking boots and picked up a jacket and a stick. 'Is Mike here today?'

'Yes.'

'Tell him to look out for anyone snooping around,' he said. She paused with the hoover in hand, frowning at him, watching as he swapped the stick for a heavier one.

'Is it tinks?'

'Yes, perhaps.'

The rain was off and he walked quickly, over the Ash Bridge and on past the *The Misty Glen*, which was lightless and silent. The path branched off from the road soon after this, and the tracks of a dirt bike could still be seen in the mud. He followed them through birch and oak woods on the lower slopes but soon he was on the open hill; at first yellow grass and crushed bracken, then out onto the heather. When he was half way to the top he paused to smoke and look back at Duncul, in its park of beech and elm, and the village, the gulag a little way off, every day of his childhood laid out before him; the church, the school, the Tarr and the Ash, the fields of Burnum, the crofts, the loch to the east of the castle. Every path and house and field and ditch remembered, every child and adult, his whole story, all innocence, all of a remembered future, when the world had been bright and full of dreams. Days when he had run home to his mother with minnows in a jar. Days when he had planted appleseeds in the lane behind the school with Angus McPherson, and Joel Kennedy. From here he could slip into it again, he thought, if he stayed here, now, smoking amid the heather, and did not move again. But the check pattern of the bike tracks in the mud led up, and he followed.

By late morning the wind had lessened and Lillian had awoken, groggy from the sedative. She wanted to go up onto the deck but Vanneck advised against it.

'It's still a bit rough,' he said.

'I can feel that,' she said. 'Where's Paula?' Paula was her nurse. 'And Anthony? What has happened to Anthony?' Anthony was her steward. Vanneck had never once lied to her. He had concealed things, but never lied to her face. He was not going to start now.

'We've left them behind.'

'What? Why? Where?' He brought her a tray with her pills and some water.

'In Lisbon. We've left all the crew behind.'

'What? Who's running the ship?' She always called *Rage III* a ship, and he never corrected her. She was right; it was better to be on board a ship than a boat.

'We are. Well, Brighton is. He knows about boats. I mean ships.'

'Brighton? What about Captain Bartlett?'

'We left Captain Bartlett behind too,' he said, and he saw her face darken with the same kind of fear that had kept her from boarding a plane.

'Sam, what are you talking about?' He offered her the water for her pills. 'What's going on?'

'We had to take the boat, Lily.' He had to tell her the truth, but he could not tell her everything. She could never know everything, never. She waited for him to continue. 'We have to go somewhere and Captain Bartlett wouldn't come. He couldn't. I couldn't let him. He didn't want to anyway. He refused.' She waited. 'He refused. He said the weather was too bad for this boat in the North Atlantic at this time of year. Now…' he held up his hand to stop her. 'It's not. Brighton assures me it's not. This ship is as solid as a rock. It can sail through hurricanes. Not that there is going to be any hurricanes. It's better that he didn't come anyway.' He felt that he had dug himself into a hole, and attempted to start again. 'Look. This is about hope. It's about hope for you, for me, for a lot of people. It's bigger than any of us. It's bigger than anything I or we have ever done. It's more important than anything *Lilco* has achieved. And it's our last chance.' She had been sitting up, and now she lay back into the pile of pillows and he saw, as he hated to see, overlaid on the face of Lillian, the face of that old strange woman, the old woman who had somehow come to inhabit her.

'Do you want me to guess?' she said, with a weak, mirthless smile.

'Yes,' he said, returning it.

'Sam, I don't know anything about it. You never told me.' And before he could reply; 'It's about Adam, isn't it?' He nodded. A wave made the boat shudder.

'How much do you know?'

'I know that you went back, after the war. You never told me what you found. You never told me what you did.'

'After the war. I went back. The Singa were almost all gone. So many of them had been killed. There were only eighty left. And they were dying; starving. Their whole way of life was gone. I tried to save them. I had a plan. I tried to take them out of Congo, but it's Africa. Things went wrong. Like Adam. Some of them died.'

'But it wasn't your fault,' she said.

'Perhaps. If I had never tried perhaps they would have all died. Millions died in that war, and after it. But, what I did, caused some of them, many of them, most of them, to die.'

'Sam,' she said, so gently; an exhalation that was an expression of horror as well as sympathy. He wanted her to reach out and touch his hand, but her hand stayed still on the bedcover.

'But some survived, and they went to Scotland,' he said.

'You took them to Scotland?'

'Yes. Not me. I paid people to take them to Scotland.'

'Why Scotland? Why not Belize? Why not Montezuma?'

'It was the way things worked out. Scotland is a safe place, for refugees. We found a way of working them into the system there, so they were secure.'

'So, they're safe?'

'Yes.'

'What does this have to do with us, now?' she said, and he had to think before he answered. He spoke with an attempt at brightness.

'There was a miracle. There are children, and I, we, suspect, hope, believe that there is something of Adam in them.'

'How so? How is that possible?'

'That's what we need to find out. That's why we are going there.' He made an excuse then, and left her because now he could not look her in the eye. For the first time in his life he had lied, brazenly to her face. There was a miracle, he had said. There was no miracle, only crime; only crime upon crime.

CHAPTER EIGHT

As Eamon climbed, patches of snow began to appear amid the heather, lying more deeply in the hollows. It was cold on the top, but there was no wind and the sun was breaking through clouds to the south. He saw a ptarmigan sprinting through the rocks ahead of him, and a herd of deer off to the west. A long time ago he had shot one; only one. When the neighbouring estate had been bought by one Mohammed Mahoud, billionaire from the Gulf, when Eamon was still a boy, his father had leased him the whole of the Glencul shooting, so it was twenty years since Glencul had been a shooting estate. Even his father had considered the entertainment of stock-brokers and retired colonels to be a bore, and a waste of time for what money it brought in. He had refrained from selling the hill ground however; that would have been a kind of sacrilege. And his instinct had been right, because then the whole green-energy thing had come along and the Glenfashie dam. On the eastern horizon Eamon could see the wind-turbines that Mohammed Mahoud had put up, as if he didn't have enough money already. They were still now, in the windless day, pointing a hundred metres into the sky.

It was a three mile walk over the moor before he paused to look down at the dam for the first time. It was a silver sliver of light, reflecting the low sun. There was the long, low line of the dam itself, and the steel pipe leading away to the west, now disappearing beneath the peat bog, now emerging again, down six hundred metres and three miles towards another sliver of silver, the head of Loch Houn, the long finger of the sea stretching some twenty miles in from the West Coast. This path over the hill was a short-cut to the dam, as the road from the village to the head of Loch Houn led along the face of the hill he had climbed, going much further to the west and then doubling back to the loch head, ten miles either way. From the head of the loch a dirt track had been made, leading up to the dam, and then carrying on beyond, around the dam loch and into the hills. About half a mile before the track reached the dam, half concealed by a fold in the hills, there was a collection of porta-cabins around a steel-clad shed and a yard with diggers, pickup trucks, pallets of cement, lengths of pipe, and a white van, all surrounded by a chain-link fence. Lazy smoke was rising from a chimney. The path he was following led down, back and forth across the hillside, then across the peat bog and the dirt track to the camp. Eamon sat and smoked. He wanted to stay up on the hill. He had not climbed a hill for so long, and he wanted to keep climbing. He moved along the face of the hill and came to a ring of standing stones; small stones barely visible in the heather, a taller one in the centre. The work of men long disappeared. The work of ghosts. He looked down again at the dam and the camp. As he watched a car came up the track from Loch Houn. It was a small car, moving slowly. It was a Fiat, a grey Fiat.

The car drove past the entrance to the camp and on, towards the dam. It stopped, and Eamon could just make out a figure, tiny from this distance, getting out and walking along the top of the dam. The figure paused, then moved, paused, then moved. Then it carried on to the other end of the dam, and paused. Then it climbed down to the base. Eamon wished he had brought binoculars. The figure, a man he presumed, was carrying something. He was taking photographs. He spent perhaps half an hour taking pictures of the dam. Then he got back into the car and drove back down the track. He stopped outside the camp, and got out.

Eamon began walking quickly down the path.

He had reached the bottom of the hill and was crossing the peat bog when he saw the man return in a hurry to his car. Eamon began running. Seeing the car beginning to move he ran downhill, away from the camp, trying to intercept it. He reached the track ahead of it and jumped out holding his hands up. The little car accelerated towards him. He could see the driver, a young man with eyes open wide and mouth half agape. He drove straight at Eamon, forcing him to dive off the road into the deep ditch. When he climbed out the car was bouncing down the track at full speed. He walked back up the track to the camp gate.

The chain-link fence was ten feet high and razor wire curled along the top. The gate was shut but just inside there was a small shed from which heavy boots, legs, and a belly in a bright yellow jacket protruded. Eamon called out and the man leaned forward in his chair, revealing a heavy, square face with a beard. The man looked at him for a few seconds, as if deciding if Eamon was worth the trouble of getting out of his chair, then he got up and came over to the gate. He stood so close that Eamon could smell his sweat and deodorant but he did not extend any kind of greeting.

'Is the manager here?' said Eamon.

'No.'

'Who is here? Why is this camp here?' The man turned his back on him and took a two-way radio from his belt. He spoke into it in an Eastern European language and Eamon did not understand. Behind the guard, on the other side of the camp, another man in a yellow jacket came out onto the platform in front of a porta-cabin. He replied into a similar handset as he looked towards the gate.

'Manager busy,' said the guard.

'He doesn't look busy to me.' Eamon waved at the man at the porta-cabin. The man spoke into his radio and the guard's radio crackled with his voice.

'You must make appointment, you want speak,' said the guard.

'Can I come in?'

'Is not safe. You not wear safety,' he gestured at Eamon's clothes, 'Health and Safety.'

'How do I make an appointment?' The guard spoke into his radio and the man at the cabin replied. The guard ambled over to his hut and came back with a card printed with '*Enerpro Energy Solutions*', and a website address. 'Thanks,' said Eamon. He took out his phone and dialled Edgar Dupuy's number but there was no signal. 'Where can I get a signal?' The guard shrugged and pointed down the road towards Loch Houn. Eamon walked, looking at his phone and cursing. He had walked a mile before he got through to Edgar's recorded message.

'Edgar, this is Eamon. Call me immediately. I've been to visit the dam, as you suggested. It is a lovely walk, but why is there a construction camp still here? I look forward to hearing from you.' He called Rona. 'How did you get on?'

'A lot of strange stuff. No-one knows anything about the car. But there's some odd things about the woman and the child, and what Joel did.'

'What?'

'Well, she never came out. Joel brought her groceries. The child was seen occasionally playing in the garden, but they say it was sick, a weak child, and very pale. Obviously the father was white. Then it wasn't seen for a good month before the murder. And then the morning of the fire, before Joel lit it, people were watching; he did some sort of strange ceremony before he struck the lighter. He was moaning and crying they said, and he walked round the shed first one way, then the other, stopping and bowing, and getting down on his knees, and going round and round, and then he lit the shed on fire and just sat there in the garden, crying his eyes out, waiting until the police came.'

'But the police know all this?'

'Yes, of course, they took statements from everyone.'

'What about Mrs Drummond, did you speak to her?'

'Yes. What she meant, by "You should know", is that you own the house. At least Glencul Estate owns the house, and two others in the gulag.'

'Who lives in the others?'

'They're empty. Been empty since they were bought.'

'Where are you now?'

'Feeding cattle.'

'I might need a lift, is it OK if I call you later?'

'Sure,' she said, and he could tell she was smiling.

He tapped the screen and straight away it rang. It was Edgar.

'Hello Eamon. I'm glad that you've been to look at the dam. It is splendid isn't it? Where are you now?'

'I'm almost at the head of Loch Houn.'

'I'll come and pick you up. I'll explain about the camp. It's actually a good thing that it's still there. I'll be there in about an hour. Toodlepip.' He ended the call. Eamon carried on walking. Even over the phone Edgar could communicate that strange mixture of breezy good humour and anxiety.

Pyotr Tiranasov, an old man, sat behind a desk with metal legs and a surface of plastic veneer. The unexpected winter sun was low beyond the window behind him, lighting up his unkempt hair like a halo, casting his face into shadow and catching the whorls of cigarette smoke that rose, turned, settled and coated the walls, the plans of the dam on the walls, the calendar with the picture of the half-naked woman and everything else in the cabin, with a yellow nicotine tinge. The room stank of cigarette smoke. He smoked three packs a day, and instead of using a watch, he counted; one every fifteen minutes unless he was agitated, but he was rarely agitated now. He had timed himself once and found it remarkable how regular his smoking was. He was on number twenty eight. It was about two o'clock. The young man in the ski jacket and orange hat leant back in his chair against the wall. Pyotr remembered a time when he had held some affection for this young man, James Peery, a few years back, when he had first met him. He had had an inkling of paternal feeling for a foolish, lazy, young man, always grinning and smoking too much weed. Happier days. Days before Flieber, days before the dam. Days before Peery had become Sigurson, and his smile had become cold. Pyotr drew heavily on number twenty eight. All of it was Flieber, not Sigurson. Guilt. Up to our necks in guilt. What can be done? Long ago he should have drowned Flieber in a bucket, like a puppy. But he didn't do things like that anymore, not himself. And Flieber had paid, a lot; not so much now, but perhaps he would again.

'He's asking you to close things down for a while,' said Sigurson, 'Especially the next shipment.'

'It is not possible,' said Pytor. He had a cigarette-stained voice and an accent, but his English had been aquired with the benefit of a grammar book.

'He wants you to know that he'll offset the costs.' Pyotr laughed.

'He is very good at offering what he does not have. Let me see my costs on the table, in cash, then I will think about it.'

'He says you have to shoulder some of the blame, because of Grigor.'

'Let him come here and talk to my face.'

'He's trying to keep his head down.'

'The assumption, the mistake, is that my business is somehow secondary in importance to his business.' We sacrifice everything for money, he thought. Everything to this God. 'Somethings can't be stopped when they have begun, you know; they have a certain momentum.'

'He says he understands that.'

'It can't be stopped,' said Pyotr. 'It's too late. There are other factors in play here, not just you and your shit.' He spat out the last word. Sigurson was silent for a while, looking at the floor, then he shrugged.

'It was a request, not a demand.'

'Where is Grigor?' said Pyotr.

'Grigor's laying low.' The young man shifted his wieght and the material of his jacket and trousers made a hissing sound.

'What you going to do about all this?' said Pyotr. Sigurson shrugged. 'What are you going to do about your woman? The police are watching her now.'

'Social Services.'

'Police, Social Services, newspapers.'

'You don't need to worry about that.'

'If you have a problem, I have a problem. I don't want a problem.' There was silence as Pyotr stared at the tendrils of the last draw on number twenty-eight. He closed his eyes and held the bridge of his nose between thumb and forefinger. 'James,' he said, 'You know, what you are, what you become, is never anyone else's fault. You do know that?' He opened his eyes. Sigurson looked at him and dropped the smile, revealing a face that Pyotr had come to revile; hard, afraid and certain. 'Do you remember when I first met you what it was you wanted? You remember? Jamaica. You wanted to live in Jamaica, in a hut on the beach, with a girl and a big bag of weed.' Sigurson looked at the floor, then up again at Pyotr with the smile returned.

'I was an idiot then,' he said, and his clothes hissed as he stood up to leave. 'I didn't know anything. I didn't know who I was.'

Before long Eamon smelt the sea. The tide was high and had risen through the band of brown weed and beyond the shore of stones to cover the short grass at the edge of the loch, and air bubbles were percolating from pockets trapped beneath the stones. 'The devil boiling his kettle,' he had been told as a child. A new pier had been built at the head of the loch. Thick concrete piles led out fifty metres to the deeper water, to where the tide never left. The old stone jetty and boathouse that he remembered from childhood fishing trips lay further along the northern shore. He walked to the boathouse. It was ramshackle. Sheets of rust red corrugated iron had been blown off the roof, but the door was still held shut by a rusting chain and padlock. He peered through a hole into the gloom. She was still there, amid a mess of ropes, buoys, beer cans and upturned fishing crates; the 'Mirabelle', the dinghy they had used for mackerel fishing, looking as if she had been tossed there by a storm. He tried the chain but it was fast. He resolved to repair it all, fix the roof, take her fishing again, one day. He walked back and out to the end of the pier where he smoked and waited. Half an hour passed. The sun began to descend towards the top of the mountain on the southern shore. Edgar Dupuy pulled up at the end of the pier in a Land Rover, effusive and too cheerful.

'Splendid isn't it?'

'What?'

'The pier. *Enerpro* built it so they could bring materials in. Otherwise they would have had to rebuild the road from here to Glencul.'

'So *Enerpro* built the dam. But that was two years ago. Why are they still here?'

'They kept the camp going because they were supposed to put up wind-turbines further up the glen. But there's been problems.'

'What problems?' said Eamon. They got into the Land Rover.

'Mainly Lampreys. *Lampetra Fluvialis* to be precise. A rare kind of hideous eyeless fish, discovered in the upper reaches of the Fashie burn. So the whole thing had to be put on hold while they do a scientific study. Pain in the arse, but rules is rules.'

'Why didn't you tell me about all this when I was in the office the other day?'

'Well,' said Edgar, keeping his eyes on the road. 'I suppose I'm used to running things without your input. And your father was so ill for the last couple of years. I'll show you the site now. If you want to know all the details, all you have to do is ask. It is your estate.'

'It's my estate but the security guard at that camp wouldn't let me in.'

'Latvians. They're all Latvians. He probably didn't understand what you wanted. Nor who you were. We can go there now. No problem.'

'Yes, let's,' said Eamon. Edgar drove quickly and they were soon at the gate of the camp. He got out and spoke to the guard. Eamon watched him smiling and gesticulating. The guard spoke into his radio. Edgar raised his voice and pointed back at the Land Rover. Up at the porta-cabin the other man came out, stood in the doorway and spoke into his radio. The guard replied and Edgar came back without his cheerful grin.

'Sorry old chap, they don't seem all that keen on letting us in. Health and Safety you know.'

'Let me get this straight; you employ these people, am I right?'

'Not strictly speaking. It's a partnership.'

'But this is estate land, this camp?'

'Yes, but there's a lease,' said Edgar, 'They lease it from you. The guard is only working under orders. There's nothing he can do. Why do you want to get in anyway? There's nothing to see.' Eamon drummed his fingers on the dashboard. He thought about telling Edgar about the man on the bike and being thrown in the river, but as he stared hard at his factor he realised that Edgar could not meet his gaze. He was staring ahead out of the windscreen and Eamon felt a mixture of curiosity and a surprising pity as he saw that droplets of sweat had appeared on his forehead. Edgar was literally squirming. 'I can speak to the boss,' he said, 'tell him who you are, if you insist. Let's leave it for now. I'll show you where the turbines are planned.' He gunned the engine and they lurched on up the track.

First they stopped on the dam. The two of them got out and walked along its hundred metre length. It was a long, low dam, no more than thirty feet high at its highest above the peat on the dry side. It was as if Edgar couldn't stop himself from talking, about megawatts and head heights, prices per unit and feed-in tariffs, policy and government changes. They went back to the Land Rover and carried on up the glen. A couple of miles past the end of the dam loch they saw a large stone house on the other side of the glen from the road, set among some pine trees. The building was an old one, but the stonework was clean and freshly pointed, and there was a long extension at the rear. The windows were new too, no astragals, but blank sheets of tinted glass, and everything was encircled by a new, high concrete wall.

'What happened to Tarvin Lodge?' said Eamon. He remembered the former shooting lodge as a ruin; his grandfather had had the roof removed to avoid taxes.

'Amazing isn't it, what they did. Talk about money.'

'Who?'

'An American company bought it out of the blue about five years ago. It wasn't even on the market and they paid a good price too. Your dad couldn't believe his luck. Then they spent millions doing it up.'

'Was this *Enerpro*?'

'*Enerpro* did the construction work, but the company was…*Glenpro* I think. An American company.'

'What's it for?'

'Some sort of shooting, fishing lodge for an American billionaire I think. I don't know because it has never been used for anything. No-one has visited since it was finished. Maybe he died.' They drove up, switch-backing as the road rose until the Land Rover was crunching through a recent snowfall. Edgar stopped and pointed out to the moor where the turbines were to go. They could see the scar of the track half obscured by the snow. It led across the peat but then stopped, a job cut short.

'The whole thing awaits the lamprey study,' said Eamon. Then, pointing to dark eastern clouds; 'We'd better turn back. Snow coming in.'

They drove in silence for a while as Eamon debated how, when, and how much he should confront his factor.

'Edgar, why didn't you tell me that I owned the house where the child was killed?' He watched the knuckles whiten as they gripped the wheel.

'You didn't ask. Do you want to know about every tenant you have?' There was even a note of anger in his voice this time.

'Since when have we owned houses in the gulag, and why?'

'Since about three years ago. Social Services came to me. They were looking for housing for refugees. I had nothing empty but at the same time these three houses came up for sale; repossessions, very cheap, no-other buyers. It was too good a deal to turn down. Guaranteed rents. Government money. I bought them.'

'My father bought them?'

'He wasn't really taking an interest by then,' said Edgar. Eamon smiled at the euphemism. By then the booze had pretty much addled his father's brain. Not enough for him to be declared incompetent, but enough for *de facto* power of attorney to be in the hands of the Dupuy's.

'But two of those houses are empty.'

'Yes. Well it turned out not to be such a good idea. The council only took one. But I'm reliably informed that they will be taking the other two, soon.' They bumped down the road, past Tarvin Lodge, past the dam and past the camp towards Loch Houn. When they reached the tarmac of the road to Glencul the tyres hummed as Edgar sped up. 'I know your dad hated the gulag. But it was my job to keep the place above water. The dam was still at the planning stage back then.'

'It's fine Edgar, don't worry about it.' Eamon was tiring of the effort to work out when Edgar was lying and when he was not, and he hadn't eaten since the morning. 'What about Stevie Van? Did you find out anything about that?' Edgar was suddenly grinning again, beyond suspicion.

'Aha! Bit of a mystery there. Here.' He took a large envelope from the door pocket and tossed it onto Eamon's lap. Eamon took out a photocopy of a map that was paper-clipped to a handwritten letter. 'I must say I think I may have a hidden talent as a detective. That took some finding, I can tell you.'

The map showed the edge of the village and the quarry where Stevie lived. A red line was drawn around the whole quarry, including the track that led from the village road. There was no other writing, only a reference number next to the red line. The letter too was a photocopy. It was written in a relaxed copperplate, handwriting learned in an age before computers. It was from Torquil Dupuy, Edgar's father, to Richard Blackwell, the family lawyer. It was dated June 1990.

'Dear Richard,

Enclosed please find the relevant plan as discussed last week, (compliments to Molly). I have given the matter some thought and I can accept that there are things above my pay grade; nevertheless, it bears repeating that in my opinion this chap is the wrong sort.

Your humble and obedient servant,

Torquil'

'That's all you've got?' said Eamon.

'Turn it over.' Eamon turned the letter. There was a note on the back in the same handwriting.

'Phone call re. the above RB last night, emphatic, "Leave Steven Reid alone."'

'If you want more you'll have to take it up with Richard,' said Edgar.

When Edgar had dropped him at Duncul, Eamon went to the tower door. It was locked, but there was a note. *'Key under pot,'* it said. He made a mental note to talk to Kirsty about security and another to take a key with him when he next went out. In the study he called Rona. Twenty minutes later she arrived with sausage and chips from the café in the village.

'So what have we got?' she said as they sat by the fire, chips on laps.

'I don't know. I'm completely confused.'

'Maybe we need a big board, with photographs and drawing pins.'

'Maybe a large dram will do.' He rose and poured two from the decanter.

'We need to decide what it is we want to know.'

'Well for a start I want to know who threw me in the river, and why. That leads to *Enerpro*. Then I want to know who tried to knock me down in a car, and why. He was scared, of me, or perhaps of the *Enerpro* people, perhaps of the man on the bike who was in that compound. Then I want to know why he was photographing the dam. I also want to know why Edgar Dupuy is such prolific liar.'

'Hasn't he come clean now?'

'Has he hell. He sat in his office and told me rents don't pay etcetera, but three years ago he was buying up houses to rent out to the council. That doesn't make sense. He's leasing ground to these *Enerpro* people, and they won't even let him into the camp. He pretends that makes sense but I could see he was pretty pissed off about it.' He drained his glass and refilled it. 'I want to know why a multimillion-pound building with no conceivable use has been built in my back yard. I want to take Edgar Dupuy and stick his head down the toilet, the little shit. Then I want to know why the mother of the child, Isabel, had a stone that is almost identical to the one beneath Duncul that almost nobody knows about. How and why? Then I want to know why Joel Kennedy killed a child, and what that strange ritual was all about. Was he just mad? You see Stevie Van is right. Drugs aren't enough to explain that. And what was Isabel's relationship with Joel? You said the child was pale, it must have a white father. Perhaps Joel was the father?

'We need to speak to Isabel,' said Rona.

'I tried that. Social Services are impenetrable. Like talking to a brick wall.' He took another gulp and paused. 'And I want to know what's going on with Stevie Van and those loons at *The Misty Glen*. They're as fishy as hell.'

For a long time they sat by the fire. Eamon wanted her to leave and wanted her to stay. Ten years ago he had treated her like dirt, and still niether of them had mentioned that. It was an elephant in the room, for him at least, but he could not bring himself to remind her of how he had behaved. And did she not care that he was perfectly capable of doing the same thing again? He felt exhaustion reveal itself in a kind of terror that he had grown to accept as familiar. It was an experience of the fragility of the world, as if all that made sense, all sanity, all order and all love, lay poised on the edge of an abyss and all that embraced us was a horrifying beauty, an ice-cold nothingness. It was the sensation that nothing lay beneath nor above, save shadows, reflections and chimera. He stared at the flames, drinking in their light like an antidote. He became aware that she was watching him, but did not return her gaze and let his eyelids close.

'It was bad, wasn't it?' she said. He opened his eyes and saw this beautiful girl, the light shining from her lips. What did she want? She did not want to know. No-one that is sane would ever want to know. And yet she asked. Yes, she had met death, but not killing. Killing was something different. Killing was seeing into the world that should not be seen. 'What was your job over there?' she asked. He had dreaded that question when he had first come back from Afghanistan. He had anticipated it for years before realising that no-one ever asked, not even Kate, especially not Kate, and he had come to accept and regret that no-one ever would. Now, here was Rona McColl, the girl from next door, asking. 'You were in the Paras weren't you?' She was asking. When he closed his eyes again all he could think of was Joel Kennedy, circling the shed, weeping, groaning, round this way and round the other, bowing to the ground, raising his hands to the sky.

'Yes, for a while,' he said. Raising his hands to the sky, pouring petrol, setting fire. 'Then I was in something else. Reconnaissance. Letting the air force know where to drop their bombs.' Setting fire. Child sacrifice. Sacrifice for what? That was hard to tell. Killing terror. War on an abstract noun. How do you do that? Fighting fire with fire. Terror with terror. 'Then I went on to moving trucks around. Logistics. I wasn't very good at that.' He looked up and smiled. Hopeless in fact. 'Then they found something I was good at. Telling the difference between the truth and a lie. There were a lot of lies in Afghanistan.' He closed his eyes again. When he opened them the fire was out, there was a blanket over him, and she had gone.

CHAPTER NINE

The night suffocated the land. The street-lights struggled towards an impenetrable sky, like votive candles against the darkness, and the lights from the windows of the village and the castle barely emerged from the thick drizzle. The moon and the stars were dead memories. A few cars stirred on the roads. Marie McPherson driving to a night shift in Inverness with thoughts of children and patients. Malcom Henderson coming home from Aberdeen, after three weeks on the rigs, with thoughts of twining limbs and beer. Gavin and Glyn Stott, their van creeping like a wounded beast, rattling and growling up the steep hill on the road to Loch Houn.

'You need to fix that fookin' heater,' she said, shivering in a tracksuit, her arms folded on the roll of fat at her waist.

'He says don't spend money.'

'Fixin' a heater int spending money. It's a bloody necessity.'

'Do what Pyotr says is a bloody necessity,' said Gavin, and the words turned both their mouths into thin lines. They drove on in silence. The road twisted and the engine whined on the slopes.

From the top of the hill they could make out the tiny lights below. 'Ere, you won't need heaters in Fuengirola,' he grinned, and she grinned, and then as they descended their mouths hardened into lines again.

Lights shining out of a black loch and a black sky. Lights moving on the water. The smell of diesel smoke and sea and the sound of an engine from the depths and the sound of sea whipped to foam by propellers. The grinding of steel burnt black by oils. The whispers of men. The screech of steel hawsers and the straining of steel beams, lights swinging, lights probing. Men in yellow jackets and thick boots. There are three black pickups lined up at the end of the pier and the *Eloise*, a small cargo vessel sits light in the water, its sides high above the pier, leaning against the fenders and making them squeak. A white cube in a metal cage, the size of a small car is lowered onto one pickup. It roars off into the darkness, and the headlights swing along the track up the hill. A white cube in a metal cage is lowered onto the next pickup, and the next. Then the lights go out and there is silence. Gavin and Glyn rattle to a stop at the end of the pier and walk into the darkness towards the boat. Glyn holds her sides and keeps her legs together as she walks, as if this posture will keep out the cold. Gavin wears a cowboy hat because he always does. 'Get back to the van,' they are told, and they get back, and sit breathing in smoke as if that will keep out the cold. Offloading a boat is a difficult job and there are tides to think about. The pickups roar back down the track from the hill, big engines spinning, mud flying, back along the pier, and the white cubes in metal cages descend from the darkness into the arc lights and onto the pickups again. Men shout whispers at each other and signal to the crane driver. Hawsers creek, fenders squeal, the cubes bump down into the pickups and they roar off into the night again. Then a pallet of cement bags is lowered onto the pier and the plastic covering sliced open.

'That's us,' says Glyn, and Gavin reverses the van along the pier. They listen as a thick voice counts off.

'One, two, three, four...' the voice expressing the strain and the numbers coming slower as the effort of lifting mounts. 'Ten, eleven,' then the thump in the back of the van for 'twelve, thirteen, fourteen,' up to twenty as the van settles down onto its suspension.

Rona counted the steps from the bed towards the door of her mother's bedroom. On the third step, two before the door would be reached, her mother would speak. On the third step the silence she kept all through the long, clumsy indignity of being washed and dressed would be broken, and the tension released, every morning.

'How is Eamon?' said Harriet McColl, on the third step. Rona stopped.

'He's well,' she said, without turning, and took the fourth.

'You should go on the pill,' said her mother. Rona's hand grasped the door handle. She turned.

'Not really necessary, mother.'

'Just a thought, dear.' She waved her daughter out of the door. Rona did not stop in the kitchen where the kettle was boiling on the stove. She walked straight out to the yard and thumbed the quad engine into life. She drove too fast through the gate and down the track towards the river. In the river field she turned off the engine and sat smiling into the sunlight and rain that fell on her cheeks. She tapped a number into her phone. A young female voice answered;

'Social Services Highland.'

'Hello,' Rona said in her best voice; clear, smiling, authoritative; her mother's expensively educated debutante voice. 'I wonder if you could help me. I'm trying to get in touch with an Isabel Mtetu...' They put her on hold, and gave her Vivaldi, and 'can I take your name?' and 'I'm afraid I can't give you that information.'

'Of course, I quite understand. I wouldn't dream of asking you to break any rules but perhaps you could pass some information on to whoever is dealing with her case. I am the owner of the house she was occupying in Glencul, and while we were cleaning it out for the next tenant I came across some letters, which I can only imagine belong to her. Is there some way we can send them to her?' She was served up Vivaldi again, then;

'Hello, Mrs McColl, can we take a number?'

'Yes, of course.'

The wind and the sea had lessened during the night, as if pondering calm, but then the dawn seemed to bring some deep antagonism to the depths,

and the waters heaved, as if on the point of vomiting something up, and
the air began to growl around the boat like a hungry animal. Vanneck had
cooked breakfast and laid a table. He led Lillian through to the salon, but
his plans were defeated by the lurching of the boat, and they both sank
into armchairs with cups of coffee. He had asked Brighton to join them,
an attempt to manufacture an air of civility and normality for his wife's
sake, but when Brighton came down from the bridge an awkward silence
descended, save for the rattling, quivering, and muted wind and rain
beyond the thick glass. She had never liked Brighton, perhaps mirroring
her husband's mistrust or for some mysterious feminine reason. Vanneck
signalled with his eyes for his captain to leave. When he had gone the
silence lasted a long time, until she broke it.

'Sam.'

'Yes.'

'I want you to tell me what you are not telling me.'

'What do you mean?'

'What I mean is, I know you are lying. How did they die? Why? I want
to know how the Singa died.'

'God, Lily, some things should never be told.'

'I want to know. You can't keep all this to yourself. If it is something to
do with us, with me, I want to know. What happened?'

'They died on the boat. What can I say? I wasn't there. Something
happened, on the way. There was trouble, fighting. People got shot.
When the boat arrived in Scotland they were all dead.'

'People got shot? By who? Why?'

'The people running the boat! For God's sake, Lily, it's not a simple
thing, taking eighty men, women and children, incognito out of Africa
and sending them to Europe. It's illegal, and that's only the start of your
problems. What kind of men do you think I could find to do that sort of
thing? Huh? This wasn't P and O cruises. People smugglers. They were
gangsters, thugs. Men out to make money by any means necessary. Men
with guns. Men with blood on their hands.' He paused, but she did not
reply.

'Look, there was trouble on the boat. I paid for everything to do be
done properly, but I wasn't there! I trusted people. I couldn't get too

close. I had three governments bearing down on me anyway because of the Wiseman patent. Do you remember that? The whole thing was done in secret, in the dark. Something happened, off the coast of Spain. That's all I know. There was an argument, a fight, and there were shots fired and the Singa...' he trailed off. 'The Singa were locked in the hold. They were locked in the hold for two weeks. Christ!'

'By the time they got to Scotland, they were all dead, all except three. Three women. Three women survived. That's it. I dropped it, then and there. Everything. I told Flieber I wanted nothing more to do with it.'

'Flieber?'

'Yes, Flieber. Remember that scruffy little Yank?'

'Yes of course I do. I liked him.'

'Yes, well, he was running the whole show. Still is.'

'Running what?'

'He's obsessive. Determined, ambitious. He refused to come back, refused to close it down. I cut him off. He used his own money. He carried on with the programme, with the three women.'

'What programme?'

'Lily...' he said, and tears were falling.

'What happened to all those bodies?'

'Lily... I don't know. I cut him off. I stopped it.'

'Stopped what?' she yelled with her weak voice, but at that moment an immense shudder passed through the boat, a vibration from bow to stern, and they were almost thrown from their seats as the whole structure paused and seemed to move backwards for a moment. At the same time there was a grinding roar from somewhere beneath and behind them. Vanneck jumped up and held her, then ran up the stairway to the bridge and Brighton.

'What was that?'

'Nothing, just a big wave. There's a heavy gale coming in.' He pointed to a screen that showed a swirling satellite image. 'It's moving west to east and we are going north so we'd best just keep going. I'd say about ten or twelve hours of rough, then it'll ease off.' Vanneck watched Brighton's calm face watching the sea. He felt soothed by the view from the bridge, the shifting bows ahead, adhering to a rhythm that made sense, whereas in the salon the rolling and shuddering of the boat appeared random and meaningless. The screens and buttons and switches gave the impression at least that there was an element of control, and down there there was a woman and questions that he did not want to engage with, not now; maybe when they were in calmer water. He went back down to her.

'It's going to be rough for a while. It's better if you sleep through this.'

'I don't want to sleep,' she said. 'I want to talk to you, Sam.' But her voice was weak and she offered no resistance as he placed the pills in her mouth and held the glass to her lips.

Eamon's knock on the door of a house on the edge of the village was answered by Ira Mack, a small woman with short hair. She looked annoyed. Eamon apologised for disturbing them and asked for Finlay. 'Finlay's here,' he was told, 'unfortunately.' Finlay had not been to work since the fire.

He was a solid man of a similar age to Eamon, lying in jeans and a t-shirt on a couch and watching a game show. He stood up to shake Eamon's hand and invited him to sit down but did not switch off the television. Their conversation was punctuated by clapping, laughter and the promise of great prizes. Finlay sat with his head in his hands.

'I can't get it out of my head,' he said. 'I see it in my sleep.' Eamon asked him if he had known the boy and Finlay objected. 'Why do you have to ask me that? I did know him. I saw him when I was down at my brother's. Skinny wee thing. Sad wee sick-looking thing, playing in the garden. Not playing football or anything, just sort of poking around with a stick, standing about, looking up at the sky.'

'Was there anything unusual, when you found him in the shed?'

'Unusual? Burnt to death, that's unusual.'

'I mean, was there anything strange about what was in the shed? Any strange objects, or writing, or drawings or stuff?'

'It was burnt to hell. It was just a normal shed. Tools, a freezer, a workbench, he was on the workbench. The only unusual thing was the branches. There were branches, burning, all around the workbench. Like he'd set a bonfire.'

Rain and sleet hit Eamon as he left the Mack's house. The beginning of a gale coming in from the west was roaring in the tops of the trees. He walked into the gulag. The police tape around the house had snapped and was flapping in the wind. The white tent had gone, revealing the black spars of the burnt-out shed. *His* shed, he realised. He entered the garden.

There was no work-bench, no freezer, no tools, no branches, only what remained of a wooden floor and half of the walls, blackened, broken and soaked with rain and sleet. He peered through the windows of the house. *His* house, he realised. He tried the back and front doors but both were locked. Edgar must have the key, he thought. He took out his phone to call him. As he listened to it ringing he looked up at the steel pole that supported the prison camp lights and the camera, fifty feet above the ground, pointing directly at him and the house, like an accusing eye. Edgar Dupuy wasn't answering.

As he walked up the drive to Duncul he saw Mike Mack working with a chainsaw among the beech trees. He cut the engine as Eamon approached and their conversation was accompanied by the whistle of the wind.

'Did Kirsty speak to you, about the tinks?' said Eamon.

'Aye. Been a while since we've had any trouble from them.'

'What trouble? When?'

When he was inside Eamon found Kirsty standing on a chair in the hall, dusting paintings.

'Why didn't you tell me about the break in?' he said. She stopped dusting and looked at him as if she was about to clip his ear.

'Nothing was taken. We didn't want to trouble you. It was just after your father died.' He asked her to show him the window that had been broken and she slowly got down from the chair and led him to the basement. 'Mike said it was tinks, but they don't usually break in. I think it would have been boys from the village. Probably the Brights from the gulag.' She switched on the fluorescent tube and pointed to one of the slit windows high above. 'It goes out to the kitchen garden. It would have been a boy. Only a boy could get through. But what is there to steal in here? They didn't take anything. The only damage was the window and the padlock on the door to the stone room. We replaced them both.'

'Clarice Wright,' said Rona, breathless from her ride in the wind from
Burnum. 'Phoned me this afternoon, she seemed very anxious that Isabel
should get her letters back. She's her social worker.'

    'Did she say where Isabel is now,'

    'No, but she said someone would be coming to pick them up today
or tomorrow.'

    'Then what?' said Eamon.

    'It's a name. It's something.'

Richard Blackwell was a huge man, more than six feet tall, with an
enormous stomach and a bald head like a watermelon. He had gappy
yellow teeth, bulging eyes, and spoke with a thundering, self-amused
voice. 'I'll arrive in time for supper,' he said on the phone, and duly
did, in a tiny car. He held the sherry glass between sausage like thumb
and forefinger, drank from it with a pout, swilling the wine around his
mouth and smacking his lips, and had three refills before he got through
the fishing to be had at Buie, his cousin's estate in Sutherland, and *La
Traviata*, which he had witnessed in Inverness.

    'Well,' he said, 'I think perhaps we should direct our attention to
Steven Reid. Or as he is cryptically known in these parts, "Stevie Van".
Somewhere in the vaults! The vaults! There are papers!' He held out his
glass for another sherry. 'Thank-you. Are you sure you want to know?'
he chuckled. 'Actually there is nothing like that. It's all a bit of a muddle
really. Rather disappointing you'll find. Stevie moved up here, summer
of '89. Plonked himself in the quarry. Dupuy senior wanted him moved
on, *immédiatement*. Tried to do it himself, as was his wont, then called the
local constabulary. But *pater tuus* declined to pursue the issue. Deputy
Dupuy was pretty pissed off. He asked yours truly to intervene. Your
father and I enjoyed a fantastic supper in town, at the station hotel I
seem to remember. He was in the mood for charity, which, God bless
his memory, was not his habit. He said he didn't see the harm in Stevie
staying for a while.' Richard paused to slurp, leant back in his chair and
looked about the room with a satisfied smile.

'That's it?'

'Yes. He understood that Deputy Dupuy was not going to be happy with a hippy on his patch so he asked me to come up with a ruse, to keep his factor off Stevie's case.'

'Hence the plan of the quarry?'

'Zigackly. I had another splendid dinner with Dupuy next time he was in the toon, compliments of my dear departed housekeeper. Those were the days! Anyway, I informed Dupuy that it was all hush hush and *sotto voce* and all that, and nudge-nudge wink-wink, and he was to draw up a plan of the locus concerned and it was all to be swept under the table.'

'What was?'

'Aha, that was the genius of it! Nothing, Duncul, nothing! There was nothing to be swept; so I swept away, and under the table it went. Dupuy sent the plan, and the note you saw. End of story.'

'So he has no title to the land?'

'Mmm,' the lawyer rocked his enormous head from side to side. 'Yes and no. In the final analysis he has thirty years of occupancy.'

'Does that count?'

'It counts for as good as, under Scots law.'

'So he does own the quarry?'

'You're very keen on the definitive my boy. Don't be so. It's not all black and white. He does and he doesn't. We can leave it at that.'

'Can I evict him?'

'You can try. But you'll have a hell of a job, and in the end you'll fail.' For the first time Blackwell's expression was serious as he stared at Eamon over his sherry glass. Eamon met the gaze and remembered the note Dupuy had written on the back of his letter: '*Phone call re. the above RB last night, emphatic, "Leave Steven Reid alone."*' That was his father's instruction and RB, loyal beyond the interference of the grave, was still enforcing it. 'Probably easier to shoot him. Though as your lawyer I advise against it.'

'He's a drug dealer.'

'He's an entrepreneur!' grinned Blackwell.

'You've heard about the murder, of the child?'

'Marijuana madness? You think? Come on, you'll have to dig a little bit deeper if you want to find the source of that particular tragedy. The police are.'

'What do you mean?'

'Something a little bird told me.'

'What?'

'Still playing detective are we? Thought you'd retired. Take up fishing if I were you. It's good for the soul.'

'What do you know?' said Eamon. Blackwell raised his empty glass in reply and Eamon obliged.

'More of a big fat bird, actually. My friend Thomson Breavis, of university days. Always thought he was a bit of a loser meself, but one can never tell in this day and age. Do you know who he is?'

'Haven't a clue.'

'He's Procurator Fiscal Inverness. And I probed him, knowing I was on my way here and having a family interest and all that. I'm very good at probing you know. But I'm telling you this under the seal of the confessional you understand?'

'Of course.'

'Prejudicial to the course of the law and all that. According to him, said unfortunate infant was not killed in the fire.' Eamon took the news in silence. 'Said unfortunate infant was deceased…'

'I know, four weeks before.'

'How the devil did you know that?'

'They said it on the news. The date of death was given as the first of November, not December, which was the date of the fire. Why would they make that mistake?'

'Well, there you go, I didn't tell you a thing.'

'So where was the body, for those four weeks?'

'Do I need to tell you?'

'In the freezer?' Blackwell gave a ponderous nod. 'Cause of death?'

'Acute anaemia.'

'So, not a murder at all then, a natural death, an illness?' Eamon could not conceal the hope from his voice.

'Not so fast, my boy. Acute anaemia can be caused by a chronic iron deficiency. But then why wasn't that picked up by Social Services?'

That evening, after Richard Blackwell had devoured the better part of a baron of beef ('a labourer is worth his wages my boy!') and had departed northwards into the dark, Rona rode in on her noisy beam of light. They talked in the unlit hall.

'So it wasn't a murder then,' she said. 'It was a cremation. What about the Kennedys? Do they know?'

'Apparently not. And they can't be told. The police are building a case.'

'But that's horrible! They think Joel did it!'

'What's to say he didn't?' Eamon was surprised at the harshness in his voice. 'It could still have been Joel! He could have killed the child and then put the body in the freezer.'

'Then why did he burn it? Why do that whole ceremony thing in full view of everyone?'

'I don't know!'

'You have to tell the Kennedys!'

'Do you remember what I asked you, when you came over that night? Can you keep secrets?' She was quiet.

'Where does it leave us?' she said, peering at him through the gloom.

'I don't know.'

'I'm going home.'

'I'm sorry. Come up and have a drink.'

'No,' she said, making for the door. 'Mother is expecting me back.'

CHAPTER TEN

Early the next morning the priest from Aberfashie arrived on a bicycle. He was a thin Pole wearing spectacles and bright green lycra. Kirsty showed him into the hall, and he sat on the edge of an armchair, cradling his helmet and admiring the vaulted ceiling thirty feet above. It was a pip above freezing in the hall, and Eamon put on a hat before he went down. The priest was thin-lipped, nervous, but with a steely purpose, as if he had summoned courage to enter a den of iniquity. Eamon supposed that he had found out, as every Aberfashie priest eventually did, that the Ansgars were Catholic and he was intent on recapturing a fidelity that had been lost with Eamon's father. He wanted to know if Isabel had been Catholic, perhaps assuming the possibility from her Congolese origins. Eamon, unable to offer even a guess, felt a mixture of pity and irritation. Yes, there was something predatory about him, seeking the gain of a soul from the devastation of grief, using death as a recruiting agent. But then written on the small face behind the round lenses, behind the nervousness and determination, there was something else. Nothing so much as an answer; perhaps only a question. Eamon imagined how every day the man must meet the stolid indifference of the young and the cynicism and mistrust of people like himself. In a world that was gradually, inexorably, abandoning faith, how did he persist in his own? How did faith persist amid the onslaught of the rational? Perhaps it was just the last flicker of a dying light. Perhaps he was only at the cusp of the long slide into self-pity and indulgence, drink-sodden and tormented by an imagination only weakly fought, the marks of the older priests that had passed through this house. He left, awkwardly, after long silences, clearly disappointed at not having been invited to dine nor return.

Later, the American novelist, Trib Rugleef, came to visit. When he had first visited, Eamon had been both irritated and intrigued. He was a short, young man with a mass of black curls, and an amiable and determined expression, a face of ambition and confidence, a face with a future. Later Eamon had idly googled the name, but had found nothing, not one hit, not even a Facebook page, and he had lost interest. Now he felt his mood darken when Kirsty announced that 'the writer' was in the hall.

As Eamon descended the stairs, the American greeted him with a voice emerging from somewhere behind the nose. He was wearing new brogues and a tweed jacket, like a tourist that has been to a 'Scottish' shop.

Eamon shook his hand a little too firmly. 'How is your writing going?' he said. He did not want to offer tea, and he dreaded the emergence of Kirsty from the shadows, bearing the tray.

'Well, I think,' said Rugleef, as if he was not in the habit of thinking about it. Eamon, being as rude as he was able, waited for him to carry on. Trib, being an American, found no difficulty in obliging. 'Glencul is an inspirational place. Where I'm situated I look over the whole village; I can see the river and the loch and of course this place. It's beautiful! And I think I'm really finding my voice here. And I'm getting to know people and the people are inspirational too, not that I'm writing about the village or the people, but in an oblique way, you know, events, everyday things are helping to move my imagination.' He paused, nodding his head, making the curls bob.

'That's good,' said Eamon.

'For example, I know it's a sad thing, but the murder, you know, of the

African child, has made me think a lot, not just about the plot but about the whole purpose of the book, what the deeper meaning is.' He pursed his lips and gazed into the empty fireplace. 'Did you know the child?'

'No.'

'Do you know the mother?'

'No,' said Eamon, wishing he could ask him to leave.

'I have to say, the whole thing is mystifying,' said Rugleef.

'What do you know about it?'

'Only what I've read in the press, and gossip, around the village. What do you know? I would have thought in your position people would talk to you more. I mean, what's intriguing about this part of the world is that there is still a kind of feudal structure. You know, perhaps you might consider yourself to have a kind of…paternal relationship with the people in the village. I know this is old-fashioned, but your family has been here a long time.' Eamon looked at him across the few feet of cold air that separated them. This was an American thing of course, straight-talking, pointing out the hidden obvious. The silence was broken by the arrival of Kirsty and the tea. Eamon, still reluctant, gestured to a chair.

'Maybe,' he said, looking at the floor. 'There might be some truth in what you say. A lot of them are tenants of mine.'

'That's what I thought. So, like, it's a terrible thing that happened, for the village, and for you personally.'

'Yes,' said Eamon. He poured and they drank.

'And are the police sure of their man? Is it, Kennedy, Joel Kennedy?' There was no question of letting Trib, of all people, know anything. Eamon already regretted telling Rona what Richard Blackwell had said.

'As far as I know. I'm not involved in the police investigation.'

'Oh, they haven't questioned you? I know it's gossip, but I heard that you owned the house where the child was killed.'

'No, and yes, I do own the house, but all that is handled by my factor.'

'Oh, I see, there's a level of separation of course. You know, I actually knew Joel.'

'Really?'

'Yeah, I met him a few times when I was out walking. We talked. He was a very odd guy.'

'In what way?'

'It's hard to put my finger on it, but I had a feeling about him. He was secretive, evasive, and I don't like to defame the dead, but there was something sinister about him. I know he's from here and I'm sure you knew him when he was younger but recently, he was scary crazy. I'm sure the drugs had a lot to do with it. I mean I've nothing against pot, but he was doing some serious stuff, I hear.' As he spoke Eamon felt an unnacountable rage rising. Now he wanted the American to leave, the nosy little shit. He yearned for an excuse to end the conversation, and found one in the distant ringing of the kitchen phone.

'Excuse me,' he said. He answered the phone but did not recognise the voice nor reply to it. When he returned to the hall he told Trib that he was sorry but he'd just been reminded of an appointment.

'Oh sure. I've gotta get back to work anyhow.' He got up. 'It's been great, I love this place, and anytime you want to come over to the caravan you're welcome, come and shoot the crap, watch a movie or something. I'm a great cook, even on the little shitty stove I got there.'

'Thanks,' said Eamon, crushing the offered hand. 'I'll keep it in mind.' He moved his guest towards the front door.

That evening, in a light rain, he once again found himself walking towards the quarry and once again turning around, and walking back towards the village. He paused at the entrance to the gulag and looked up under the lights to the camera. Of course the police would have the recordings. Perhaps they had the recordings from the beginning of November when the child had been put in the freezer. Perhaps. Perhaps the mother had killed the child. It happens. Perhaps Joel had discovered the body in the freezer. Why had she given him the stone? Was she simply mad? Driven mad by her own sin? Nothing could explain the man on the motorbike though, nothing but Clarice Wright. Clarice Wright would come and then what? Tell them nothing? He walked back towards the quarry, without any idea about what he was going to do there. He was on the dirt track, almost at the gateway, and he could see the caravans when he saw the door open and Stevie Van come out. He was dressed in a cagoule pulled tight around his head. Eamon stepped into the hedgerow and let him pass. When he was a hundred yards down the track he followed, conscious that Stevie only had to turn his head to discover him.

Stevie walked through the village and into the darkness on the other side, past the gate to Duncul and across the Ash Bridge. He was going to the *Misty*. Eamon hung back. There was no point in being spotted. There was no point in following, he thought, but he followed. When he reached the bar he paused on the road, debating whether or not to go in. He went into the courtyard behind which was surrounded by dilapidated and unlit sheds. On one side of the courtyard stood the white Transit van, and he recognised it as the one he had seen in the compound by the dam. Eamon went over to it and looked through the window at the crushed coffee cups and sweet wrappers on the dashboard. He walked around to the back of the van and was about to try the door when he heard footsteps and voices.

It was the voice of the woman from the bar with the northern accent and a voice of a man on the other side of the courtyard. Eamon sensed a movement and turned to find Stevie standing next to him. They both froze. Then Stevie took a hand from his jacket pocket in a slow movement and raised a finger to his lips. With his other hand he pointed twice towards a doorway in the shed behind the van. Eamon slipped into the shadows. He heard the van door open and saw shards of a torch beam flicker around the yard. The man, the woman and Stevie stopped talking. Eamon could only hear their footsteps and the rustle of Stevie's cagoule. He thought he could smell the woman above the damp air of the yard; a faint whiff of deodorant and a deeper note of unwashed flesh. He felt an intimacy with them and a strange warmth towards them, three other humans, standing so close. There was shuffling and then the sound of boots scraping on the metal floor of the van, something heavy shifting, then finally the voice of the woman.

'Good as new,' she said. Then the van door closing again and the sound of their footsteps towards the door of the bar. Eamon waited several minutes before he moved. He turned the handle of the van door by increments. It was pitch dark. He felt with his hand and crept forward on the metal floor. There was a smell of oil and dust. There was a paper bag; several, heavy, fat and square. Cement bags. They had had pallets of them at the camp. He crept out of the back of the van and closed the door. Then he walked in the shadows out of the yard, past the door to the bar and quickly along the darkness of the road. As he approached the Duncul gate he was about to turn in. He was going to call the police and tell them they could find a shipment of drugs in the back of a van at the *Misty Glen* bar. But the memory of that finger to the lips prevented him and he walked on, through the village, to the quarry. The door to the caravan was unlocked.

The gas-cylinder stove was lit and hot. He sat in one of the armchairs and lit a cigarette. When he had finished he thought again about going home and calling the police. But again he changed his mind, and to kill time he began to look through the books behind him on the shelf. When the door opened he spun around to see Stevie undoing his hood.

'See anything that interests you?' Stevie took a small packet from the pocket of the cagoule and put it in his jeans pocket, then he took off the cagoule and hung it on a nail next to the door.

'Slightly esoteric for my taste.' Eamon replaced a copy of *The Celestine Prophecies*.

'You've got a library in Duncul,' said Stevie. 'Have you considered staying at home and reading your own books. You could wrap up in a velvet dressing gown and have Kirsty bring you a glass of port.'

'I've only one question before I call the police. Why the finger to the lips? Do you think that's all it takes to keep someone quiet?' Stevie took off the heavy-knit jumper. Beneath he wore a t-shirt that was stretched tight over a lean, muscular chest. He hung the jumper on the nail and sprang across the room, knocking Eamon from his feet. Eamon felt the back of his head hit the bookshelf and heard the books fall around him. Stevie placed one hand on his throat, sat on his chest and struck him once, twice, three times in the face with the other. Eamon felt with his right hand and grabbed something metal. He brought it crashing against Stevie's temple. He saw the reddened face wince with pain and he rolled his body, pushed back with his arms and threw Stevie off. Stevie landed on the coffee table, snapping all four of its legs. He stood up and backed to the other side of the room. Blood streamed from the wound on his head. He felt it, looked at the blood on his fingers, and shook his head slowly in disgust at Eamon, who was brandishing the crude iron poker from the fireplace. Eamon tossed it aside. He took off his jacket and rolled up the sleeves of his shirt. He gestured to the door, but Stevie charged again, wrapping his thick arms around Eamon's neck. Eamon wrapped his own around his opponent's waist, and the two men, of equal strength, thus locked, bleeding, wrestled around the room, breaking, turning over, smashing everything in their path, breaking the lamp so that they rolled in darkness, heads pressed together, tasting blood, sweat, fear and rage. After a while they lay locked on the floor together, neither able to move. Eventually Eamon felt Stevie's body relax and give a strange shake. It took a moment for him to realise that Stevie was laughing, an uncontrollable chuckle, with his mouth next to Eamon's ear.

'I'll stop,' said Stevie, 'if you'll let go.' Eamon let go. Stevie rose, cursing, and switched on a fluorescent strip above them, illuminating the wreckage. He found the poker, used it to open the stove door, and put a log on. Eamon stood up. His shirt was ripped to a bloody rag. Stevie went into the kitchen and came back with a can of beer, opened it and sipped. He sat in an armchair with a broken arm and took out his tin of rolling tobacco. Eamon looked for his jacket among the debris. He turned over the remains of the coffee table and looked behind the couch. Stevie drew heavily on the cigarette.

'They'll kill you,' he said. Eamon looked up.

'Who will? The cowboy and the barmaid?'

'No. The people they work for.'

'The people you work for,' said Eamon. Stevie snorted.

'I don't work for anyone. Come to think of it they'll probably kill me too.' Eamon saw his jacket under the upturned couch and crouched to pick it up. It was covered in broken glass and scraps of paper. Photographs. There was a photograph of his father. His father as a young man, and another of his mother, his father and himself, a young boy. Eamon held them up.

'How did you get these?' For a moment Stevie's mouth hung open, motionless.

'Sometimes when you see stuff it's better to look the other way,' he said. Eamon looked at the picture. He and his mother were smiling and his father was serious. His own blonde hair was sticking up and he was shrugging his shoulders; he was laughing. He could remember when the picture had been taken. It had been his tenth birthday. 'Skeletons,' said Stevie. 'Everyone has skeletons. Sometimes it's better to keep the cupboard locked.' It was as if the words lit something deep within Eamon and rage escaped him, like vomit. He felt his voice rise, out of control.

'Fuck you Steven Reid! Fuck you! You're all fucking liars! Why the fuck are you here? Why here? Why don't you fuck off to some other shithole! Did you know this? The police are lying to the Kennedys about their son! Joel Kennedy didn't kill that boy! Didn't kill him! He was burning the body! Why have you got these fucking photographs!' Stevie looked up at him with a sinister snarl.

'Tough being lord of the manor is it?' Eamon dusted the glass off his jacket and put it on.

'These are mine!' he said. 'I'm taking them.' He bent down. There were other photographs. Duncul in midsummer. Himself on a bicycle.

'No they're not. Your dad gave them to me. Sit down. Calm down, have a beer.' He offered the one he had opened for himself. 'You want the truth. Sit down. Or is it too much for you, big man?'

'You've got to be fucking kidding,' said Eamon. Stevie raised his eyebrows and drew on the cigarette.

'Welcome to the real world.'

'You've got to be fucking kidding.' Eamon tossed the photographs on to the floor and walked out into the night.

Stevie Van. Steven Reid. Drug dealer. Pot-smoking dole-scrounger, living in a beat up caravan in a quarry. Eamon couldn't even think the word. Not possible. Full of shit. Phone the police, now. Bring the whole thing crashing down, now. He could have stolen those photographs. He was some sort of weird stalker. How could he have got hold of those photographs? Phone the police, now! Why was Richard Blackwell lying? He was lying. He was putting him off the scent, just as he had put old Dupuy off the scent all those years ago. Why was he allowed to live in the quarry? It made too much sense. It made no sense. His father had been a bastard, that was true. A ruthless alcoholic bastard. His father had driven his mother to an early grave, driven her mad. He had made her ill.

He had always known that. But this? Well, what was so remarkable about this? He wouldn't have been the first Ansgar to have an illegitimate child. In fact there was something of a tradition. He called Blackwell but there was no answer. He called Rona.

'Bit of a problem in the ongoing saga of the eviction of Stevie Van,' he said, and saying the words felt like jumping off a cliff. 'I think we might be related.'

Vanneck and Brighton had watched the storm build throughout the day. Neither man suffered from seasickness but Vanneck began to feel a turmoil in the stomach that echoed that of the sea, and a tension approaching cramp in his limbs. Again, the onslaught of fear. There was a vindictiveness in each gust of wind and each wave that slapped against the bows. The storm was attacking him. It was directed against his mission. It made sense, after all; he was Prometheus, stealing fire from the Gods. It made sense that the Gods would be angry. There was fear of the sea, and then there was Lillian, below, in the darkened room, another knot in his stomach.

He had been down several times during the day, to check her shallow breathing and to make sure that she was safe in her bed. But he did not want her to wake up. She wanted to bring it all to light. She wanted to drag it all up from the depths, but he was convinced that she would not understand. She had understood everything up until now. She had understood when he had wrestled his patent for Spartanone from the clutches of the University of Michigan. 'It is your work,' she had said. It had been clear and simple to her, 'as much as one of my poems is mine. No-one else contributed, no-one else even thought about it.' She had understood about gene patents and she had understood about embryo modification and derivation, when entire nations had been outraged and governments had hounded him, baying at the gates of Montezuma. She had understood about Adam, even the death of Adam. She had mourned him as a man, of course, but she had never questioned the morality of taking him out of Congo; of taking this old, old man away from his family and life in the forest, away from everything he had ever known, everything that had ever made sense to him, and putting him on the other side of the Atlantic in a laboratory and subjecting him to test after test, needle after needle; NMR scans, cognitive tests, physiology tests, all performed by people in white suits and face masks, and all the while keeping him in a sterile environment, in a plastic tent. She had understood that. Would she, could she, understand what he had planned for Tarvin Lodge? 'What programme?' she had demanded, from a dry and vitiated throat. When was the last time her voice had been raised in anger? Vanneck could not remember. He did not want to see her awake. No, he would sedate her again. He would deal with all that after Loch Houn, when they were on their way home. When there was a human face to it all she would understand.

CHAPTER ELEVEN

Grigor had been living in the bed and breakfast for five days and was hating it. He was sure that somehow the accommodation was making him ill. It was not that it was unclean, although he suspected that there were hidden pockets of germs in the cushions on the couch in the living room and in the mattress beneath his sheets. It was something more subtle, more pervasive than germs. He had decided it was to do with the mentality of the owner. Décor, he reasoned, was an expression of the mind of the decorator, the soul of the decorator, and the relationship between a person's mind and certain illnesses, especially cancer, was well documented. The woman who ran the bed and breakfast, who had arranged the cushions on the couch and the sheets on his bed, was giving him cancer. He had felt it since the afternoon he had arrived; a general sense of being unwell. There was no specific ache or nausea or rash, but nonetheless he was certain that he was absorbing a subtle and cumulative poison.

The bed and breakfast was an old house, perhaps once an important house belonging to a wealthy family, but it had been chopped and changed; walls demolished, walls built, and toilets added. His bedroom was a half or a quarter of what had once been a reasonably sized room, and after it had been filled with the bed, sink, chest of drawers, wobbly little table holding a kettle, cups and a saucer holding packets of coffee, miniature tubs of milk and tea bags with strings attached, television stand and television and wardrobe full of rattling plastic hangers, there was just enough room to stretch out on the thick purple carpet and vigorously exercise his stomach muscles. It was a combination of these factors, he had decided, the incoherence of the whole, and the incongruity of the things, the thousands of things that she had filled the house with, that was making him ill. It was perhaps a purely psychological effect, he thought, but then perhaps it was also a physiological effect of the combination of all the unnatural chemicals that were contained and emitted by the things. And then, had not colour both a psychological and physiological effect?

There were cushions everywhere. There were three on the bed, of three different reds, that he had to throw on the floor when he slept. There were more on the shelf above the cupboard. In the lounge, cushions littered the couches and armchairs. There was too much furniture; so many nests of tables, side tables and coffee tables, all cheap, cheap veneer polished hard or glass topped. There were too many chairs, none of them matching, and too many fire extinguishers. There were too many faux leather couches in the lounge. There were far too many pine dining table and chair sets set too close together in the vast dining room. It was as if she was running a furniture auction. It was as if she was expecting a hundred guests to descend at once. Meanwhile, she had one. And then on the tables, ornaments; and beneath the ornaments little mats or crocheted lace circles. Brass cows, china shepherdesses, bowl after bowl half-filled with dried rose petals, little drums brought back from Spanish holidays, varnished tree roots that looked like contorted faces, a row of cowbells hanging from leather straps on a cast-iron frame, a miniature brash gong, a collection of bright gnomes, sitting on a toadstool catching fish, playing pan pipes, male gnome batting eyelids at female gnome, and then on the walls, mirrors. He counted twenty mirrors in the public rooms alone, and t-spoons with coats of arms on their handles mounted on varnished wooden plaques, paintings of mountains and peasants on carts, horse brasses, paintings of blue-eyed boys and girls with over large heads, photographs of nondescript children in school uniforms, photographs of the Eiffel tower, the Leaning Tower of Pisa, hung upon off-white paint with a rough texture, hung upon green and gold striped wallpaper, hung upon a wall of thin planks of pine, hung upon white wallpaper embossed with velvet ascending tendrils. The owner, a middle aged woman with hair cut in a straight line across her forehead, with a shapeless figure and a limp, seemed incapable of resisting the temptation to add. She even added to the butter, (curls of butter) at breakfast; a small purple flower, in the butter. He could not eat any of the food. Butter, curled, with a flower in it, could not be eaten by Grigor Semyonovitch. He had gone to the first breakfast. It had been served with a smile that he had not reciprocated. Bacon and eggs, beans and toast, cold on a cold plate, and there had been no lemon for his tea. He had retired to his room, to a ten-kilogram tub of vanilla *Hardbody 3000* and a tub of vitamins. How long could he last on *Hardbody*? It was an interesting experiment, but his shit was already turning to pebbles. He needed a lettuce, some avocados, tuna, even a steak. But Sigurson had said no going to shops. He had said meals inside, as few people seeing you as possible. Don't go back to the camp, the police are looking for you. Don't go to the camp. Where to go? Get back on the boat. Get out. Fucking Sigurson. Fuck Sigurson! That had been strange behaviour up there in the woods. There was something not right about it. Something false. He had been so precise about where the box was. He had had the location on his phone. There was something odd about that. Certainly. Grigor performed another set of thirty crunches.

No signal. That was it. No signal for his phone, no signal for any phone up there in the forest. Sigurson had used his phone to find the location of the box. Sigurson had been lying.

Clarice Wright looked in the mirror at her straight grey hair and pinched grey face. Clarice Wright had never been beautiful; her face had always had too many angles. But not long ago, she had been young. What was the point of looking in the mirror? But he had that effect. Some men had that effect, they made you look for a mirror, and straighten your hair. He would be here any minute. She unzipped a folder and took out the charts and placed them on the side table. The flat was ugly and bare, with old, cheap furniture, just like the last one. There was a knock on the front door. She opened and there he was, wearing those stupid clothes and carrying a heavy black holdall. She smiled and he smiled but it was a cold smile from him. She could see Sigurson was not in a good mood.

'Where is she?' he said. She gestured to a door. 'Where's the charts?' he said, and she led him to the living room. He put down the holdall and studied the papers for a few moments while she took out a syringe from her handbag and placed it on the table. He picked up the syringe and left the room, closing the door behind him. In a few moments he returned and sat down on the worn looking couch, taking the hat off his long blonde hair.

'What now?' she said.

'Five minutes.' He smiled steadily at her.

'No I mean, is she going to stay here or go back or what? I'm just asking 'cos it'll have to be arranged. Paperwork and all that.'

'Here for now.'

'Who's going to stay with her? Ah cannae. I've got to go back.'

'No you don't,' said Sigurson.

'What do you mean?'

'You don't have to go back.'

'I've got a job to go to.'

'Sit down, Clarice,' he said. She looked at his strange, pale face. He was smiling but so thinly; a smile that she could not understand. Suddenly she felt her vulnerability. She was alone in a flat with this man, this cold pervert. That's what he was, he had to be. He was a wierdo.

'I'm goin' to the toilet,' she said.

'No you're not. Sit down.' She stood still. He stood up. He was a head and shoulders taller than her. He grabbed her thin wrists and she moaned in fear as he pushed her back towards the armchair. Then he hit her hard across the side of the face. The smile had contracted to a thin line and he was breathing through his nose. She had been hit before. She told herself she could take it. She drew her knees up to her chest, closed her eyes and covered her face with her arms. He hit and hit, snapping a nail off her pinkie and spattering blood. She felt the flat of his hand again and again against the side of her head until the pain stopped and there was just a numbing and the bang inside her skull as each blow fell. Then he punched at her face, trying to reach the eyes and nose. She could hear his breathing. Then he kicked down on her legs and her side with his hiking boots. Where does this end? Maybe it ends when you're dead. But he stopped and after a while she opened bruised eyes.

He was on the other side of the room, breathing heavily through his nose and opening the holdall. He took out a baseball bat and threw it across the room at her. Then he took out a circular saw and threw it at her and she yelped in pain as it hit her shin. Then he took out a keyhole saw and threw that at her, but carelessly, and it bounced on the floor before the chair. Then a thick role of tape and a heavy role of black plastic bags. This hit her on the head. Then a full set of kitchen knives still in their plastic box. He did not throw this, but sat back in the armchair and held it on his lap. He was smiling again.

'Can you see,' he said, 'what all this is for?' She nodded. 'Time to go,' he said. She did not move. 'You've got about five seconds,' he whispered. She got up and realised she was only able to see through one eye. She found her bag and one of her shoes on the floor and looked for the other. 'Leave the shoe,' he said. She caught sight of herself in the mirror in the hall as she limped to the front door, the black eyes, blood streaming from the nose, the torn lip. She did not recognise the face.

When she had gone Sigurson looked at his bloody knuckles and licked them. He sat still, feeling his heart and breathing slow down. He realised how hot he was and took off the jacket and trousers to reveal a wiry torso and long, thin legs. Then he went to the kitchen in his underpants and t-shirt and took a long drink of water. He gathered the scattered tools and found Clarice's shoe under the couch. He put it in the bin in the kitchen. Then he went through to the bedroom where Isabel lay on the bed, curled up asleep on her side. He moved her so that she was flat on her back and opened her legs, lifting up the nightdress. She was wearing white panties with a little heart on the front. He looked down between her legs, and up at her face. She would be unconcious for hours. He looked down between his own legs but there was no bulge there.

He pulled down her nightdress and covered her with a blanket. Then he thought about chopping her up. He could put her in the bath and bleed her out before she woke. 'Jamaica, in a hut on the beach, with a girl and a big bag of weed,' Pyotr had reminded him. Now he wanted to kill someone. But not her; not now. Shit. His head ached. His throat was dry. He should have killed Clarice but it was too late now. He felt the need to get high, an itch that had been at the back of his mind all day. High and drunk. But he hadn't brought any grass with him. He got dressed and left the flat.

Joshua Malafu walked on the beach. The wind whipped spray from a green, grey, dark sea under a low cloud. This sea did not sparkle and there were no pretty boats bobbing at anchor, no children laughing, no amusement parks and sandcastles, no hawkers selling sunglasses and baseball caps and handbags. The beach stretched ahead and behind to a flat horizon. They told you, again and again, as you travelled north towards the sea between France and England, by train, by car, by bus, by foot; you will never get across the sea. Every black face from Fuengirola to Barcelona to Toulouse to Paris. You will never get across the sea. They have put up wire. The truck drivers are using baseball bats and chains. You will be killed in the tunnel by a train. You will be arrested and sent back to the forest where you belong. Don't go to Calais, they had said, so he had not. He had taken the bus out of Paris to Boulogne and walked onto the beach, and slept, and walked. The wind was cold and the sea was liquid ice, like needles on the hand. He had walked out of Boulogne past a marina, looking at boats; boats with sails and boats with engines. He had no idea how to make either of them work. He could see ships, far out, dark and slow, creeping between sea and sky. The wind whipped the sand against his legs. He had to walk, to keep moving, even if it was only to fight off the cold. North, in spite of everything, towards Calais.

Vanneck was sure he could hear new sounds coming from the boat; a creaking deep within, then a thumping, a creak, then a thump. The weather was relentless. However, Brighton persuaded him that they were making good progress, pointing at the big screen in the centre of the console. They were still south of Ireland, heading north-west, 'making sea room,' said Brighton, whatever that meant. But the ten hours of storm he had predicted had lengthened into fifteen, and even on his bright face Vanneck could see the grey hue of exhaustion. 'The storm,' explained Brighton, 'is taking the same course as us.' The Gods, thought Vanneck, are on our case. 'We could turn to the south-west; we would be out of the weather in a couple of hours.'

'We can't,' said Vanneck. 'We have to keep on.' Screw the Gods. 'What's that noise?'

'Something loose somewhere. It happens in storms.'

'Is that serious?'

'Not necessarily. We'll see in the morning.'

The fire was unlit in the study and a dull grey light from the window carried the cold of the morning into the room, chilling the furniture, chilling the Persian carpet and numbing the fingertips that held the cigarette. Eamon was smoking inside, taking short, sharp breaths as he stood leaning on the mantelpiece. Rona, seated in a wing back chair and wearing a fleece jacket against the cold, reminded him of the prohibition, but he frowned at her and pulled hard on the cigarette and flicked ash into the grate.

'If he is your brother,' said Rona, 'then really, he's the one who has the right to be upset. Think about it. He's been treated abominably.'

'He's a fucking drug dealer!'

'So what? So he sells pot. He sold it to you when you were younger; he's sold it to half the people in the village. None of us are saints.'

'What about what his drugs did to Joel Kennedy?'

'You don't even believe Joel killed the child. You should go and see him.' He looked at her steadily. He could see that she was right. Christ, she was right. He left her in the study, opening windows to get rid of the smell of tobacco.

He knocked on the door of the caravan but there was no answer. Stevie was not in the wrecked sitting room. He found him in the bedroom, curled up in a flowery duvet and asleep. There was a pool of vomit on the floor. Eamon knocked on the wall and Stevie stirred.

'Jesus,' he groaned. He sat up against the headboard. 'What do you want?' Eamon sat on the bed.

'Those photographs. Why do you have them?'

'Work it out.'

'Stevie, are we related?'

'Does it matter?'

'How?' said Eamon. Stevie snorted.

'Same way as always. Daddy had a girlfriend. Probably more than one come to think of it.'

'Why didn't you say anything?' Stevie looked at him for what seemed like an age.

'Fuck off, Eamon,' he said, and Eamon nodded.

'Is that your mother?' Eamon looked at a framed photograph on a shelf behind the bed. It showed a thin, fair-haired woman with a wide smile holding a baby on her hip. Stevie turned the picture face down on the shelf.

'That couple,' said Eamon, 'at the Misty. I'm going to go to the police about them. They won't harm me.'

'Don't be stupid. Do you not see that you're involved?'

'How?'

'You're laundering their money for them, Eamon.'

'How?'

'The dam.'

'I don't get it.' Stevie got out of bed and went to the kitchen in his underpants. He came back with a cloth and began to clean up the vomit.

'Drugs come in through here, then down to Glasgow, money comes back up here and into construction; dams, small turbines, pellet boilers, all that green shite. The guys that run the drugs, that's your camp over the hill.'

'Does Edgar Dupuy know about this? Is he in on it?' Stevie shrugged in reply.

'Probably not. Nobody knows more than they need to know.'

'So, what am I supposed to do? Let it carry on?'

'Fucked if I know. All I know is you don't want to mess with these guys.'

'Who are they?'

'Latvians. I suppose you could call them mafia, or whatever.'

'What about Joel? Does this have anything to do with Joel? Was Joel working for them?'

'Who the fuck knows what Joel was doing. Sneaking about. Keeping secrets. He bought his weed from me and bit of speed. Spent most of his time up the hill working for Duncan Fraser.'

'Who's Duncan Fraser?'

'Fencer. Old guy, lives way up at the end of Glenfashie.'

'Maybe he knows something, about Joel,' said Eamon. Then he told Stevie about the child being in the freezer and the fact that the fire had not been the cause of death. 'Don't you want to know what was going on with Joel?' Stevie heaved a sigh and a curse.

'Come on,' he said, picking up his trousers. 'It's a long walk.'

Again the morning brought no respite. Vanneck had tried at one point to sleep on the bed next to Lillian, but had been unable to even close his eyes, and had returned to the bridge to keep watch with the now visibly worried Brighton. The creak and the thump had grown louder with each repetition, and by the rising of a frail sun behind them, the light picking its way through the crests of sharp waves beneath a tumultuous grey sky, they were able to see the cause. On the port side, the side that was taking the brunt of the weather, a gangway had come loose. It was a heavy, elaborate, stainless steel confection. With each roll of the boat it came crashing against the hull, swinging on a tangle of wire rope. Both men stood peering down from the bridge, and winced at each collision, each seeming more violent than the last. Each time a wave washed over the deck the gangway was brought with it, and crashed into the superstructure. It had already destroyed a section of the hand rail around the lower deck and was hitting one of the salon windows. The way it moved, swinging out and down, was like a deliberate effort to punch a hole in the side of the boat.

'I'm going to have to cut it loose,' said Brighton. Vanneck did not reply. Brighton left the bridge for a while and came back wearing a bright red and yellow suit and a harness, and carrying a bolt cutter.

'Will that do it?' said Vanneck. The bolt cutter wasn't very big. The boat rolled and the gangway came down on the deck with an almighty crash.

'It will have to,' said Brighton. 'I'm going to fasten a long line to the starboard rail, but if I fall overboard you have to stop the boat.' He pointed to a big red button on the console. 'I'll pull myself in, but as soon as I get to the ladder at the stern you hit the green button and hold it down for a count of five, 'cos once we're stopped the waves will knock the hell out of us, OK?' Vanneck nodded. Brighton went out.

Vanneck looked down at the red and yellow figure as it came around from the leeward side into the brunt of the storm. He felt utterly detached, as if he were watching a film. He could hear the wind and the rush of the sea and the rain against the windows, the thump and crash at each movement of the gangway, but the figure made no sound and it moved in short, jerky movements against the wind. He knew from the moment he saw the figure on the deck that something bad was going to happen.

Brighton crawled over to the port side and managed to fasten the mouth of the bolt cutters onto one of the cables that held the gangway. Vanneck watched him squeeze with both hands and saw the cable snap. The gangway was now held by two cables, and their length allowed it to vanish completely over the side beneath the waves, but as the boat tipped and another wave hit the gangway swung over, high above the deck and narrowly missed Brighton as it landed. He fastened the bolt cutter to the second cable and squeezed. The boat tipped and the gangway slid across the deck and disappeared over the side again. Then the cable snapped and pinged across the deck. A wave washed over the deck and Brighton was washed with it against the railings on the starboard side. Vanneck watched him crawl back, hand over hand, and fasten the cutters onto the last cable. But as he applied pressure the boat rolled and the next wave hit and the gangway swung, away towards the bow, then round, back towards the base of the bridge, and at the apex of its arc struck Brighton, pinning him against the deck. Through the roar of the storm Vanneck heard his muffled cry, but he was out of sight, below and against the superstructure. Then Vanneck saw him; the boat rolled and dipped, and the gangway slid bow-wards across the deck, a tangle of cables and shining steel, like an enormous trap, holding the red and yellow form of Brighton. Vanneck saw his face; the mouth was open in a silent scream and a spike of steel emerged from his torso. The gangway slipped over the side beneath the waves. Vanneck held his hand over the red button. The boat dipped and rolled, then the gangway swung up again, still clasping the red and yellow form, and crashed against the deck and slid against the superstructure. Again, it rolled over the side and beneath the waves. Then the remaining cable gave way and the rope that was attached to Brighton's harness stretched tight over the deck. Vanneck's hand hovered over the stop button, and he stared at the seething sea. Neither the gangway nor Brighton re-emerged. He thumped the button and felt the absence of the engine's hum.

The boat swung, bow to the waves, and rose up and crashed into a trough. Vanneck was taken aback by the violence of the motion, and his first thought was for Lillian, asleep in the cabin below. The bow rose again, and they thundered into the next trough. Suddenly the wind and the rain seemed more violent. He looked for Brighton. The rope was taught over the port side. He could see neither Brighton nor any flash of the bright steel of the gangway that held him. He waited, and again the bow heaved out of the water and crashed down the side of the next wave. He waited for one more wave, then he pushed the green button and held it down. The engines hummed through the boat, and the boat turned, and rolled, and the bright red rope that attached to Brighton stretched out behind. Vanneck's eyes seized upon an axe in a case on the wall. He tore open the case and ran down the stairs to the starboard door to the deck. Even in the lee the wind and spray came at him like a spitting, lashing animal. The rope was tied to the starboard handrail and he took one step out of the door and hacked. He missed, but hacked again and again till the last strands snapped and the line whipped away across the deck. He scrambled back inside, already soaked, and climbed the stairs to the bridge. He put the axe back in its case and sat in the captain's chair. He found himself thinking of the story of Jonah and the appeasement of the storm, and sure enough, after an hour of sitting, frozen and shivering from shock, staring alternately at the screens and out at the raging sea, he felt the wind begin to lessen.

Joshua had begun to see people on the beach, walking dogs and jogging. When he saw the port in the distance, windmills waving at the sky, cranes and oil tanks illuminated by a break in the clouds, he stopped walking and felt hope leave his exhausted body. He thought about turning back but when he looked back at the miles of beach he had walked since Boulogne he could only find the energy to stumble into the dunes and lie down. He opened his sleeping bag and slept. In the night he grew so cold that he had to get up and gather driftwood by torchlight and light a fire. Not long before dawn a dog came, looked at him, and barked. Anxiously he shooed it away, but then a woman's voice called and the dog ran back towards the beach. As the dawn light glowed over the land behind him and weak rays caught the wave tops before him he spoke out loud in his own language.

'I have come this far. I cannot walk on water.' he said, and he heard a voice reply.

'You will swim,' said the voice, clear and deep, in his own language that he had not heard another speak for three years.

'I will drown.'

'You are mine and I am yours. Death is no matter.'

'The cold will kill me like a thousand thorns.'

'I will be with you,' said the voice.

'I will never get to the Singa,' said Joshua.

'Trust me,' said the voice. 'Walk into the water.' Joshua, so cold and hungry that he could not bear to stand, zipped up the sleeping bag tight under his chin and closed his eyes again.

When he awoke later in the morning the wind had dropped. The sea was almost flat and it had retreated to far off across the wet sand. Little waves lapped tenderly at the edge of the sand, and a glowing bank of mist sat further out. Joshua packed his bag and walked to the water's edge.

'Swim,' said the voice.

'No.'

'Swim into the light. Trust me,' said the voice. Joshua put his hand into the water, into a burning cold.

'No,' he said and began walking towards the port.

'Listen to me. Take off your clothes, leave everything, walk into the water and swim.'

'I am not afraid to die. If that is what you want.' He stopped, undressed, leaving everything in a pile on the beach, and walked naked towards the sea. A dog sniffed at his heels and watched him as he walked; a tall, thin, stooped man. When he was up to his thighs he heard a woman's voice behind him and he recognised some of the words.

'*Vous ête's fou, Monsieur!*' she said. He ignored her. The water gripped his balls and he gasped. 'England is very far from here, *Monsieur*. You will die!' Joshua launched himself and struggled for breath. '*Monsieur, Monsieur! Arrêtez!* Stop!' The dog began barking ferociously, and Joshua heard a splashing behind him. He swam with bold strokes towards the glowing bank of cloud, but he felt a hand, then two hands clutch his left foot. '*Monsieur!*' Her voice was high pitched and panicked. '*Arrêtez Monsieur!* I can help you! I can help you!'

'Stop swimming now,' said the voice. 'Stand up. Trust me.'

CHAPTER TWELVE

Sigurson had been lying. Fifty press-ups, rest. Fifty crunches. This room is so fucking small! Like a prison cell. It is poisoning me. What was that shit about? Why pretend to look for a box? What was that all about? Think! You were never clever at school Grigor. They all told you you were stupid. Everyone knows you are stupid. Not stupid when you kick though. Not so stupid when you learned how to fight. Sigurson thought he was stupid. Sigurson and Pyotr, that old man treating you like a child. Tell me nothing. Go here, fetch stone. Why? Why fetch fucking stone? Go there and take this bag to car on road. Do not open bag. Why? What is in bag? All secrets, too many fucking secrets! Now dig hole in woods, for what? Think Grigor! Thirty pull ups. Break their necks with these hands. Then stop. Get in car. He doesn't want to cut the root with his stupid big knife. He looks scared of his knife. He's a big pussy that Sigurson, scared to use his knife. Get in car, he says. Then he doesn't talk all the way back.

Eamon and Stevie took the same path that had been marked by the bike tracks up the hill. On the flat at the top the hill, in the silence, before the descent to Glenfashie and the dam, they turned to the east and followed sheep tracks and deer tracks through the scatterings of snow. It did not rain, but the sun struggled weakly against the blanket of cloud. All around to the horizon lay the tops of hills, like white crested waves of a gigantic frozen sea, a sea that existed in a time beyond the pitiful moments of men, inexorably moving and falling and crashing. Stevie walked at a steady, fast pace, without pause, without a word. After two hours of walking, when Eamon reckoned their eastwards movement had taken them parallel to Glenfashie and further along it than the end of the dam loch, Stevie paused for a smoke and surprised Eamon by talking, as if his thoughts had been eased by the walk.

'Your dad took that picture of my mother and me. He used to visit us, in Edinburgh, until I was about ten. Now that I think about it, that's when you would have been born. Then he fucked off. I didn't know where he was until I was seventeen and my mother was sick and dying. She told me about this place. I was getting into trouble with the police, gangs and all that. I bought the van, drove up North; Sutherland, Skye. I was on the road for about a year before I ended up here. I was kind of circling it I suppose. I wanted to see how much trouble I could cause. I parked up in the quarry and after a week or so I summed up the courage. I was walking up to the castle, up the main drive, piss-drunk and stoned, and I saw you. You must have been about seven. You were playing in the woods on that big swing. It was like being hit in the guts. I turned around and went back to the van. I didn't know where to go but I was going to leave. Then your man Dupuy came to visit and *asked* me to leave. That pissed me off. I got stubborn. Then Daddy came round. He was as confused as I was. I don't think he knew what he wanted me to do. He asked me not to tell and I agreed. Simple as that. He used to come to the van to drink and talk. We used to get pissed, and I would always end up thinking, you're a cunt. Then he would go away and I wouldn't see him for six months. Dupuy never bothered me again. Then after I'd been there for a year or so, your man Blackwell came to visit. I was on the dole. He gave me a cheque. Been sending me cheques every month since. Why do you think I'm still here?'

'But why did you never say anything to me? I remember getting stoned with you, when I was what? Seventeen?'

'It wasn't up to me. It was up to Dad,' said Stevie, and the last word stunned Eamon into silence. They finished their cigarettes and carried on eastwards. When they began to descend the face of the hill, and the dam was behind them, miles to the west, Stevie pointed out their route to a patch of dark green on the hill ahead.

It was a forestry block, mature spruce extending in adjoining squares east and south, carrying on along one side of a glen that extended from Glenfashie. There was a faint, narrow track along the floor of the glen, little more than a path. It was a hidden place, perhaps once inhabited, now only the realm of deer, sheep, hillwalkers maybe, and Duncan Fraser, apparently.

It took them a while to find the cabin. Stevie explained that it was a while since he had visited, and it was hidden in a clearing in the trees, half-way up the face of the hill. It was a low wooden building, little more than a hut, made of lapped boards and hunkered down into the grass. It was not falling down or rotting, but decrepit in an ordered way; the boards covered in lichen and the roof covered in moss. There was a tin chimney and a faint trickle of smoke. Stevie thumped hard on the door, and called, but there was no answer.

'Might have to wait for a bit,' he said as he opened the door.

They entered a low ceilinged room lit by one small window. It served as kitchen, living room, store-room, tool shed and bedroom. There was a sink beneath the window, a dining table and chairs by the door, a bed covered in blankets against the back wall, a torn and faded leather couch, and in the centre of the room a pot-bellied stove. The room was warm and there were faint scents of creosote, drying wool, oilskins, and a stronger smell of wood smoke, tobacco, and venison. There was a gun cabinet displaying a rifle and a shotgun, an embroidered legend, 'God Bless This Home,' a framed print of a stag on a hilltop, shelves of tinned food, bars of soap, boxes of matches, tins of tobacco; a shelf of books, and a fishing rod hanging in the rafters. There were the tools of a fencer ranged against one wall; shoveholers, mells, chains, axes and wire cutters. Eamon was surprised to see Stevie fill a kettle from the sink and put it on the stove, then rattle the grate and put some logs on the fire. Then he took his boots off, sat on the couch, put his feet up on a crate and rolled a cigarette. Eamon sat at the table and took out one of his own. Once he had made the tea Stevie sat back and closed his eyes. Eamon looked at the books; old books with broken spines and faded covers, in Gaelic, and others, newer, on mathematics, annotated in the margins with tiny, neat handwriting. 'Best not to move things around too much,' said Stevie, without opening his eyes, 'just chill.' Eamon put the books away and leant back against the wall. Before long, tired from the walk and warm in the strange room, he found himself dozing.

Vanneck forced himself to think rationally and clearly, like a scientist. He did not need Brighton. The boat was programmed and the course was set. Brighton had told him; it practically sailed itself. *Rage III* would take them to Loch Houn. X marked the spot, right at the entrance to the Loch. They were still heading north. The route was far out around the West Coast of Ireland, up past the Hebrides around the north end of Lewis and in towards the West Coast of Scotland, avoiding shipping lanes. He would only have to steer the boat into the mouth of Loch Houn. The journey was supposed to take five more days. In five days he could work out how to steer the boat, surely. So far, he knew how to make it stop and go. There was a joystick on the console instead of a wheel. There were five screens; one was a radar, another for the satnav, one was a satellite weather feed, and the other two looked like operating systems for engines. There were two keyboards and a bank of switches. Once he was in Loch Houn he would have to know how to operate the anchors, how to moor, and how to lower the launch. Perhaps Flieber could help. Did Flieber know anything about boats? Vanneck doubted it. Flieber was a lab rat. But Samuel Vanneck could do it. He was one of the century's greatest scientists. He could work out how to steer a boat. He went down to his wife's bedroom.

There was a smell of vomit and perfume in the darkened room. She was lying on her side on the floor next to the bed surrounded by bottles and pots fallen from the dressing table. He rushed to her side and lifted her onto the bed.

'Not good,' she groaned. 'This is not good, Sam, where's Paula?'

'I told you, Paula…' he began. 'Paula is coming soon.'

'I want Paula, and Antony must come and clean up, he hasn't been for days.' Vanneck brought her a glass of water. 'Where are we going, Sam?' He felt her head for a temperature but it was cold.

'I've told you, Lily. Don't you remember?' She drank the water and sat up, looking at him steadily.

'I remember, Sam. You told me a lie.' He looked away and went over to the sink to pick up a towel. 'Now the storm has stopped we can talk some more.'

It was midday when Sigurson awoke. He was still wearing his jacket and trousers and was soaked in sweat. Isabel was moving around in the kitchen. Sigurson's head ached. He took off the jacket and groaned. She appeared in the doorway to the kitchen and stared at him. She was dressed in jeans and a jumper and it looked like she had made some attempt at combing her hair. He wondered how old she was. More than twenty, less than thirty. He wondered what she was thinking. What on earth could she be thinking? She went back into the kitchen and he heard the movement of dishes and the lighting of the stove. He closed his eyes again. His phone rang. It was Flieber.

'So?' said Flieber.

'S'done. All done.'

'Great. Good. Awesome. You're a fucking superhero Sig. You hear?'

'Yeah. Listen Gurt. We need to wrap this up.'

'I'm working on it, buddy. I'm in negotiation as we speak. It's all looking good. I've got him by those big old hairy balls and he knows it. I say, tonight, you do your business one more time for luck, and then we're good to go. It's all moving. Just hang tight.' Flieber ended the call. Isabel was standing in the doorway with a cup in her hand.

'Thanks,' he said, taking the coffee.

'Where is Clarice?' she said, sitting on the edge of the armchair.

'Gone. Other work. It's me now. Clarice is finished.'

'We need food. We need to eat.'

'Ok. I'll go and find a shop,' he said. We, she said we, that was funny. 'We need to eat.' Like we're a team or something. Like we're in this together. He looked at her. There was something impressive there; strength. Her son had just died. Isabel. Isabel something. He could take off with Isabel. Isabel would fit right in in Jamaica. He could take off to Africa with Isabel. She could show him the ropes.

'Don't you want coffee too?' he said.

'I had some. Why you give me...' she made a squeezing gesture, squeezing a syringe.

'Oh, yep. Sedative. To make you sleep.'

'But you are not a doctor.'

'Nope, doctor's orders. You sleep well?'

'No,' she said, 'I had a bad dream.' He smiled weakly. He looked at her hand and felt like touching it or touching her arm. He felt like doing something to comfort her. He realised he was still drunk. What was she? Part of a plan. Cargo. Product. Isabel. He put on his jacket and moved to the door.

'What would you like?' he said. She looked at him, puzzled. 'I mean to eat?'

'Some bread.'

'Bread? That's all?'

'Bread is enough. You can choose.'

He did not know the area and had to follow his phone to a supermarket. He started with a handbasket but went back out again for a trolley, because he thought he would treat her. He knew how to cook. He spent a while debating whether to do lamb or roast beef, but decided on steaks, the best fillet, and oven chips. He was sure there was an oven in the flat. Chips, steak, salad, and he bought ciabatta, freshly baked, the best in the store, and ice-cream, the expensive stuff. He got lost on the way back to the flat. All the streets looked the same; dull, grey housing blocks, bare squares of grass between the blocks, gardens with broken bikes and mattresses, some of the flats with their windows boarded up. It reminded him of his childhood in Glasgow. A shithole of a place. He had to use the map on his phone again and by the time he got back he had taken more than an hour. He cursed himself. She had been hungry and he had wanted to please her.

He had to knock the door down to get into the bathroom. The thin door splintered out of its frame completely. He had known. He was sure he had known. Before he left there had been something in the look of her. She had made a decision, and he had thought she was being brave. Her little round face floated in a bath of dense crimson. She had not bothered to undress, just rolled up the sleeves of her jumper and cut. The clothes made her heavy but he wrenched her out of the bath. The blood was still pulsing. He used laces from his boots as tourniquets, and tore strips from towels to bind the wounds. 'Isabel!' he cried. 'Isabel!' She was still breathing, just. Just, just. 'Isabel! Isabel! I'm sorry. I'm so sorry. God, God, I'm sorry!' He dragged her from the bathroom into the living room and pulled off her wet clothes. Then he picked her up and carried her to the bedroom and wrapped her in blankets. What happened now? All that blood. How much blood? Hospital, he had to take her to a hospital, but he couldn't. He called Flieber.

'Fuck!' said Flieber. 'You're supposed to be looking after her! OK, shit! Get back here now! Get in the car and drive.'

'Isn't she going to need blood? Doesn't she need blood or something?'

'I don't know. Jesus! I'll look it up. You get back here now. Just drive, keep her warm, give her a coke or something, for shock.'

When Eamon opened his eyes an oil lamp lit the room, and a man wearing a yellow oilskin jacket and trousers, whom he assumed was Duncan Fraser, was sitting on the edge of the couch next to Stevie. The man was rocking backwards and forwards and smoking a pipe. He was small, with a smooth face and a white beard, and intense, wide-open, grey eyes. Stevie was fast asleep, chin up, head resting on the back of the couch. Duncan saw Eamon move and nodded in greeting.

'Hello,' said Eamon.

'Hallo yourself,' said Duncan, looking down at the floor and puffing on the pipe. 'Did you sleep well?' And when Eamon said that he had, his host assured him that this was a good thing. His voice had a West Coast lilt.

'We're sorry to intrude,' said Eamon.

'Not at all, no intrusion at all Duncul. We're not exactly busy here.' Duncan spoke without looking at him, rocking backwards and forwards.

'We thought we might be able to ask you about Joel.'

'Yes. Joel. Poor Joel.'

'Did he work for you?'

'Not exactly Duncul, not exactly. I would say he works *with* me. That is the way I would put it myself.'

'Doing what?'

'Fencing, nothing but fencing, that's what.'

'And was he…' Eamon searched for the words. 'Did he seem well?'

'Well? You mean is he well in the head?'

'Yes,' said Eamon. Clouds of smoke emerged from the pipe as Duncan thought.

'That is impossible to say. I would say that he is troubled, yes, very troubled. He is certainly preoccupied.'

'With what?'

'Well, dark things, I think.'

'Witchcraft?' said Eamon, wondering why he chose that word.

'Could be,' said Duncan, and the room fell silent but for the stream of air into the stove. Stevie stirred. 'It's all in there.' Duncan pointed without looking to the other door in the room, set in the wall next to the shelves and tools.

'What is?' said Eamon.

'All in there.' Eamon rose and opened the latch on the door.

First, there was the smell of the forest, and damp, as if the door led outside. Eamon took a torch from the tools that were ranged against the wall. The room was smaller than the other, and littered with pine branches and brown bracken stems, and among these, sheets of paper and torn up books. A bed, a table and a chair had been overturned, and blankets and sheets thrown into the mess. The torch cast crazy shadows on the walls. Eamon felt broken glass crunch underfoot. String tangled around his ankles. He picked up a sheet of foolscap. It was covered in the same markings as the Stone of Duncul; the half-formed Y's and I's and V's, small and large circles, drawn over and over again in black ink. Another sheet was covered in circles joined by a pentagram. Books had been torn down their spines. Eamon read some of the titles: *Ley Lines*, *Standing Stones of Great Britain*, *Rites for the Modern Pagan* and *Hepatic*

Metabolism. The branches were knee deep. Eamon waded across to the upturned table and opened one of its drawers. There were pens, more scraps of paper covered in spidery handwriting, verses cut from a Bible, syringes in sterile packets, and a ligature. Stevie stood in the doorway and spoke over his shoulder to Duncan.

'Jeez Duncan, did you not think of tidying the place up?'

'It's his room,' answered Duncan from the couch. 'He can tidy it himself when he gets back.' Stevie and Eamon exchanged a look.

'Did he do this himself Duncan? I mean throw everything about?' said Eamon.

'I only looked yesterday. It was like that when I found it.'

'Was he taking heroin?' Eamon held up one of the syringes. Stevie shrugged.

'If he was, he wasn't getting it from me.'

'Are you out of stock?'

'I'm in the party business, not the fall asleep and choke on your own vomit business. Besides, this isn't the room of a smack-head.'

'Why so?'

'Too much going on. All that writing and drawing. Smack-heads don't do fuck all. They certainly don't build fences for a living.'

'We should tell the police about this,' said Eamon. Stevie shut the door and put his finger to his lips.

'You can't tell the police about this place.'

'This is evidence.'

'Evidence of what? Evidence that he was off his head? Everyone knows that. What about Duncan? He's been off the grid up here for thirty years. They'll take him and put him in a home.' Eamon looked around the room. Eventually, he realised, all this will lead the police to The Stone of Duncul. To the castle. To him. Then what? He began gathering up the papers. He found a large black bag in the corner of the room, like a soft briefcase, padded and lined with silver foil, containing several syringes in plastic wrappers. He tipped them out and began filling the bag with papers, drawings and maps. He found a photograph of Duncul, cut from a calendar, and printouts from google maps of Glencul and Glenfashie. There were pages cut from books with spidery notes in the margins and a folder of corporate brochures about *Enerpro*. He stopped looking at them, and simply put every scrap of paper he could find in the bag, even the strips of Bible verses. When he went back to the other room, Stevie was sitting with Duncan on the couch.

'Joel's in trouble with the police. He'll not be coming back for a while,' said Stevie.

'The police is it? Oh well. Yes. The police.' Duncan rocked and puffed. Stevie asked him the easiest way back avoiding the dam and the camp.

'If it's not snowing, the best way is along the top above the wood. I'll show you.'

'When was Joel last here?' said Eamon.

'Not since the beginning of November.'

'Which days?'

'It's all there, on the calendar.' Duncan pointed. Eamon turned back the calendar to November. 'Red cross for every day he worked. For his wages you see.' There was a red cross for every day in the last week of October and the first two weeks of November. He turned back to December. The twenty-first was marked with a heavy red circle.

'Why is the twenty-first marked, Duncan?'

'That's Joel's mark, not mine. Shortest day of the year the twenty-first, that's all it is.'

He took them up on a narrow path through the trees. When they were above the tree line he pointed out the way they should take. The day was turning to twilight but the sky had cleared in the west and the descending sun was casting beams upon distant hills. They could see the glimmer of Loch Houn below the sun, although the dam and the camp were obscured. On the other side of the glen before them Eamon could see the truncated road where Edgar had shown him the wind-turbine sites. There were several white cubes at the end of that road. They were tiny from this distance; something to do with the construction, he thought. Down below, on the floor of the narrow glen that led south-east from Glenfashie, he could see a bothy with a stream of smoke rising from the chimney.

'What's that?'

'That'll be the shepherd's house,' said Duncan.

'What shepherd?'

'No. No shepherd now, not for a long time. That'll be the Africans.'

'Lie still Joshua Malafu, lie still in darkness and warmth. Feel how full your belly is and sleep. I will take you down, beneath the sea, and I will raise you to the light in England. You do not like to be pitied but do not spurn her. Besides, many things can be disguised as pity. Perhaps she does not want a poor African to drown on her beach. Perhaps she does not want the dirty body on her white sand. Perhaps she would rather risk the police at the port, risk being caught carrying an immigrant in the boot of her car than see your body rolling in her little waves and glistening in her sunlight. Never forget that you are nothing, and that I carry you in the palm of my hand.'

CHAPTER THIRTEEN

By the time Eamon and Stevie had reached the bottom of the glen it was growing dark, and there was a light shining from the window of the bothy. When they had been higher up they had seen an adult standing by the doorway of the bothy, and had heard a voice calling, and there had been a child further away, among the peat hags and rocks. Then, following their path, they had gone into the forest again and the figures had been hidden. They reached the floor of the glen about a mile below the bothy and followed a track that was little more than a path marked with the wheels of an Argo or quad. When they came into view of the bothy again they saw two women, both wearing long, black dresses, standing in the doorway watching them. There were no children now. The women turned and went inside.

At first, when she opened the door, Eamon thought it was Isabel. She had the same broad forehead and short jaw; a pixie-like face. Her hair was neater, tied in corn rows. The dress she wore, under a grey fleece, was black lace, almost a ball gown, ill fitting and flaring out at the hips. She gave no sign of recognition and did not smile a greeting. Her face did not wear the terrible grief Eamon had seen in Tarr Bow, and as he looked closer in the dim light of the candle that she carried, he could see that it was not Isabel. This woman was younger, her skin smoother, but she looked resigned and worried.

'Hallo,' he said, and she nodded in reply but made no sound. She gestured along the short corridor into the house. The walls were bare, scratched plaster, and the floor was linoleum worn through to the concrete. There was a smell of dog and peat-smoke. Eamon hesitated and she repeated the gesture. He walked towards the light at the end of the corridor and entered a room lit by a single candle set upon a chest of drawers. The other woman sat with her hands clasped on her lap. Her dress was black velvet, with petticoats, over jeans, and with a woollen hat. She had the same short jaw and pointed chin. On the bed lay two children. They were boys; pale-faced compared to their mothers, with wild curly hair, but with the same features. They lay side by side with the blankets drawn up to their chests and their arms on top of the blankets with the sleeves rolled up, offering the veins in the crook of the elbow.

'Jeez,' said Stevie.

'What is this?' Eamon searched the faces of the women. 'What is this?' The seated woman with the hat gestured towards the children. The woman with the candle sat down on the bed next to the children and drew her hand over their arms. For a moment Eamon had a distinct feeling that he was dreaming, and was about to awake. He repeated his question and the two women looked at each other. The one with the hat spoke first, in a language that Eamon assumed was African. The other replied, gesturing at the bag Eamon was carrying. The strange phrases came thickly, passing back and forth and rising in tone. The woman in the hat grew angry. The language was sinuous, interspersed with clattering plosives like rain falling on thick leaves. The woman with the hat rose, covered the boy's arms with the blanket, and ushered the men from the room, back towards the corridor, smiling, grinning and obsequious. The other carried on talking and pointing at the bag. The one in the hat said something sharp to her and she stopped. The woman in the hat began pushing Eamon, and he could see through the smiles to the urgency and desperation on her face. He pushed Stevie before him along the corridor and out of the bothy. The door slammed shut behind them and they heard a bolt slide. Outside in the dark and the cold they moved away from the door, sat on a rock and smoked cigarettes.

'I don't think we are who we're supposed to be,' said Stevie.

'Or we didn't do what we're supposed to do.'

'Which is what?'

'I'm not sure. We'd better start for home.'

'We're not going to go over the top in the dark,' said Stevie. 'We're going to have to walk back along the glen and sneak past the camp. You can call one of your servants to pick us up from Loch Houn.'

Grigor could see the single light burning far out in the water. The water was cold and dark, but calm and clean. It would cleanse him of all the filth he had absorbed, and he would burn off fat. He stripped off his clothes and stuffed them into his backpack, then he put the backpack into a black plastic bag and tied the neck. He put this into another black plastic bag which he blew up and tied. Then he tied a length of cord around the neck of the bag and the other end of the cord around his own neck. It was no more than a kilometre to the boat. He waded naked into the water, without flinching, until he was swimming and the black balloon floating behind him.

The water was good and pure; he would absorb the salts. We came from the sea. The sea is where we were born, aeons ago, and then we crawled out.

It is colder than he thought. Keep moving towards the light. Got to get out of that house. It is making me sick. Swim, Grigor, swim. My God it is cold. Swim towards the light. Keep swimming. One, two, three, four. What is he looking for in that hole? Why is he lying about the hole? He didn't know where he was digging. He was just digging. To bury something. To bury something that comes in from the boat. The boat is bringing in drugs. To bury the drugs? Guns. They want to bury guns. Swim you stupid fucking Grigor. Swim! Swim towards the light. Swim!

By nightfall the sea had shed itself of all but a ripple of disturbance and *Rage III* sped on her wake towards a Milky Way that sprang like a firework from the horizon. Vanneck cooked his special spaghetti and vegan meatballs and opened a bottle of alcohol-free red wine. After much experimenting he found the controls for the roof of the salon and they dressed in furs that she had bought in Paris to sit beneath the stars. Lilian was in such a good mood that she even asked for Brighton, and Vanneck had to explain that he had not slept at all through the storm and was sleeping. She smiled at him as she sipped her wine but he found it hard to return the smile.

'Come Sam,' she said, 'You look like a guilty schoolboy. Tell me what you did. Tell me about the programme.' He toyed with his spaghetti.

'First, I want you to promise me something,' he said. 'Promise me you won't ask me to turn back.'

'Ok. I promise.'

'Fine. Adam. It starts with Adam, as you know. Adam was a mythical beast, according to his stories. It wasn't us who found him. It was a German journalist who was writing a book about Henry Morton Stanley and following his route along the river Congo. Away up in the north of the DRC he found a man who could remember Stanley and that meant he had to be a one hundred and thirty year old man, at least. Well, the German told a colleague and the colleague knew someone who knew someone who worked for me and we made the trip. One hundred and thirty two years old. So he said. So the Singa said. And that wasn't the only remarkable thing. He was sure of his age, because, unlike all the other tribes around them, some of the Singa could read and write and they kept a kind of calendar. So, according to them, he was the oldest human being on the planet. As far as we knew he was the oldest man who had ever lived. So we took him to Montezuma, and we found something remarkable. We found the holy grail.'

'I know all that.'

'We found a component in his blood, a protein, an immensely complicated molecule, that was acting as a sort of super antibody, an anti-aging serum, or at least, that was what we assumed. We did not have time for this to become definite, we did not have time to do all the tests that we wanted, because he died.'

'I know all that too.' She looked steadily across the table at him, hiding her hands from the cold in the folds of fur.

'What you didn't know, and I didn't know then, was who his father was. I wanted to go back straight away, but the war came and for seven years we couldn't get in. When we finally got back, as I told you, the Singa had been decimated. Their way of life was in ruins, and they were asking, begging for help. And whereas before they had been reticent and suspicious of us, now they were willing to tell us everything, and of course the mystery of Adam's lineage came up. It had been obvious from the beginning that there was some European blood in there. His features, the paleness of his skin. What came out this time was that he had had siblings, and that they had both lived until a few years before we found him. You understand how remarkable this is? It was a sign of a definite genetic component to his longevity. His mother was a Singa, we were told. Then there was the question of his father. This is where the whole thing became incredible. They had his things, things belonging to his father, in a metal box, that they kept in a cave, and they were so desperate for help, they gave me this box, which amounted to a sacred object for them. "Adam's father," they said, "this is Adam's father."'

'What was in it?'

'I have it here.' He rose from the table and went to a panel in the wall which slid back to reveal a safe. He unlocked it and took out a metal box about the size of a shoe box. He moved aside her half-eaten meal and placed it on the table in front of her.

'Have a look,' he said. She took off the rusty lid. Inside there were three books, a pair of spectacles with a silver frame, a leather belt with a silver buckle and several buttons. She opened the topmost book. It was a Bible, and the pages were well thumbed and annotated with tiny handwriting in pencil. She placed it on the table and took out the second book. It was bound with brown paper and the pages were tied together with string; a home-made book. On the fly-leaf there was a circular design of half formed letters and circles and lines, Y's, and upside down V's.

'Do you remember Adam's stone? The one he wore around his neck?'

'Yes, this design.' She ran her finger over the pencil marks.

'All the men and boys wore them. It was a kind of talisman, a sign of their tribe.' She turned the page, and read out loud the long, looping copper-plate handwriting. '"Cosmic Salutations and the Breath of Life. A treatise on the Energetic Exhortations off Plasmageroid Interior Pictogrammatical Functions of Continental and Local Effect. By His Most High Holiness, Adam Sigurson." Good Grief. What's this?' Vanneck smiled. She turned a page. There was a diagram; lines connecting symbols like the ones on the flyleaf. She turned another. '"I Adam Sigurson, being an exhalation emitted unto this planetary sphere on the second day of 1818 by the calendar of Christ humanised, and thus on the first day of the first month of the first rotation of the new era, do hereby dedicate this treatise to the transfiguration of what is known as man..."' Vanneck silenced her with a shake of his head.

'Don't go on. I've read a lot of it. It doesn't actually say anything. Although later on it does become a little more poetic. I think he might have been eating mushrooms.' The third book was much slimmer than the others, also home-made, but the brown paper cover had acquired a dark patina, and the pages bore smudged finger-marks. It was a much used book, and written in an African language;

'"Njambe apala ngondo na ngenjo..."' she read, stumbling over the words.

'We had this translated from the Singa,' said Vanneck. 'It's a sort of prayer book, like an office, or an order of service. It's a mixture of the Bible and Sigurson's own peculiar theology which makes him out to be some sort of Christ figure. Some of the male Singa could read this, and they used it for funerals and weddings and baptisms. The point is, Adam's father was Adam Sigurson. You can google him. He's on Wikipedia. He was from Shetland, born in 1818, went to school there, became a minister in the Church of Scotland, got married to one Jean Peery, and then got a bit of a reputation for funny ideas. He was into what would later become known as ley lines, and was fascinated by standing stones and ancient Pictish knowledge, numerology, ancient codes in the Bible, all that stuff. He was a proto-hippie, ahead of his time by a hundred and fifty years. This did not go down well with the good folk of Shetland, plus, he was a hippie in another respect; into free love. He was bedding every woman he could, all over the islands. Jean Peery, being a God-fearing woman, and with the support of her family, escaped, and he took up with another woman, apparently a bit more to his way of thinking. She had a reputation as being a bit of a witch. Anyway, they were shunned, cast out of the church, and after some time on the mainland they took off for Africa, intent on setting up some kind of heaven on earth. They were never heard off again. Ever, until now.'

'Wow.'

'Wow indeed. He went up the Congo river before any other white man. Before Henry Morton Stanley. Quite an achievement, especially considering he was basically bonkers. That in itself makes for an interesting story, but it is not the point. The point is, he was Adam's father, and apparently the father of at least two others who lived to be older than other human beings ever, ever, as far as we know. Now this is the crucial bit. He was Adam's father. No doubt about that. Now the Singa, as we already knew, are a genetic island. They were an isolated tribe, rarely mingling. They're like pygmies. They have very peculiar and easily identifiable unique genetic markers. But they don't live particularly long. It seemed that what had happened was that Sigurson, nutcase from the far North, breeding with this particular gene-pool had created this freak, Adam, and his siblings. I know, it's crazy.'

'It is crazy,' she nodded.

'Crazy but true. However, Sigurson was dead. Adam and his siblings were dead. We still had the Singa, what was left of them. I went looking for the Sigursons. It wasn't easy. I looked at his lineage. It appeared he was the last in his line, until I looked for Jean Peery. She never remarried, but sure enough she had had a son. Born in 1858. John Peery, taking his mother's name. John Peery married and had three daughters and a son. None of the daughters married, none had children, no idea why. The son moved to Glasgow and had two daughters and a son. That son, Mathew Peery, had a son. We found him. James. James Peery. Rather an odd character. We told him about his famous great-great-grandfather and he was excited by the news, and changed his name to Sigurson, officially. James Sigurson. We took his DNA. He thought it was a 'cool' idea. No problem. We studied the hell out of it.'

'And?'

'And whatever. What does DNA tell you? Truth is, not much unless you know what you are looking for. We had the protein, the magic antibody. We had DNA from Adam. We had DNA from this descendant of Sigurson's, and DNA from eighty Singa. It didn't tell us how to make the protein. Life is not that simple. If only. That was when Flieber came up with the idea that was on everyone's mind but no-one dared say it, not even at Montezuma, where we are all supposed to be so open with each other. It took Flieber, a first year doctoral student, to say it.'

'Let's breed another Adam.'

'Yes,' said Vanneck, and his tone changed, and the room with the open roof was suddenly freezing as her face darkened. He rose and went to a console on the wall behind her to close the glass panels.

'And did you?' she said. He looked at the back of her head.

'No. I told you, it went wrong. The whole thing. It was a disaster.' He sat back down.

'But that was the plan.' Her look was stern and without a trace of that frailty that he had become so used to. She was the old Lillian, the young Lillian, the one who had spent her life trying to pierce the heart of things, trying to get deep inside. He put the books back into the box and put the box back in the safe.

'Yes, that was the plan.'

'How?'

'Artificial insemination. We built a facility, to accommodate the whole tribe.'

'The plan was to get the women pregnant, with this, this Sigurson's sperm?' He forced his eyes to meet hers.

'Yes.'

'With their consent?'

'Yes.'

'How?'

'It was an issue that we never had to confront, because they never got there.'

'How did you plan to do it?'

'We had someone that knew the language. We were going to explain things to them.'

'What if they didn't want to?'

'We were considering alternatives, other surrogates. It's a moot point.'

'And the men, the Singa men. What did they think of this idea?' He was silent, poking at congealed spaghetti with a fork. 'Sam, I can see why you told me nothing about this. You knew this was wrong.'

'What I was doing had the potential to change the world. For me, for you, for my investors, for everyone that is old. I didn't tell you because of this. This conversation. You are the same as everyone else. The same as the governments that tried to stop me patenting genes, that tried to stop the embryo research. Are you another fucking ethics committee? It's the same shit, Lily. Get this into your head. Sometimes people need to make decisions that are difficult. Yes, sometimes people suffer. War. People have to be sent to die in the trenches. That's a fact. In order for humanity to go forward, there have to be sacrifices.'

'The difference is necessity. A war, a justified war, is a necessary thing. This is different. It's not a war. It's different, Sam.'

'How? It's a war against death! We're trying to cure ageing! We are talking about curing you, curing me!'

'You're talking about living forever?'

'Don't be silly.'

'What then? Another ten years? Twenty? And then? We die, we all die in the end.'

'I'm talking about taking a step. When did you object to the work we've been doing on Alzheimer's? What's the difference? Do you have a problem with cancer research? What is cancer research about, if not prolonging life for old people!'

'But these people, the Singa, they're uneducated, innocent.'

'Pah! Innocent? What? The noble savage? I'll tell you what these people are, on the one hand they are nothing. They're dying, the detritus of a forgotten war. They were starving to death out there, in the fucking jungle! Nothing, and on the other hand they contain something incredible and precious. The possibility of a cure for ageing, and God knows what else. What am I supposed to do? Let them die in their grass huts?'

'And in the end you killed them.' He stood and swept his arm across the table, smashing the plates and glasses to the floor.

'Yes, Lily, I killed them! I killed them. I tried to take the men off the boat! Then I locked them in the hold for two weeks when they fought back! I starved them and shot at them when they tried to get out! That's me, mass murderer Samuel Vanneck! Do you think that's what I will be remembered for? After everything I've done! After everything I've done for humanity, everything I've done for you!' She was silent. He paced the room and then went out onto the deck.

'I want to go back to my room now,' she said. He heard her and stood in the doorway.

'Go on then. See if you can make it on your own. Or perhaps you need help, perhaps you need medicine.'

'Where's Brighton?'

'Brighton? Oh, I forgot to tell you. He's dead. I killed him too.' He watched as she stood unsteadily, holding onto the table, then turned her back on him and walked, slowly, supporting herself on the furniture, back towards the bedroom.

Rona guided her mother's Volvo swiftly away from the pier back towards Glencul, with Stevie in the back and Eamon in the front seat, both of them so exhausted they were hardly able to talk.

'So Joel couldn't have killed the child?' she said. 'It's impossible if he was up there all that time. Impossible.' Eamon watched her face glowing in the light from the dashboard. The walk down Glenfashie had taken them three hours. They had crept in the ditch for a full mile past the camp where there were arc lamps and machinery moving. They had had nothing to eat since the morning. Eamon felt that familiar terror, the world tipping, the hollowness of everything. They were tin men, rattling on the surface, and empty within. For the second time he found refuge in her face. Smooth, round cheeks and excitement in the eyes. To her it was a game, an adventure. She had never witnessed what lay behind it all, behind every crime. Or had she? Did she know about the banality of evil? How the death of a child, the mangling of life into a corpse, was the product of nothing more than the touch of a button, the difference between a one and a two. Behind all this, whatever was going on in the bothy at the head of the glen, behind whatever had happened in the mind of Joel Kennedy, in the gulag, in the camp, at the *Misty*; nothing more than the difference between two digits, nothing more than a pixel on a screen. At Nuremberg they had revealed that behind the mountains of corpses there stood men with clipboards. She kept talking, swinging the big car around the curves in the narrow road. He watched her hands on the wheel, her bright face, lips and teeth moving.

'I've been looking up the planning permissions for the renovations to Tarvin Lodge. Very mysterious. The agent was none other than Edgar Dupuy. He was acting for a company, get this, based in the Cayman Islands. *Glenpro Holdings.*' Eamon said nothing. She glanced from him to the road, back to him. 'Well isn't that odd?' Odd, thought Eamon, but it didn't tell them anything. 'It's one of those things, shell companies, where people don't want you to know who it is that's doing the work, don't you think? They're trying to cover their tracks.'

'Perhaps,' said Eamon. The car skidded and swerved to a stop and Eamon lurched forward against his seatbelt. 'What?'

'Didn't you see that?' the car whined in reverse.

'What?'

'That man! There's a man!' She pulled up alongside him; a tall, thin man with a lopsided appearance, carrying a backpack. Beneath the hooded jacket there was dark skin, a short jaw, a broad forehead. Eamon wound down the window. The man stared blankly at him. He held his hands in his pockets.

'Hallo,' said Eamon. The man nodded and carried on walking past them down the road in the direction of Loch Houn. 'He's one of them. He's got the same face. Hold on a minute.' He got out of the car and jogged after the man and grabbed his arm. He was met with the same blank expression, neither hoping nor fearing, expecting nothing, offering nothing. 'Do you speak English?' The man shook his head. *'Parlez vous Français?'* The man shook his head. He had the same eyes as the women in the bothy, as Isabel Mtetu. The man moved his arm slowly out of Eamon's grasp and turned to walk on, into the darkness. 'Isabel. Isabel Mtetu,' said Eamon to his back. The man stopped, and turned. 'Isabel Mtetu,' said Eamon.

'Isabel,' said the man, in a whisper. 'Isabel Mtetu.' His eyes glistened in the red car lights.

'Yes. Isabel. I know her. You know her?'

'Isabel,' said the man, taking a step forward. He took a hand from a pocket and pointed at himself. 'Joshua. Joshua Malafu.'

'Come, Joshua, get in the car.' As he opened the door for him he could see that Joshua's eyes were wet with tears.

Your face that never ages; sunlight in a garden, and the limpid air pierced by the scream of a telephone. It is never a good thing, thought Pyotr, surfacing like a swimmer from the dream. A phone ringing at midnight; an accident, a fuck up, a death. Perhaps all three. It's a call from the boat. They have Grigor. 'What do you mean?'

'About an hour ago Sasha hears a knocking on the side of the boat. He thinks it's a piece of driftwood, but it's knock knock knock, knock knock knock, bump, bump, bump. Like it's alive. Something alive knocking on the boat, so he says it's a seal and he goes to get his rifle. It is a still night, no waves, and dark. He's pointing down into the water and he can hear the thumping just below him. He's just about to pull the trigger when the moon comes out and he sees white. A white seal? No, a white body. It's Grigor, drowning, trying to grab onto the side of the boat but there is nothing to hold and he's thumping with his fist.'

'Christ.' Pyotr sat up on the edge of the bed and rubbed his face.

'"Grigor!" we are shouting, "Hey, Grigor!" But he is not saying anything. We let down a ladder and he grabs hold of it. He is naked. It is fucking cold you know? He can't climb the ladder. So we lower the dinghy. We get down to him and try to pull him into the boat, but you know Grigor is a big guy. We can't get him in and he's cold like a stone and mumbling and still thumping his fist against the boat. Shit we had problems! Then we get him into the dinghy and pull it up, then out onto the deck like we caught a shark. I think he's dead but he's still moving. Lev says he's frozen so we put him in blankets and stick him in a bunk. What we gonna do boss?'

'Keep him warm. Leave him. Phone me in the morning. If he wakes up.'

'Sherry?' said Edgar, with a winning smile. Eamon declined. They were in the kitchen at Grey Acres, lulled by the heat of the Aga. There were children's toys on the floor and the plates of breakfast on the polished marble table. Ginny was off to a gymkhana with the girls. They had the house to themselves, and that was good, thought Eamon, in case he had to knock Edgar about a little. 'You're probably right, a bit early for the sherry. We can wait until lunch. You'll stay for lunch won't you?' Eamon sized up Edgar, silently. He had spent most of the night trying to talk to a man who seemed to have only seven words of English. His name, *Eloissey*, Isabel Mtetu, Singa, (that was himself, he was Singa) and Loch Houn. Apart from this he spoke a few words of pidgin French and a few words in Spanish. He had a map of the North-West of Scotland, a computer printout, with the word *Eloise* written on Loch Houn. Eamon assumed that this was the *'Eloissey'* he kept repeating. Then, while he was stuffing porridge down his throat as if eating for the first time in months, Eamon had noticed the coloured string around his neck and had asked to see the stone. It was identical to the one Isabel had shown him, and Eamon had taken the incomprehensible African down to the dungeon. But Joshua had refused to enter the stone room. Eamon had been unable to make him understand, and had given up. The man had left the basement ahead of him.

'I need some answers, Edgar. Clear answers.'

'Yes, yes, of course. What about?'

'Quite a few things. One. Who is leasing the properties in the gulag?'

'Back to that old chestnut is it? I told you. Social Services. Highland Social Services. Social Services Highland, whatever they call themselves these days. Your friendly local council.'

'I want a name. Who do you deal with?'

'I can look that up for you. It was a while ago. I'll have to check the files. What's so important about this?' He reached for the sherry bottle. Here comes the narrowing of the eyes and the knot on the forehead.

'Edgar. How long has your family worked for mine?' Edgar stopped short of uncorking the bottle.

'Yonks.'

'Your father, and his father, and if I'm not mistaken, his father before him. You seem to have done rather well out of it.' Eamon gestured around the brand-new kitchen.

'Oh come on, Eamon, what are you implying?'

'It's a lot better than my kitchen. The point is, do you want to be the one who causes the connection to be severed?' Edgar got to uncorking the bottle.

'No, of course not, God forbid!'

'I want a name.'

'Christ.' Edgar's shoulders slumped. 'Wright. Clarissa or something.'

'Clarice Wright?'

'Probably.' He knocked back the sherry in one gulp.

'Right. Number two. Are you aware that the men you hired to build the dam are drug dealers?'

'No.'

'How did you begin? How did they get the contract?' Edgar drummed the marble with his fingertips.

'This is my father's time you understand. It was nothing to do with me. *Enerpro* was a recommendation. I think. They've done others. Farr and Glenmoriston. What makes you think they're dealing drugs?' Eamon debated the wisdom of letting Edgar know what he knew.

'Nothing. It's a suspicion that's all. Moving on. Number three. What do you know about the Singa?'

'The what?'

'Black people, staying in the gulag, the murdered child, the women and the children in the bothy, up beyond Glenfashie? What do you know about all that?'

'The bothy? What bothy?'

'Do I have to bring out a map Edgar?'

'If you are talking about the one way up beyond the forestry it's nothing to do with us. No-one has lived there for twenty odd years since Gavin Matheson died. It's Mohammed's ground. Blessed be his holy name. Not yours. Not my problem. Look, there are refugees everywhere now, all over the country. They're coming in like rats. The Social Services look for accommodation; I provide accommodation. It's not my business who they put in the properties. I've told you all this.' He reached for the bottle again.

'Question number four. Who owns *The Misty Isle*?'

' Not you. You haven't owned that for a century.'

'Who?'

'An English couple. I don't even know their names. It's nothing to do with us. They bought it from the Jameson's about five years ago.'

'Number five. Tell me about Tarvin lodge.'

'Christ. I've already told you. What do want to know?'

'You were the agent for the planning permission. You didn't tell me that.'

'They were looking for someone with local knowledge. I was a middle man, that's all.'

'You were paid to do what?'

'File applications. Deal with the council. I know the right people.'

'And who or what was the client?'

'An American. I never met him. Flieber. Gurt, Bert, Dirt, Flieber. Dealt with him over the phone. That was years ago. What the hell are you aiming at Eamon? If you think *Enerpro* are dealing drugs why don't you go to the police?' Eamon sighed.

'And this Flieber. Did he have anything to do with *Enerpro*?'

'No. Yes. Not at first. *Enerpro* did some of the work. They were in the area. They had the machinery and they were bringing in materials for the dam.'

'Have you got a contact for Flieber?'

'Somewhere I'm sure. I'll have to look.'

'Now. I want to know now. I want everything you've got on him and Tarvin Lodge, and I want all your papers on the dam. Everything you've got to do with *Enerpro*. And I want a number for Clarice Wright. Now. Let's go to the study. I'll keep you company while you look it all out. And I'll think I'll have that sherry, thank you.'

As Pyotr was inhaling the last centimetre of his twentieth cigarette of the day, heavy sheets of rain came rattling against the window behind him. The room was cold, in spite of the electric heater drying out the air. The telephone on his desk rang and he answered. It was Gurt Flieber.

'To what do I owe the honour? No, let me guess. You are coming to deliver a suitcase full of the cash to compensate for the disruption of my business.'

'Less of the sarcasm Mr P, I'm doing you a favour. You've got a problem which I suggest you do something about. Do you know who Eamon Ansgar is?'

'Yes.'

'He's been snooping around, and guess what? He suspects a certain small scale renewable energy company of smuggling drugs in at Loch Houn, under the cover of shipments of construction materials.'

'Now, let me see. I don't suppose his interest in the activities of *Enerpro* might have been engendered by the strange and unfortunate death of a child in his village?'

'More likely the strange and unfortunate behaviour of your imbecile nephew,' said Flieber. Pyotr paused and lit number twenty-one, early, putting him off his rhythm.

'Ah yes,' he said. 'That reminds me. Do you know where Grigor is?'

'He's laying low.'

'That is what Sigurson said. Where?'

'He's in a guest house, nearby.'

'He doesn't answer his phone.'

'I told him to switch it off. I'll get him to call you if you're so anxious.'

'Yes, do that. Now you tell me, what do you know about what Mr Ansgar knows?'

When he had finished talking to Flieber, Pyotr called the boat.

'He's sick boss,' said Lev. 'First he was too cold, now he is too hot. I give him paracetamol and hot lemon. He's shivering like crazy, talking shit.' Pyotr told Lev to call him when his nephew made sense, and dialled the number Flieber had given him.

'Mr Ansgar? Pyotr Tiranasov, managing director at *Enerpro*. I think perhaps it would be a good idea if we met.' We sacrifice everything to this God. Mammon. Every scrap of kindness, every tenderness, all hope, all love, all honour. It devours everything. Let us see if Eamon Ansgar is also a worshipper.

CHAPTER FOURTEEN

Eamon was on his way home from Grey Acres when he got the call. An old man with a deep, resonant voice. A voice that was used to being obeyed. The voice of a calculating mind. It reminded him of his father's voice, but it did not have the note of exasperation. Pyotr Tiranasov was calmer and more persuasive. Eamon pulled over into a passing place.

'So you're the man in charge of the drug importation business?' he said. Pyotr laughed.

'Perhaps you are jumping to conclusions. That is never a good idea. Apparently you were here recently at the camp and they wouldn't let you in. I apologise for that. They did not know who you were. I would be happy to show you around.'

'Perhaps you would be happy to show the police around.'

'Of course. Why not? I am sure I can persuade you that we have nothing to hide.'

'We'll leave that to the police, I think.'

'As you wish. I would like to suggest a little prudence though. You can call the police, bring them down on my camp and have them investigate my business if you like, but the police happen to be very concerned about a little thing called evidence. The end result may only be a very irritated police department and a very irritated *Enerpro*, and nothing more. A waste of time and money for all. I think we should meet first, get to know each other, see what kind of men we are. You might find me very reasonable.'

'What does that mean? A cut of the profits?'

'You are already profiting handsomely from the endeavours of *Enerpro*, Mr Ansgar. Glenfashie dam is only the beginning.'

'Not interested.'

'Besides, I might be able to help you out on the question of the whereabouts of a certain African lady.' Eamon was about to reply, but paused. 'You see, drugs are one thing, boring really in comparison, but this, this other thing, is really far more interesting.'

'What do you know about her?'

'Let us meet, Mr Ansgar, or may I call you Eamon? Let us talk a little. In the meantime, do not go to the police. It is not worth it, trust me. Especially for her.'

In the end it was perhaps as simple as this; Lillian was a woman and soft-hearted; useless when it came to making difficult decisions. The irony was, after the fight with Lily and sitting up all night on the bridge, watching the screens and the stars, he had missed Brighton. Brighton had been against the whole project from the start, but only because he considered it too much of a risk. He was not against it on principle. He had made an assessment, and his assessment had been that they would get caught.

At dawn, in blue light turning to yellow over a flat calm, Vanneck put on shorts and a t-shirt and did fifty rounds of the deck, then finished off in the gym with some free weights. He ate a breakfast of wheat-grass juice and goji berries. He showered, changed, and went back to the bridge. They were north of Ireland now, a hundred miles to the west, making good time. There was a front moving towards them, but it was still far out in the Atlantic, south of Greenland. He resisted the urge to call Flieber. There was no need. He took out some fishing gear and cast off the stern deck. It was a perfect day for fishing, a beautiful day, but the boat was going at full speed, twenty knots, and probably too fast for fish. He went into the salon where the plates and glasses and food still lay on the floor, and tidied up, throwing everything into the sea. Seeing the glasses he was overwhelmed by the desire for a drink. He went into the crew's cabins and rifled through the drawers. In the third cabin he found what he was looking for in one of the lockers; three bottles of malt. It was late in the morning before he checked on her, and he was half drunk. She was sleeping, perhaps sedated. He checked her pulse. It was so weak it was hard to find. He did not try to wake her. What was the point?

'You agreed to meet him?' said Rona, wide-eyed and incredulous.

'Why not? What do I have to lose?'

'He's a gangster. Stevie said they'd kill you.'

'He may be a gangster but he didn't sound stupid. Why would he offer information about Isabel? No, he's probably going to offer me money, to buy me. It's a chance to find out, to make sense of all this.' He had spread out the papers from Joel's room on the floor of the study; drawings, symbols, maps, pages of barely legible handwriting. 'Then there's these.' He tapped the pile of files from Edgar's office. 'Planning permissions, contracts, plans, letters between his dad and *Enerpro*. And this.' He held up a memory stick. 'All the emails between *Enerpro* and Edgar's dad. I still think he's holding out on me though. How come this *Enerpro* guy phones me as soon as I've been to Grey Acres? Edgar must have let him know. Here's a thing. *Enerpro* didn't do *some* of the work on Tarvin Lodge. They did all of it, every brick. And it started at the same time. Everything at the same time, the dam, the lodge, and the pier.'

'What does it all have to do with Isabel, and Joshua?'

'Something, but I don't know what. I've got a number for Clarice Wright, but it goes straight to voicemail.'

'Clarice Wright dealt with Edgar, Edgar deals with Tarvin Lodge and the American, Flieber. Edgar deals with *Enerpro*. Edgar ties it all together. You know what that means don't you?'

'What?'

'It's you. Edgar works for you. He's only a factor for the house of

Duncul.'

'Yes, Duncul. And Joel was obsessed with the Stone of Duncul. Look at these drawings. But how did he know about it?'

'The break-in,' she said. 'It must have been Joel.'

'He was small enough. But how did he know it was there? Why would he break in? Why did he kill himself? Why did he burn the child?' Eamon lit a cigarette.

'But people in the village know it's there. Kirsty, for example, and Mike. They've worked in the castle all their lives.'

'So Joel knew about the stone, but couldn't have known what was on it until he broke in.'

'We need to go over everything,' she said. 'Every scrap of paper. Every email. The answer is in here somewhere. I can stay late. Mum's gone to her cousin for the week.' Eamon watched her, on her hands and knees, trying to decipher Joel's handwriting. He would, he could, invite her to stay the night. Tonight.

'I'm going to meet Pyotr. I'll be back in a couple of hours.'

'I don't think you should go alone. Take Stevie with you.'

'I agreed to go alone. Besides, Stevie won't help. He's practically one of them.'

'Be careful, don't you have a gun or something?'

'A gun only gives people permission to shoot you.' She smiled at him as he left.

He had refused to go to the camp, an instinctive rather than a rational reaction. He should have insisted on a public place, he reflected, as he drove up the hill from Glencul towards Loch Houn.

The car park, at the top of the hill, just before the road began its long winding descent to the Loch, was just as potentially dangerous as the camp. Maybe even more so. It was sheltered by trees on three sides, and the fourth framed a view over Glencul; the farms in the glen to the west, the village and castle, the loch to the east and the winding Ash. It would be a good spot to kill someone, as long as no tourist happened along the road, which was not likely late on a freezing winter's afternoon.

The car was already there when he pulled in. As Eamon stopped he saw an old man with thin white hair wearing a black overcoat get out and light a cigarette. Eamon took out one of his own as he approached and Pyotr stepped forward to light it.

'A pleasure to meet you, Mr Ansgar.' He had long yellow teeth and his lips were dry. 'You know, I met your father. We met on several occasions. I liked him. He was a practical and serious man.'

'My father would never have had anything to do with this.' Pyotr shrugged.

'Perhaps not. But after all, what is this?' He sat back against the bonnet of his car. 'Business, business, business. Money, money, money. That is all. How did your family come to own all this? All this land, all these buildings?'

'A very long time ago.'

'But you know, don't you, your own history? You fought for it. Blood was spilt. Which side did your family fight for at Culloden? No, don't tell, because I know. Your ancestor sent one son to fight for the Stuarts and one son to fight for Cumberland, so that whatever happened he would be on the winning side. Now you, Ansgar, the descendant of pirates, of Vikings, raping and pillaging, want to be a principled man. You want to run to the police because you suspect, and I emphasise, suspect, I may be running drugs through here. I can read books, Ansgar. I know where your money comes from. Not from your inadequate dabbling in The City. It's all old money, money from the colonies. Money from the opium trade, money from the sugar trade, money from cheap labour in Bangladesh. You want to be a man of virtue? "Give everything you have away to the poor and come follow me."' He laughed. 'Your money, Ansgar, has more blood on it than mine.'

'I'm not responsible for any of that. This is now. What you are doing now is illegal.' It sounded pathetic though, that word, 'illegal'. He sounded like a child complaining, 'you're breaking the rules'. Pyotr smiled.

'Yes, I know, what I do is illegal, so you say, but what you did in Afghanistan was legal, was it? Killing women and children? Was that legal? I'll be honest with you Ansgar. I have killed men in my life. Only men, and only with a knife or a pistol. I know exactly how many. I looked every one of them in the eye. I will tell you how many if you tell me how many you have killed. But you can't, can you?' Eamon did not reply. He knew that he had made a mistake in coming, he could feel it as if the ground was shifting underneath his feet. 'I knew it was a good idea to meet,' said Pyotr. 'You can tell a lot when you see a man's eyes. You see, you are right, there is a difference between you and I. We are on opposite sides of a line, now, at this point in history, and that line is the line of the law. It is not the line of right and wrong. What is the house of Duncul but a long line of gangsters? What is at the heart of Duncul? Blood and murder, like every great house in every land. Come over here to this side of the line, and you can see what I am talking about. But you won't, will you? Of course not! You have your principles! Your nobility. That is good, because I am not going to offer you money. I have looked into your eyes and I can see that you won't take it. I look around at all this, and all this is yours. I am not Satan, I cannot offer it to you, and you already own it. What I am going to offer you is something else.' Eamon heard a rushing sound from behind him and at the same time he recognised the smell that had been tingling the edge of his senses for the last minute. Petrol. He turned to see a pillar of flame rising from his car, the flames sucking at the air, drawing in the world towards them, and the sight was so strange, so unexpected, that for a moment he had the eerie feeling that the old man with his white hair and his long coat was a kind of magician, and that a dark art had drawn the flames up from the earth or down from the sky, until he saw behind the flames a man dressed in black and wearing a ski mask, holding a petrol can. The flames were boiling through the interior. Eamon backed away from the car. The old man lit another cigarette.

'That, my friend, is called arson. Listen. If you go to the police I will do the same thing to your castle, and I won't be too concerned about who is in it at the time.' The three of them watched the flames from the edge of the car park and for a moment Eamon had a bizarre sensation of conviviality. They were like three men standing around a bonfire. He almost laughed. They stepped back, expecting the car to explode at any moment. It crackled and popped, and the roof buckled, black smoke swirling into the low sky. Sleet began to fall, hissing into the flames. The tank went off with a roar rather than a bang. Eamon remembered that there had not been much in it.

'What about the African woman?' he said. 'You said you would tell me something.' The old man stared into the flames.

'I will tell you the most important thing. Look there, look into the flames. What do you see?' Eamon looked at the melting plastic, twisting metal and cracking glass.

'Pain,' he said.

'Hell is what you see. That is hell. You don't want to go there, do you?'

'Is she alive?' Pyotr found the question funny.

'Alive? What is alive? That woman has not been alive for years now. Nor the others.'

'So you know about the others?' Eamon tried to read his eyes but Pyotr turned away, concentrating on the fire. It was growing dark. 'You said something just now, about us being on different sides of the law, but that is not the same thing as right and wrong. Are you sure that you know the difference?' Pyotr did not reply, but beckoned to the man in the ski mask with a twitch of his head and went to his car. He flicked his cigarette butt to the ground and they drove off in the direction of Loch Houn, leaving Eamon standing in the thickening sleet, warmed by the flames. He stood for a while, in the growing dark. It was a ten mile walk to Duncul. He reached into his pocket for his phone. 'Shit,' he said. It was in the car.

Rona had stared at the symbols and the inscrutable handwriting on the scraps of paper for hours. There was certainly something wrong with the mind of Joel Kennedy. What she could decipher from the writing was more philosophical than anything else. *'The nature of truth…What is a fact? A fact is not a thing. A thing exists before a fact. There are no facts without things. We cannot know any truths unless they are true. God pre-exists all things. What comes first? Facts or things? Perhaps facts come before things. A thing must be thought of before it exists! Things only exist because we know them. But things exist independent of us, therefore another mind has brought them into existence. Thus God exists, but only beyond us…'* and so on. By the time she reached the end of a paragraph she had forgotten what the start was about. She tried to be systematic. She collected what she deemed 'Philosophy' into one pile, then 'Symbol Work,' into another. He was trying to decipher the markings that appeared on the Stone of Duncul and the stones that

the Singa wore. He lined them up, and allocated meanings. Was the tri-
forked Y a tree? Was the upside down V a mountain? The straight line, a
man? He lined them up in different formations, like words. What if they
were letters, an ancient alphabet? But there were only six of them. Then
he joined them together to form pictograms. The Y on top of the upside
down V was a man. The small circle was the sun or the moon. Was the
large circle the sea? Rona marked another pile 'Stones'. This consisted of
maps of Glenfashie. She knew some of the stone circles; the two on the
face of the hill above Burnum, crude circles a few yards across, a ring of
stones no more than knee height and a larger central stone. She had not
realised there were so many others, at least according to Joel. There were
fifteen according to Joel, three on the top of the hill behind Burnum,
five further up the glen, another one apparently covered by the water
of the dam, another one right where the dam itself stood, (this he went
over and over again with a pen) and another three further down the glen
towards Loch Houn. He joined them with lines, east to west, north to
south, lines criss-crossing over the maps like spider's webs, with the dam
at the centre, circled round and round and round.

Then there was the pile of papers she marked 'Duncul and Glenfashie'.
These consisted of notes on the history of Duncul. *'Slave ownership in
the Caribbean. Ansgar plantations still exist.'* Half of them were illegible.
*'How long? Witchcraft in Glenfashie? Burnings? Ansgars since twelve hundreds.
Fifteenth century? Reformation and Catholic families...Follow the lines of
blood...It is all about blood. All they care about is blood.'* She thought about
how he had killed himself, by slitting his wrists, letting the blood soak
into the blankets in his cell. Then in clearer, larger handwriting; *'Eamon'*,
repeated again and again. Then *'Eamon, Asgard, Ralph, Angus, Dominic,
Asgard, Eamon'* in a column, and in rows, the first letter of each name
circled. Then the letters jumbled up and mixed in with the symbols from
the stones. Then a big sheet of paper, *'WHAT IS TIME?'* scrawled in the
same biro, gone over again and again. There were several big sheets of
what looked, to her memory, to be copies of the stone in the dungeon.
She wanted to go down there to check but did not know where the keys
were. She went down to the kitchen and called for Kirsty but she had
gone home. The wind was rising and heavy sleet was lashing against

the windows. She tried to call Eamon, but the phone went straight to voicemail. She went back upstairs to the study and put some more logs on the fire. Then she began to go through the files on *Enerpro*, Tarvin Lodge and the dam.

This was boring, but at least the Dupuys weren't unhinged. There were letters back and forth about sewage arrangements, water and electricity supplies. Every step needed about ten letters to and from the Highland Council. Tarvin lodge was not on the grid. Electricity supplies were by generator and a proposed micro hydro scheme. The micro hydro scheme on the burn behind the lodge involved a study of the flora and fauna, and an archaeological survey had to be carried out. The maximum number of residents of the lodge had to be specified; seventy was specified. This would require a sewage treatment plant. Permission for the sewage treatment plant had to be separately applied for. A botanical and zoological study had to be completed before permission could be granted. An archaeological study had to be carried out on the site of the proposed treatment plant...and so on, back and forth. She spread out the plans for the lodge. The extension was vast, more than double the size of the original building. It was designated a 'hostel,' with accommodation for fifty, in tiny rooms containing several beds each. There was a sheaf of letters concerning the 'perimeter wall', which the planner objected to, citing aesthetic reasons. He argued that the wall should be lower, '*so as not to inhibit the view from the ground floor windows*'. Dupuy argued that the security concerns in such a remote location were significant, and pointed out that it was possible that the hostel would not be open for large parts of the year. The planner replied that '*notwithstanding the security concerns, you are not building a prison*', and so on. They came to a compromise on the hieght of the wall. She turned to the folders on the dam. These were same sort of thing, plans, estimates of output, and letters back and forth about such things as the height of the handrails on the walkway or the design of the building housing the transformers. '*To be amenable to the local environment we insist upon a local stone for cladding.*' There was a tree planting programme to be implemented. Endless scientific studies, an argument about newts, and whether the pipe down to the loch should be buried, to the possible detriment of the peat bog.

There was an entire folder about archaeological surveys. *'It is noted that construction of the access road from Loch Houn has been commenced without the requisite archaeological surveys having taken place.'* Dupuy replied with a long spiel about an agreed schedule of works and *'the impossibility of gaining access to the site in order to conduct an archaeological study when there is no access road'*. Back and forth, back and forth. A demand to cease all work pending archaeological study of the proposed route and site of the camp, back and forth, then, after all that, *'The planning authority considers the archaeological study to no longer be a condition of the permission'*. Victory for Dupuy.

There was a collection of photographs of the building of the dam. The foundation trench on the bedrock beneath the peat, concrete swelling out of steel caissons. Unsmiling men in yellow jackets and hardhats. Huge tracked diggers, cement mixers, a mesh of steel. A picture of Asgard Ansgar snipping a ribbon, the only one smiling. It was getting late. The fire was warm, she thought about falling asleep on the couch and waiting for Eamon to come back. She called him again but there was still no answer. She stretched out on the couch but could not close her eyes. She wanted to go and find him, but her mother's cousin had taken the car and she only had the quad. She would have to fill the tank back at the farm to make the trip up the road to Loch Houn. She turned back to the drawings and papers in order to stop thinking about Eamon. She wanted to go and find him. She wanted to be near him. She wanted to touch him. She had not touched him, she realised, since that stupid, drunken night ten years ago.

It was a short but nasty trip along the river bank on the quad, through lashing rain and sleet. At the farmhouse she noticed that the lights were out. She was sure that she had left the outside one on, and thought there must have been a power cut. She did not see the small black car parked at the gable of the house as she went to the front door.

Sigurson was tired from his long drive and all the checking and re-checking to see if Isabel was still breathing, and checking and re-checking the bandages on her wrists. He did not want to waste time. When Rona opened the door he kneed her hard in the stomach and she fell winded to the floor, blinded by the pain. Before she could speak he was winding duct tape around her head, over the eyes and mouth, leaving only a gap for the nose. Then he carried on with the tape that he had intended for Clarice, around and around her body, so that by the time she came round from the shock of the kick she could hardly move; she could hardly breathe.

CHAPTER FIFTEEN

The walk was definitely more than ten miles, thought Eamon, more like fifteen. It was pitch-dark and he was soaked through before he arrived back at Duncul. The fire was low in the grate. He called Rona from the landline, on her mobile, and at her mother's house. He let it ring but there was no answer. He cursed himself for not inviting her to stay. When he had showered and dressed he began looking at the piles of papers that she had made, and he fell asleep staring at the endless scribblings of Joel Kennedy.

He was awoken by a knock at the door when the room was cold and a meagre grey light was creeping from the windows. Kirsty entered. 'The police are here to see you,' she said.

There were two of them in the upstairs sitting room, standing at the window and looking out into the grey light. One was thin and dressed in a black overcoat and a grey suit. His nose was long and belonged to a face in its fifth decade. He had short, black, neat hair that could have belonged to a much younger man. The other man was younger, almost unbelievably young, with a fresh round face, wearing a neat grey suit;

a boy dressed up as a man. The older man watched Eamon with clear grey eyes, a piercing look, made all the more intimidating by an element of gentleness. Kirsty introduced them as 'Detective John Maclean, and Detective William Boyd.' She spoke with a kind of pride in her voice, as if the men were priests or ministers. As she left with a promise of tea Eamon was sure she gave a subtle curtsey. He shook the thin hand offered by Maclean and the plump one offered by Boyd, and indicated that they should sit.

'We've spoken,' said Maclean. 'About ten days ago.' He had the soft accent of the West, but with precision and clarity; a voice with the habit of exactitude and candour. Eamon nodded. It was a voice that was used to discovering the truth, like a medical instrument.

'How can I help?' said Eamon, and as he said the words he was overcome by the desire to tell the man everything, to hand it all over to him; to show him all the papers spread out upstairs across the floor of the study, to take him, now, without a moment's hesitation, up the hill to the camp; to take him to Grey Acres and hand over Edgar Dupuy; to take him to the basement and show him the stone; to bring out Joshua, who was at that moment upstairs in one of the attic rooms asleep; to tell him about the car still smouldering at the top of the road to Loch Houn. But at that moment the telephone rang on the little table next to the couch, and he picked it up.

He did not recognise the voice. There was no Eastern European accent; it was Scottish, and there was a hint of Glasgow, but also American. It was a voice that could not make up its mind what it was, and certainly the voice of nothing more than a boy, speaking words that could only be expected from the most hardened of men.

'You won't tell him anything, Eamon. I have Rona here with me now, and I'll cut her throat if you speak. Nod if you understand.' Eamon looked around the room, half expecting to see the owner of the voice somewhere in the shadows. He looked at the face and clear eyes of Maclean, and the bright eyes of Boyd, and beyond the two of them to the treetops, the rooftops of the village and the hills and woods. 'You need to nod now if you understand,' said the voice. Eamon, deferring to a sense of unreality as much as the request, nodded. 'Good,' said the voice. 'You won't speak; you won't ask any questions about who I am or where I am. Listen.' There was a scuffling sound, a gasping for breath, then her voice, only one word, 'Eamon!', then the voice of the young man again. 'You need to know only two things. One, I have her, and two, you are being watched. When the police have gone I'll call you again.' The phone went quiet. Eamon put it down and met the eyes of the policeman.

'Trying to sell me new windows,' he said. Maclean nodded.

'That could be expensive in a place like this.' Eamon didn't hear him, he was listening to her cry again, echoing in his mind. 'Eamon!'

'I was saying,' said Maclean, 'the other day, you called.' He took out a notebook.

'Yes,' said Eamon.

'You were asking about the woman who was with Isabel Mtetu. The woman that you mistook for a police officer.'

'Yes, I suppose I was.'

'It was remiss of me; I think perhaps I should have been a little more curious at the time. May I ask why you were asking?'

'I was trying to get in touch with Mrs Mtetu, to see how she was doing.'

'She was your tenant was she not?'

'Yes, apparently. It's dealt with through the estate office though.' Eamon sat down. Joshua. Joshua was upstairs and he mustn't come down.

'Yes, Edgar Dupuy, your factor.'

'Yes.'

'The woman, the one who you thought was a police officer, is this her?' He took a black and white photograph from the notebook. Eamon looked at the picture of the woman with the grey hair and pinched face.

'Perhaps. I can't be exactly sure. It was a rather dim room.' He could have asked her to stay. She had said she could stay. He hadn't wanted her to spend the night. Too complicated. The policeman frowned.

'The thing is, we need to speak to Isabel. Do you have any idea where she might be?'

'No. I don't.' Where would they have taken her? Who had that been on the phone? It wasn't Pyotr. Why would Pyotr have taken Rona? They had had an understanding. How did they know the detectives were here?

'You told me Social Services were taking care of her,' he said to Maclean.

'You mentioned a man,' said Maclean, putting the photograph back into the notebook, 'a man with the policewoman. Could you describe him?'

'A man. An ordinary-looking man,' said Eamon. Maclean frowned again. How could they see him nod? Had they a camera in the room? He looked around the room but could see nothing out of the ordinary. He got up and went to the window.

'Ordinary?' said Maclean. 'Was he tall? Short? Black? White? Can you remember what he was wearing?'

'Ordinary. Normal. White, trousers, jacket.' Eamon looked out over the treetops to the village. They were looking through the window. From where? The hill? A house in the village? They couldn't see through the trees. A rooftop in the gulag? He picked up a pair of binoculars from the bookshelf next to the window and scanned the village.

'Looking for something?'

'Foxes. There's a problem with foxes.' There was no way they could see from the hillside. Then he saw it; the camera on the gulag light pole, fifty feet above the ground, and pointing directly at him.

'Mr Ansgar,' said the detective from behind him.

'Yes,' said Eamon, putting the binoculars down. They, he, them, they were controlling the camera.

'For how long was she your tenant?'

'I don't know. I wasn't here when the property was leased.' The policeman tapped his fingers on the arm of his chair.

'How well did you know Joel Kennedy?'

'Not well. I hadn't seen or spoken to him for years. Not since school, really.'

'You are aware that he committed suicide in the police cells in Inverness?'

'Yes. I was sorry to hear that.' You know nothing, remember that, nothing at all. You are a concerned neighbour, that is all.

'It's quite a difficult thing to do, to kill yourself in police custody. The officers take away laces and belts. There are no sharp objects permitted in the cells. Least of all razors. Joel Kennedy was visited in the cells by this woman,' he took out the photograph again, 'on the evening before he died. She works for Social Services and she was delivering a prescription of methadone. So you can understand why we are very keen to contact her as soon as possible. Take another look.' He held out the photograph but Eamon did not take it.

'What is her name?'

'Clarice Wright.'

'It could be her. I can't be sure.'

'Nice place you've got here,' said Detective Boyd, standing up. 'Do you mind if we take a look around?'

'Why?' said Eamon, thinking of Joshua and the study full of papers.

'No reason in particular,' said Boyd. 'It might be interesting, that's all.'

'Is it necessary?' Boyd exchanged a glance with Maclean.

'No,' said Maclean. 'If it was necessary we would have a warrant.' He stood up. 'Clarice Wright and Isabel Mtetu; we need to find them. If you think of anything that might be helpful give me a call.' He handed Eamon a card and smiled with straight false teeth. Eamon rose and Kirsty came in with a tray of tea and biscuits.

'That won't be necessary, Kirsty,' he said. 'Just show them out.' She put the tray down and Boyd took a handful of biscuits from the plate as he passed. Eamon went to the window and watched as they got into their car. The phone on the table rang as soon as the car was moving.

'Well done,' said the voice.

'Who are you? What do you want? Let me speak to Pyotr.'

'He's not here.'

'If you harm her I'll kill you.'

'Nobody's going to get killed if you stop doing what you're doing. Leave it alone, for a week. Just stop, for a week. Then she'll be let go, and you can do what you like about Pyotr, go to the police, whatever. Understand?' Silence. Eamon heard only his own heart and breathing. 'Eamon, do I have to send you an ear or something?' Silence. 'Are we clear?'

'Clear,'

'One week from today. Stay in, read a book, watch telly.' The line clicked dead.

In spite of the blankets twisted around him, Grigor could feel the hum of the ship's generator in his bones. It had taken him a long time to realise where he was. He was on board the *Eloise*, back in the safety and the warmth of the boat, encased in cream-painted steel, among the plumbing and wire ducts. The light flickered. There were no portholes in this cabin. He was in the womb of the ship, but he had no memory of getting here. He had been swimming towards the light through the black water and his arms and legs had been getting numb. He could remember nothing after that. He felt weak and stiff. He climbed out of the bunk but as soon as his feet hit the floor his body was wracked with coughing and he began to shiver. The effort to climb back into the bunk and cover himself exhausted him. His teeth began chattering. When he closed his eyes he was back in the forest standing at the edge of the clearing watching Sigurson. He was holding the long curved knife and his eyes were wide with madness as he stabbed it again and again into a body, blood spurting up into the air over his face and clothes, getting in his mouth. Grigor cried out and he was back in the room. A dark shape came towards him and he cried out again.

'Grigor!' said the shape. 'Grigor, it's me, Lev. Calm down, taken it easy.'

Before the moment that Sigurson took her, Rona had not experienced the ultimate betrayal of a man. The moment when out of the ranks of protectors, fathers, brothers, lovers and friends there emerges an enemy. The moment that lust, hatred, or the simple desire to do evil, blinds them, and they are filled with that dogged brutality. But like all women she had had reason to imagine and plan what she would do. In her imagination she had kicked out, always at the testicles, at shins with hard boots, and she had stabbed with whatever sharp thing was at hand, always at the eyes, to blind their blindness. But when it had happened, she had barely had time to look at him before feeling the knee in her stomach, and the pain had passed through her like a blade. And there had been another effect. She had never felt the strength of a man used in that way. She had collapsed, yes, winded, but it was more than that; a hypnotic effect. It had defeated her utterly. She had not realised that they could steal your spirit too. She did not fight. Perhaps, she was later to reflect, it was a survival instinct. Let it be done unto me as you will, because otherwise you will kill me. As she had felt the bonds of the duct tape tightening she had gone limp, and had felt the sensation of no longer inhabiting her own body.

The tall man with the blonde hair and orange hat had picked her up without effort. He took her to a car, and she listened to the whine of the engine as it negotiated a winding road, rising high into the night and descending again. She knew where she was going. She made sense of the long descent, the smell of the sea and then the thump and rattle of the dirt track.

She heard voices and the creaking of a big gate opening. She could see the glow of bright lights on the tape over her eyes, then darkness, then rain and wind on her hands and face as the strong arms lifted her from the car, then darkness again; cold but no rain and the smell of a cave. Then the smell of paint, bright lights again, and she was lying on cold steel. Then darkness, and she lay still for a long time. Her mind fixed on every sound, like the hands of the drowning reaching for the surface. The lights came on. 'Sit!' A man's voice. 'Quiet!' Footsteps, shuffling, more than one person. Heavy steps and lighter steps. Voices in a strange language, like a babbling stream. Then a loud bang and darkness, women shouting; then the light on again, silence, except for the hum of a machine. The women's voices came in whispers. 'Shh, shh.' A child whimpered. Then again footsteps approached, the movement of a creaking steel bolt, a bang, and the heavy breathing of a man, *the* man, gasps and cries from the women. 'Isabel!' The man cursing, 'Quiet!' Then the door banging, and the bolt creaking and clanging shut. Then the voices of the women, together, solicitous, gentle and urgent in that strange, fluid, soothing language. Rona could do nothing but wait and listen. The door scraped and banged, and the man came back in.

He pulled her upright on the bench and she felt the cold of a blade on her wrists as her arms were loosed. She did not fight. He pulled her arms behind her and she felt a cable tie around her wrists as he tied her to the bench. He slid the blade between the tape and her body and cut her torso free. He cut her legs free but left the ankles taped. Lastly, she felt the blade on her cheeks and forehead as he cut the tape from her face. She blinked in the bright light that shone from behind the head and hat. He was smiling a thin-lipped, wide smile.

She was in a long, high ceilinged, narrow room; walls, ceiling, floor, bright white paint. They were inside a shipping container. Herself, the blonde man, two African women, two children, and another, a body perhaps, lying on a pile of blankets at the end of the container. The women were kneeling beside the body, and the thin, sick-looking children were huddled together on a bench against the opposite wall, watching. The man stood up, looking down at her.

'A wee glimpse of the future Rona,' he said. 'Keep quiet, or I'll come back and zip you up again.' She nodded. He went out, slamming the doors, and the women's eyes, suspicious and opaque, met hers.

By evening Vanneck had drunk half a bottle of Macallan and was feeling ill. He had spent a desultory day staring at the sea and the screens on the bridge, and re-reading Sigurson's book in the salon, trying for the hundredth time to find sense in the craziness. For a long time he sat watching his wife, remembering her youth and cursing her illnesses, before making his way back to the bridge and willing the incremental movement of the boat icon along the course line. The satellite phone beeped.

'Flieber?'

'You don't need to call me that. Call me Foxtrot.'

'Foxtrot?'

'I'll call you Sigma.'

'Sigma?' Vanneck chuckled.

'What's funny?'

'Nothing.'

'Where are you?'

'A hundred miles off the coast of the Hebrides, heading due north.'

'How long till you get here?'

'Seventy-two hours.'

'Good. We need to get out of here as soon as possible.'

'Why? What's happened now, Foxtrot?'

'You don't need to know. Let's just say the situation is delicate.'

'There's a delicate situation here too.'

'How so?'

'I don't know how to drive this boat, and Brighton's gone.'

'Gone?'

'Fell overboard in the storm. Washed away.'

'What?'

'Do I need to repeat myself?'

'So how are you driving the boat now?'

'It's on autopilot, right until we hit the end of Loch Houn. Then it goes to manual. I have to drive, sail it up the loch.'

'I'm sure you'll work it out, genius that you are. So it's just you and Lillian?'

'Me and Lillian. Two octogenarians in a hundred and fifty-foot boat. Ship. Two old dying people, and there's another storm on its way.'

'Sam, keep it together. Think about what we're doing here. Keep your mind on the goal.'

'Don't you worry, my mind is on the goal. And it's not "Sam", it's "Sigma".' He reached for his glass and drank.

'Sam. You're saving them. Think of that. The last of the Singa. The last of the Sigursons. What we're doing here is salvation, for them and for us.'

'Sure, salvation. That's a good one. I'll try that on Lillian.'

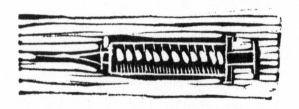

CHAPTER SIXTEEN

Eamon's first instinct was to call Stevie, but he hesitated. He was not sure what they could see or what they could know. The camera was still pointed directly at the castle. It could probably see through all the windows on the north-western side, and it had a clear view of the front door and drive. It could not see the tower door, but he considered that there could easily be another camera somewhere in the woods. Cameras were tiny now; they could be anywhere. They could be inside the house, and there could be listening bugs too. Likewise, the phones could be bugged, and now he only had the landline since the mobile had gone up in smoke. The only safe way to communicate was through Kirsty or Mike. Kirsty could take a message to Stevie, for example, but what if she was being watched? For Rona's sake surely the safest thing was to do as they said and wait for a week. Let them do whatever it was that they wanted to do, for one week, and she would be let go. He paced, and smoked. But what about the women and the two children? This was all to do with them. What did they need a week for? Whoever it was that had taken Rona, they would be gone in a week. That was the implication. He went to the study.

Rona had left a sheet of paper on his desk. *'It all leads to Duncul,'* written in Joel's handwriting. He looked at Joel's papers. According to his maps of the glen all the standing stone circles were arranged to converge on the dam. He was obsessed with the dam; his diagrams and maps infused it with some mysterious symbolic meaning. And he was obsessed with finding hidden meanings in names. There were pages of names: *'Eamon Ansgar, Ansgar Duncul, Asgard Ansgar'*, the letters jumbled up and rearranged; *'Sgansra, Cunlud, Monea, Enerpro, Proener, Roperen'*, the symbols from the stone interspersed with those letters; words in columns, words in rows, grids of words; his own name, *'Joel Kennedy'*, with numbers assigned to the letters, numbers totalled in columns. *'Duncan Fraser'* and *'Lachlan Kennedy'* given the same treatment, *'Isabel Mtetu'*, and names Eamon did not recognise, *'James Sigurson, Luelmas Girsuson, Gurt Flieber, Bert Geflier, Terb Rierglef'*, and on and on. Did any of it mean anything? Eamon took out a pen and paper from the desk and tried to clear his head by writing.

'Joel Kennedy: Dam: Stone: Maps: Needles: Injecting Drugs?

African children: Offering arms for drugs. Drugged for ceremonies? Child abuse? Child Sacrifice? Why Africans?

Stone: Ancient rituals? Performed by who? For whom? Pyotr?

Pyotr knows, but it is not his thing.

Pyotr: Drugs, Money laundering, dam.

Joel: Dam, all about the dam.'

Eamon felt he was going around in circles, like Joel. There was a knock at the door. Kirsty put her head in and looked at the papers but made no comment. 'Mr Rugleef here to see you.'

'Oh no. Where?'

'In the hall.'

'No tea, thank-you Kirsty.'

'Hi!' said Trib Rugleef as Eamon descended the stair. 'Howya doin'?'

'Bit tired at the moment, thank-you.'

'Oh? busy day?' The American was carrying a pack of beer.

'Sort of.'

'I'm sorry to disturb you, but I kinda needed someone to celebrate with, and I thought you might like a drink. Beer?'

'What's the occasion?'

'I've reached a milestone in my novel. It's a major achievement for me. It's been a long, hard road, and I feel like I need to congratulate myself.'

'The end?'

'No, not quite, but the beginning of the end. You know the part when everything is coming together, beginning to be sown up. I'm pretty sure it's all downhill from here. I feel like I'm cruising now. I'm feeling good.' He held out a beer. It took all of Eamon's will to reach out and receive it. It was dusk outside. There were no lights on in the hall and it was cold. Surely the man would not stay for long? Rugleef opened his can and drank to his health. Eamon sat and played with the ring pull. Rugleef sat without an invitation. Eamon pulled the ring on the can and took a sip of the warm beer, persuading himself that drinking with Rugleef would at least stop him thinking about Joel's manic scribbling.

'What is your book about?' he forced himself to say.

'Well, in a sense that's a hard question to answer, specifically. I could say it's about life, and death.' Rugleef smirked, as if he had said something profound. The room was growing darker by the second, and Eamon could hardly make out his guest's face.

'What genre, would you say?'

'Fantasy, I guess, but like the *Harry Potter* books, you know, it's fantasy but also set in contemporary reality. The two worlds intermingle. It's about a quest for an elixir of everlasting life. A long hard journey, many difficulties, but the determination and courage of the hero never failing, perhaps stumbling, but never failing, slaying the dragons and eventually reaching the goal. That's where I'm at now, just getting to the goal.' Eamon took a deep gulp of beer. This was worse than he had anticipated. Rugleef could have at least have been a decent writer. Eamon had never been a fan of that sort of fiction. He had read *The Lord of the Rings* as a boy, but nothing else. But he tried to seem interested, and asked questions, and his guest wanted to talk. When they were almost in pitch darkness he even deigned to switch on a sidelight. The beer was the worst kind; warm American lager, almost as bad as the beer in the *Misty*, but Eamon felt a craving for the facile absolution that alcohol bestows, and he was on his third can, beginning to be immune to the cold, when Joshua came in from the kitchen.

Eamon had given him slippers, pyjamas, and one of his father's dressing gowns. Since his arrival the man had eaten, solidly, anything that was put before him. Eamon had made it clear with pointing and miming that he could make himself free in the kitchen and larder. After all the frustrating attempts at interrogation and explanation there seemed to be only two points at which they understood each other. These were that Isabel Mtetu was real and significant, and that Joshua should eat if he wished. When he had understood about the eating Joshua had given his only, faint, smile. Since then he had eaten, and slept, and eaten, and whenever he met Eamon on his journey from attic room to kitchen and back again he would say 'Isabel Mtetu', with an expression of profound but obscure meaning.

He came into the room behind Eamon, and Eamon did not hear him. He was watching the face of Trib Rugleef as he evinced the necessity of conflict in every scene in a novel. Eamon was watching his face, because he was bored of listening to the voice, and he saw the blood drain from it, and the jaw drop as the voice faded to a halt. Trib was staring over Eamon's shoulder, at whatever had come into his view on the edge of the pool of lamp light. Eamon turned to see Joshua's dark, sad face and yellowing eyes framed by the raised collar of the immense dressing gown and his woollen hat. The face was, as always, inscrutable, as if his eyes saw beyond the yellow pool of light, through the face of Trib Rugleef and beyond the walls of Duncul into some other deep darkness.

'Joshua,' said Eamon. Joshua was holding a large mug in one hand and a thick sandwich in the other.

'Isabel,' said Joshua, 'Mtetu.'

'Yes,' said Eamon, 'Isabel.' Joshua nodded, turned and the darkness of the hall swallowed him. They heard his soft tread on the stairs.

'A friend of yours?' asked Trib, and Eamon noticed the change in the tone of voice. He was no longer affable, attempting wit. It was as if another man had been brought to life by the appearance of the face from the darkness; an urgent man, no longer a dilettante novelist.

'Yes.'

'He knows Isabel Mtetu? Where did he come from?' Eamon saw the deliberate return of affability. 'I mean, is he a relation of hers?'

'I've no idea. He was walking, on the Loch Houn road. I think he's looking for her. But he doesn't speak English, so I can't get much else out of him.'

'Did he say how he got here?'

'He doesn't speak English, nor French. He seems to know a couple of words in Spanish, but I don't speak it so…' Eamon shrugged.

'What is he planning to do?' Eamon shrugged again. Trib did not want to talk about his novel any more. He frowned as he drank the remains of a can. 'You said the police were looking for her. Did they speak to you?'

'Yes, they were here, this afternoon.'

'Why were they talking to you?'

'I don't know. I suppose they're talking to a lot of people, trying to find her.' Trib stood.

'I have to go,' he said. 'The ending awaits.'

When he had gone Eamon stayed in the hall. The beer had made him lethargic and when he turned his mind again to the papers upstairs the symbols, letters and numbers swam chaotically. He looked at the clock to see that it was only just past five, but he felt only half awake. He closed his eyes and Rugleef's inane conversation about structure and pace and the use of idiom intertwined with Joel's writing and drawings. Eamon cursed himself; he was drunk, at least half drunk, and Rona was in danger somewhere and he could do nothing. About the only thing that made sense, was, strangely, Joshua Malafu, with his sandwich and cup of tea, in a dressing gown, going to bed, and his gentle repetition of the name, 'Isabel Mtetu.' Kirsty came into the hall wearing her overcoat and scarf, on her way out for the night.

'Do you know where Stevie Van lives?' said Eamon.

'I do.'

'I've got a big favour to ask. I know it's out of your way, but do you think you could go there now, and ask him to come here?'

'Has he not got a telephone?'

'He has, but I've lost his number. I know this might sound strange, but

I want you to ask him to come now, tonight.'

'Yes.'

'Tell him not to phone and tell him to come in by the tower door, from the wood at the back. Tell him that I need his help.'

At first Rona tried to talk to the women, but in reply she received only blank stares and silence. Then they began talking among themselves, and after a sort of argument took place the woman wearing a hat approached her. There was a plastic beaker and some plastic cups on the bench next to the children and the woman offered her some orange juice and held the cup to her mouth. Rona thanked her. She had not realised how thirsty she was. The sweet juice and the tenderness of the woman holding the cup to her mouth and cupping her other hand beneath her chin released the tears that she had been holding back. Her mouth twisted and quivered. The woman made no effort to comfort her, but backed away, wary of the unrestrained emotion, and Rona stopped herself, swallowed and apologised, steadying her breath. The woman went back to the makeshift bed where the injured woman lay. Rona saw that the wrists of the woman on the bed were wrapped in bandages stained with blood. She looked around the featureless room. The humming noise was coming from a fan in the top corner above the bed. The sensation of being in a dream would not leave her, in spite of the pain in her stomach and the biting of the tie on her wrists. She had moved into another universe as easily as one moves from one room into another, and part of her mind would not accept it. She had stepped into a world that before now she had only known as fiction; she was in a horror film. She felt light and hollow, as if she had swallowed some strange air that overfilled her lungs and stomach and was trying to lift her up, so that she would not have been surprised to find herself looking down upon the bright, white room, the woman on the bed, her two attendants and the silent, still boys wrapped together in a blanket on the bench opposite, and to have seen herself, forced to sit upright against the wall. At the same time she was consumed by a panic of thoughts, a gabble of voices in her mind, and the tension of terror through her whole body. She was overcome by the insidious power of malevolence; the power to unhinge the mind and drive a wedge between the perceived and perceiving. The world had been turned over and she could see the obverse now, the worms beneath the sod. It reminded her of the day her father had died, but there had been no ugliness in that, only unfathomable sorrow. Now with every breath she drew in evil, like the smell of the paint.

'Rona,' she said, and the word, coming out of silence, took on the coldness and hardness of the metal walls. The women looked at her, and turned away, and looked up as the door clanked and ground on its hinges and the blonde man came in. He emerged out of darkness, and with him came a gust of damp air; the smell of a cave, the same smell as the stone room beneath Duncul.

He did not look at her. He was carrying a metal tray. He set it down on the bench next to the children. She was unable to stop watching as he knelt and the boys presented their arms to him in turn. He tied a length of rubber hose above the bicep, then he flicked at a vein, tore the wrapper of a syringe and inserted the needle. The dark red filled the syringe and he took off the vial, leaving the needle attached. He filled a second vial, withdrew the needle and placed a cotton ball on the wound. He repeated the procedure on the other boy, deftly, like a nurse. The boys were acquiescent and pale. They were anaemic. He stood up, his clothes hissing with the movement, and walked past her carrying the tray; this time he looked and smiled. At the threshold, with his back to her, he stopped. Then he turned and walked back and squatted with the tray before her; vials of blood, needles, a drop of blood on the tray, rubber hose and stained cotton buds.

'Do you know what this is?' he whispered. Rona shook her head.

'Blood,' she said.

'Precious blood.' He smiled again and left the container. She could hear him moving about in the darkness beyond. He came back in with two lollipops for the boys, left again, and returned with an armful of grey blankets. He tossed two to the women and one at Rona. It fell at her feet and he paused, drew a long blade, and approached. She smelt deodorant as he leant over her, and felt the warmth of his leg against hers. He cut the cable tie and she rubbed her wrists.

'If you make a noise, if you cause trouble, I'm going to cut you, understand?' She nodded. He went out, slamming the doors. Then the light went out and in the darkness a boy whimpered and a woman gasped, but after a few seconds the light flickered on again.

Rona unwrapped the tape from her legs. 'Rona,' she said, pointing to herself. The women watched her but when she walked over to them they put their fingers on their lips and gestured that she should go back to her bench.

'You sit!' said the one with the hat. Rona sat back down.

Stevie entered the study from the tower door carrying a rifle. Eamon invited him to sit in one of the armchairs in front of the fire. Stevie propped the gun against the wall. 'Have you got a licence for that?' said Eamon.

'Maybe,' said Stevie, looking around the room. 'Can I smoke?' Eamon tossed a packet to him.

'Why did you bring a gun?' Stevie shrugged.

'Dunno. Just a feeling. It's your Dad's anyway.' He lit up. 'He loaned it to me.'

'They took Rona.' Stevie only stared at him. 'I said they took Rona.'

'I heard you. I told you not to fuck with these guys. What did you do?'

'Nothing. I met Pyotr. Do you know him?' Stevie nodded. 'Is he the boss?' Stevie shrugged.

'For now, for here.'

'He asked to meet me. I went. He set fire to my car, as a warning.'

'Did you listen?'

'Yes, but by the time I got back here she was gone. Then the police came this morning. I was going to tell them everything, but I got a call. It wasn't Pyotr. It was someone else. He threatened to kill her. Says I have to keep my mouth shut, for a week. They're watching the castle; somehow they control that camera on the light pole in the gulag.' Stevie raised his eyebrows.

'You gonna do what they say?'

'I don't know. Why do they want a week? Do you think they're bringing in a big shipment or something?'

'You say it wasn't Pyotr that called you?'

'No, a younger man. Scottish, I think.'

'It doesn't sound like it's Pyotr. He wants to be here long term, not just for the next week. Where's Joshua?'

'Upstairs sleeping, or down in the kitchen, eating.'

'Not speaking?'

'Can't speak, not anything I understand anyway.'

'You want to go and rescue her?'

'How?' said Eamon. Stevie nodded in the direction of the rifle.

'Take another one or two. You, me, Joshua. Up over the hill to the camp, bang bang bang. You're the soldier.'

'That's fucking madness. You don't even know she's in the camp.' Joshua shuffled into the room, holding a cup. He looked at Stevie and nodded, then shuffled out.

'He's going for another sandwich I think.'

'Good idea,' said Stevie, tossing his cigarette into the fire.

In the kitchen Eamon found some tinned pies and baked them while they drank tea. They sat around the heavy oak table, in silence except for the sound of Joshua chewing. He ate with purpose but without pleasure, storing up calories for some unnamed task ahead, eating as if each mouthful were a step further on an arduous climb. Eamon was reminded of hungry soldiers eating rations after a day without food. He and Stevie assented to the silence that the African somehow imposed, and they both smiled as they found themselves using signs to ask for the salt, or to offer another cup. The smell of pies filled the warm room, and they sat in a bright pool of light from the lamp pulled down over the table, but the darkness encroached from the vaulted ceiling and from the corner beneath the stairs. Eamon felt as if he was already at a wake. What was she doing now? What were they doing to her? He could not eat once he had thought of her. She could be alive tonight, and in a week, dead. Tomorrow, dead. In the next moment, as he took another mouthful, dead. The food lost all taste. He tried to inhabit the mind of the man who had taken her and the effort sickened him. She was a girl; little more than a girl. He remembered her wrists, white and slender, and thought about the man's work she did on the farm, wrestling bales of hay and bags of feed.

When they had finished Joshua gathered the plates and took them to the sink. He folded back the sleeves of the dressing gown and both Eamon and Stevie found themselves watching the measured, rhythmic way he washed plates and forks beneath the running tap. He used the cloth in a circular motion on the plates, and stroked the forks with the cloth in one direction only, away from himself towards the water, then he shook the water off each item before placing it on the drying rack. When he had finished washing he took a dish towel from the rail on the stove and dried the plates, again with circular motions, holding up each one to the light before putting it in the cupboard, and doing the same with each fork. When he had finished he filled a cup with water from the tap and nodded a farewell, then shuffled up the stairs out of the room, leaving the two men at the table in the pool of light strangely soothed. They sat for a full minute in silence until Eamon realised that he desired above all to sleep.

Once again her face. What was her face doing here? It was changing into an image of her face, printed on a banknote. A beautiful face, a beautiful feeling, like he was floating, filled with light. The phone ringing. God! Three o'clock in the morning. Pyotr fumbled for the phone.

'Flieber!'

'How did you guess? Not interrupting anything am I?'

'What do you want?'

'I want to use your boat.'

'What?'

'You owe me, and I want to use the *Eloise*.'

'I owe you? For what?'

'I took care of your problem for you. Eamon Ansgar. He won't trouble you now.'

'What did you do?'

'You don't need to know, but trust me, you'll thank me. But I need to use the *Eloise*. Not now, in a couple of days.'

'What the hell did you do? I dealt with him myself. He is not a problem. You can fuck yourself you little shit. The *Eloise* is my business. You can forget it!'

'In three days, on Saturday, I'm going to need her, for a day, that's all.'

'Fuck you!'

'Either you let me use her or I'll sink your whole fucking show, Pyotr. It's a day, that's all. Think about it. You're an old man, you need your sleep, I'll call you in the morning.'

CHAPTER SEVENTEEN

In the morning Eamon and Stevie followed the shuffling figure of Joshua to the kitchen and breakfast. Joshua made tea and porridge.

'It's not Pyotr,' said Stevie. 'If you don't believe me, call him.'

'I can't, he burnt my phone.'

'You don't understand Pyotr because you don't understand the drugs business.'

'Please enlighten me.'

'It's just that; a business. It's only about money. Whoever has taken Rona, this is another thing altogether. This is some sinister shit to do with the women, and the kids. They were expecting us to do something to them, up there in the bothy.'

'Yes, but what?'

'They were offering the kids to us.'

'It looked like that. But why?'

'Does it matter why? Some kind of crazy sick voodoo shit. Devil worship child molesting Satan-fucking. Who cares? Whatever the reason, that's what they're doing. You've interfered and they want to stop you, so they take Rona.'

'For a week?'

'For a week. Because in a week they'll be out of here. That's my guess. They're going. The women, the children, whoever is in charge, they'll be gone.'

'We have to stop them,' said Eamon. Stevie nodded and was about to speak when Kirsty came in.

'There's some people at the door. From the electricity company.'

'What do they want?' said Eamon.

'They say they need to talk to you, and it's urgent.'

There were two men in fleeces with SSE emblazoned on their breasts, and another, older man in a suit, standing in the hall. Eamon recognised one of the younger men. A fresh, open expression but with a shadow of fear cast over it, avoiding Eamon's eyes. Like a schoolboy brought to the headmaster's office. The man in the suit offered his hand.

'Gareth Tent,' he said. 'Scottish and Southern Energy.'

'What is this about?'

'This is just a courtesy call really; an apology.'

'You,' said Eamon, pointing at the young man. 'You tried to hit me with your car.' The young man was about to speak and Gareth raised a hand to silence him but changed his mind.

'Go on,' he said.

'I want to apologise for my bad driving. It was an accident. It wasn't intentional.'

'Yes it was. But that doesn't matter. Why did you do it? You were afraid of me. Why?'

'I thought you were one of them.'

'Who?'

'The men in the camp. *Enerpro*.'

'There is an issue,' said the older man, 'with the men in the camp. With *Enerpro*, with the dam. David here was threatened. Intimidated. The police have been contacted about the incident.'

'I saw him taking photographs.'

'He was doing his job, making an inspection. We've had a great deal of difficulty in inspecting your dam. I'm aware this is not your fault, but your factor hasn't exactly been co-operative. We begin draining today.'

'Draining the dam? Why?'

'In short, Mr Ansgar, it's a bad job. In fact so bad that it's a danger, especially with the weather we've been having.'

'So you're going to drain it?'

'Drain it and make a thorough inspection, and then we'll see. I'm surprised Edgar Dupuy hasn't explained any of this to you.'

'No he has not. I'll get in touch with him. Well, thank you for clearing that up. Apology accepted.' The young man smiled with relief as Eamon shook his hand.

'You won't be pressing charges?' he said.

'No. Not at all,' said Eamon. When they had left he went back to the kitchen and told Stevie. Stevie gave a snort of laughter.

'What's funny?'

'It's just that if the dam is no good, SSE are going to want to sue *Enerpro*, and so are you. Good luck with that, suing the Latvian mafia.'

'Why are they still here?' said Eamon. 'Think about it. Why haven't they, whoever they are, just taken the women, and Rona for that matter, away; gone, disappeared, if they're so worried about the attention they're getting. Why a week? Why wait a week?' He paced up and down the kitchen. Stevie watched in silence. 'Why don't they just drive, to Glasgow, down to London? Wherever? They've got a date in mind, an arrangement, in a week, sometime this week. Why are they waiting?'

'They're waiting for the transport,' said Stevie. 'The product, women and children, is hard to move. You need a specialist transport. It's people smuggling, that's what it is. And the truck has to drive from, I don't know, Latvia or something. It takes a week.'

'But they don't have to do it like that. Why don't they just put them in a car? They don't have to hide them. They had Isabel living in the gulag for months, for everyone to see.'

'But now she's wanted by the cops.'

'So they need a truck to come, or a helicopter, or a boat.'

'A boat,' said Stevie.

'They're waiting for a boat. Makes sense.'

'The *Eloise*?'

'*Eloise*?' said Eamon.

'*Eloise. Eloise*,' said Joshua, who was sitting at the end of the table cradling his fourth cup of tea.

'It's the boat they use to bring in the materials,' said Stevie.

'And the drugs,' said Eamon. 'Joshua knows about the *Eloise*. One of his maps had '*Eloise*,' written on it, on Loch Houn.'

'*Eloise*. Isabel Mtetu. *Eloise*,' said Joshua.

'Maybe that was how they arrived,' said Eamon, turning to Joshua. 'Isabel Mtetu was on the *Eloise*?'

'*Eloise*, Isabel Mtetu, *Eloise*,' said Joshua. Eamon thought for a minute. He took a roll of baking paper and a pencil from a drawer, and unrolled the paper on the table. He drew a stick version of a woman, and a boat with the name on its bow.

'*Eloise*, Isabel Mtetu, in *Eloise*?' Joshua nodded in reply. 'So they brought them in on a boat.' Joshua picked up the pencil and began drawing more figures. Stevie and Eamon leaned in to watch. The figures were tiny stick men, and he drew ten, twenty, thirty and more. Then he pointed vigorously at the figures and the boat. 'So there were more of them,' said Eamon. Joshua pointed to himself, prodding his own chest and then at one of the tiny figures.

'Joshua Malafu,' he said.

'Joshua Malafu, in the *Eloise*,' said Eamon, nodding. Joshua nodded. 'So he was on the boat too.' Joshua continued to draw. A larger figure with a big head, hovering above the boat and the tiny figures, an arm outstretched, holding a gun and then dots streaming from the gun onto the tiny figures. Joshua made a sound like a gun;

'Pich, pich, pich, pich!' and mimed with his hands.

'Jesus,' said Stevie.

'Pich, pich, pich, pich!' Joshua mimed again.

Rona looked around the container for a weapon. There were blankets, a mattress, three plastic cups and a plastic jug, some chocolate bars and a bucket to pee in. Nothing hard or sharp, only her hands, her nails, her teeth, her feet, her boots. She felt in the pockets of her jeans and her fleece, and realised with a quickening of her pulse that she still had the small blade she used for cutting open the silage bales; a pruning knife. He had not searched her; he had not thought that a girl would be carrying a knife. It was small, curved and sharp on only one edge; a good strong blade, but she could not stab with it. She would have to slice. The tip would not penetrate clothes so she would have to catch him on bare flesh, either the face or the neck. She curled up under the blanket on the bench and closed her eyes, listening. She could hear the hum of the fan and the mumbling of the women in the corner. She strained her ears but no sound came from beyond the walls of the container. She held the knife tight in her pocket and imagined the cut she would make on his white neck and the blood that would flow; precious blood.

Vanneck decided he would not go down again. He would leave her, let her learn what life was like without him. He would stay up here on the bridge. He had found two more bottles of whisky. He decided to stay drunk until they reached Loch Houn. There was no point in being sober now. The ship could drive itself. In the room behind the bridge where Brighton had changed into the survival suit, Vanneck found his captain's cap. He put it on at a jaunty angle and took his place in the captain's chair. The swell had begun again, a deep, slow rising and falling of the boat beneath him. He would stay drunk. Fuck Lillian. A light rain began to fall, raising a mist from the green sea. There were dark clouds to the west, and a swirl of white pixels moving towards the boat icon on the weather screen, but they had ridden out one storm and *Rage III* would ride out this one. 'Good boat,' said Vanneck, patting the console. 'You're a good girl, a proper girl that does what she's told. No trouble little *Rage*. Good little *Rage*. Let's go girl!' He knocked back a glass and refilled it. That was Lillian's problem; she never drank now. She needed a good drink. He stood up and steadied himself as the boat rolled and holding the bottle and glass together in one hand, he descended the stairs to the salon and entered her room.

Lillian was awake, sitting up.

'Lily!' he said, holding up the bottle. Her face was pale.

'Sam, I feel sick. I need pills. The nausea pills, on the dressing table.'

'Pills! Yes, pills. Pills for you! Whisky for me!' He crossed to the dressing table and put down his bottle and glass, but a roll of the boat toppled the bottle and it fell to the floor. He scrambled after it on hands and knees as it rolled, spilling whisky. The roll deepened and he fell forward, cracking his head against the wall as he grasped for the bottle. He groaned and collapsed. The boat seemed to tip even further, and his eyes closed and his mouth opened against the whisky soaked carpet.

Grigor stared at the bunk above him. He took deep breaths and told himself to calm down. It would all make sense soon. He was in a small room, on a narrow bunk. The walls were painted in a thick, cream, gloss paint, and there were pipes running up one corner, from floor to ceiling, and cable ducts. There was a round fluorescent light in the ceiling. He hated fluorescent lights, because he knew that they flashed at fifty hertz per second, and that that affected brain waves. Fluorescent light was poisonous light.

It wasn't a jail cell. There were no windows, and there was always a window in a jail cell; something to do with the law. There were no windows. His name was Grigor Ivan Semyonovitch. He was thirty-two years old. His mother was Olga Semyonovitch. Thinking about his mother calmed him down. There was a noise. He placed a hand against the wall and felt the vibration in the cold steel. He was on a boat, the *Eloise*. He was on the *Eloise* and he had swum to her through the black water, freezing cold. It was OK. Now he remembered. He sat on the edge of the bunk and realised he was naked. He looked around for his clothes but there weren't any; only blankets on the bed, a jug of water and a bucket on the floor. He tried the door handle. He thumped on the thick steel again and again until someone came.

'Who's that?' he said in Latvian.

'Lev.'

'Lev, let me out.'

'You're crazy Grigor. You're trying to kill everyone.'

'I'm fine now. Let me out. Give me my clothes.'

'Pyotr says to keep you locked up for now, 'til you calm down.'

'I'm calm dammit! I'm fine.'

'I've got to speak to Pyotr. I'll come back.' The footsteps went away.

Grigor cursed and took a mouthful of water from the jug. It tasted of chemicals. Poison. He spat it on the floor. He got back under the blankets and pulled them over his head to get out of the light. In the darkness he remembered the forest and digging for the box.

What had been in the box? What was so important and then not important? He imagined finding the box and opening it. Guns, pistols and ammunition, that's what. He would shoot them all, Lev, Uncle Pyotr, Sigurson, the whole crew. Why were they trying to poison him? Why hadn't they found a box, a metal box in the woods? Why had they dug a hole and then gone away and left it? A big gaping black hole in the forest, like a grave, just left there in the forest, waiting for a body. Maybe it was for Grigor? Grigor's body. Maybe that was why they were trying so hard to poison him? So they could throw his body in the grave. It would fit perfectly in the dark hole, covered in earth, away from the rain and the poison. There was no poison in the earth. It was all natural among the tree roots with the grass and branches above, natural under the sky. If only the sun would come out and clear away all these dark clouds. He needed fresh air! Grigor needed the sky! 'Lev!' he screamed. 'Let me out you bastards! Let me out!' He heard footsteps outside the door. 'Let me out!'

'You're not calm Grigor. I'm not letting you out until you're calm.' Grigor stuffed blanket into his mouth to stifle his scream.

They lit the fire in the study and Joshua crouched by it, cross-legged, as he tended the flames with small pieces of wood. Stevie and Eamon stared at the piles of paper. Eamon showed Stevie the note that Rona had left on his desk, '*It all leads to Duncul*'.

'Who wrote this?' said Stevie.

'Joel,' said Eamon.

'And you say that he broke in, to the basement? Where the stone is?'

'It must have been him, because he drew this,' Eamon picked up a large drawing of the stone. 'It's an exact copy.'

'And that's the same as the stone that Isabel Mtetu gave you?'

'No, not exactly. Here's a copy of that.' He showed him another drawing. 'The circular design is the same but the symbols are in a different order.'

'But Isabel's one is the same as the one Joshua has?'

'The same. Yes.'

'So maybe he knows what it means, what it's for?'

'You can try asking him. There's a language problem.'

'Perhaps he can draw something. Joshua.' Stevie beckoned him over to the desk and spread out a sheet of paper, the design from Isabel's necklace, and some pencils. He pointed to the design, and then handed him a pencil. Joshua looked puzzled. Stevie pointed to the blank paper. Joshua pointed to the design and took his own pendant from his neck and pointed to it.

'Yes, but…' Stevie sighed. It seemed futile. He picked up the pencil and copied one of the symbols onto the blank sheet of paper, an upside down V. Joshua frowned. 'Jeez,' said Stevie. 'Forget it.' He and Eamon left Joshua at the desk and began looking at another pile of papers.

They were drawings, crude but effective, of a kind of mound, or hut, made out of pine branches. A dozen drawings, all of the same thing. There was writing beneath one: '3 anti, 4 clockwise, 3 anti, 4 clockwise fire at dawn.' 'Look carefully,' said Eamon, peering at the drawings. 'Inside, there, he's drawn a body.' They could make out a figure, arms and legs outstretched, within the wild squiggles of branches. 'I know what this is. It's a description of the cremation. What he did on the morning of the child being burnt. The people in the gulag saw him, going round this way and then that, then bowing to the ground, going back the other way, and then he set fire to it all, at dawn, which on the first of November was about nine in the morning. They both stared at the drawings. They were a crazed mass of hatchings, tearing the paper in places. Eamon moved on his knees to another pile.

'Looks like word search,' said Stevie.

'What?'

'Word search, you know, the game where you have to find the words, in a grid.' There were pages and pages of letters and names all jumbled up.

'Is this the effect of taking speed?'

'It's never had that effect on me.' Stevie picked up a sheet. 'Here's you, *"Eamon Ansgar, monea an gras, grea monsgar."* He's doing numerology, then looking for anagrams and doing numerology. *"James Sigurson, Gurt Flieber, Trib Rugleef."* He had a lot of time on his hands.' He put the papers down.

'What did you say?'

'He had a lot...'

'No the name. You said Trib Rugleef.'

'Trib Rugleef. It's an anagram of Gurt Flieber.'

'Gurt Flieber. He's the guy Edgar was agent for, the man who paid for Tarvin Lodge to be rebuilt!'

'So?'

'Trib Rugleef. I know him. He's living in the village!'

'Trib Rugleef is not a real name. It's an anagram...'

'I know! It's too much of a coincidence. Trib Rugleef! He doesn't exist. He says he's an author but I googled him. Nothing. Not a single hit.'

'You've lost me,' said Stevie.

'The little shit! No wonder he was so curious! Trib Rugleef. He's Gurt Flieber! He's here, right here, in the village! He keeps coming round, poking his nose in, trying to be my friend! He's running the whole thing!'

'Hold on a minute. He calls himself Trib Rugleef, but he's Gurt Flieber?'

'Keep up Stevie. He's living in the village, hiding in plain sight. He told me he was writing a novel!'

'Where in the village?'

'In a caravan, McKechan's croft.'

'We can go there. You think that's where Rona is?'

'He can't be that sure of himself. He couldn't be! He was here yesterday! And when he saw Joshua, you should have seen his face! Like he'd seen a ghost. Hold on, I've got a number for him, somewhere. Edgar gave it to me.'

On cigarette eighteen the sun was obliterated by a bank of cloud above Loch Houn and the clattering of heavy rain on the window of the porta-cabin. Pyotr sucked in smoke.

'Big storm coming in. My boat is going nowhere in this. You can forget it.' He stared hard at the diminutive figure before him. Gurt Flieber was the bane of his life. Arrogant little Yank shit.

'Are you sure about that? What's your plan B?'

'What plan B?'

'I don't know if you've noticed, Pyotr, but they're draining the dam. Another day and it'll be empty.'

'And? So?'

'Doesn't that worry you a tiny tad? Considering?'

'Considering what? What are they going to find? Three thousand tons of concrete, that's what.'

'You sure about that?' Flieber waved smoke from his face. 'You were sure you knew how to build a dam, Pyotr. Turns out you got that wrong.' Pyotr blew more smoke at Flieber. The dry, acrid air was just how he liked it, as if the room was on fire.

'You know what the trouble is with the dam? You know why this all started?'

'No. Entertain me,' said Flieber.

'Handrails! Fucking health and safety guy measures the handrails, and they're ten centimetres too low. Eighty centimetres, instead of ninety. So then they start looking at other things. The fixing of the handrails, into the walkway. Something is loose, some bolt. The guy wants to test the concrete. Then it all goes to shit.'

'Something wrong with your concrete? How come? It's not rocket science.'

'You think you know about concrete? Let me tell you, it is rocket science. There are a lot of factors: moisture content, porosity of ballast, cement type, temperature, mixing time. Not an easy thing to get it right when you're making big pours, in a hurry, with fucking amateurs! With assholes who know nothing, breathing down your neck! And when you have additives, additives that have no business to do with concrete! Fuck you, Flieber!'

'Sheesh, calm down old man, you're gonna pop an artery. The question is, when they drain it, are they going to find anything? Honestly.'

'The truth? I don't have a clue. They will find what they will find, and there is nothing you can do about it.' He put out number eighteen and started on nineteen, early.

'You're lucky you've got me on your side, Pyotr. Someone with an ounce of brains. I've got an idea to stop them, even if only for a while.'

'What?'

'Eamon Ansgar. He's the owner. He can stop them. At least, his lawyers can.' His phone buzzed. He looked at the number on the screen, frowned and answered.

'Flieber.'

'Gurt Flieber? Trib Rugleef?'

'Eamon. I was just talking about you. I'm guessing you got the number from Edgar. How did you guess the name?'

'Where is she?'

'Who? What? What are you talking about? Tell you what, why don't I come and see you? We can crack open the beers. And for God's sake this time do you think you could stretch to a little heating in that pile of yours?'

As soon as Flieber had left the room, Pyotr dialled a number.

'Lev. Get ready to go, and send the dinghy in as soon as it's dark.'

'Bad weather coming in boss,' said the voice on the phone. 'It is not a good time to go anywhere.' Pyotr put the phone down without replying.

CHAPTER EIGHTEEN

Eamon and Stevie were in the study when the phone rang.

'I'm coming up the drive now,' said Flieber. 'I just wanted to make sure you understand a few things before I arrive, in case you're feeling heroic, or macho, or whatever. You listening?' Eamon did not reply. 'I've got a proposal for you, a perfectly reasonable proposal. I want to talk. If you do anything to me, the little princess is going to get hurt. Understand?' They heard his car on the gravel, then the doorbell and Kirsty's voice as she let him in.

'What do you want to do?' said Stevie.

'Nothing. We can't do anything. Eamon led the way down to the hall. 'No tea thank-you Kirsty.'

'You sure about that?' said Flieber. 'Come on, less of the hostility. Have a cup of tea. Coffee for me please, Kirsty.' Kirsty looked for Eamon's nod. 'Awesome.' Flieber sat on a couch and gestured for his host to sit.

'And who do we have here? The local pot dealer. Cool man! Whassup! Have a seat. I've been itching to get hooked up, but you know, pressure of work. Plus, I need my brain.'

'Where is she?' said Eamon.

'All you need to know is that she's fine, for now. She's in safe hands.'

'You need to know that if you hurt her I'll kill you.'

'Yeah, yeah, yeah. Tough guy. Nobody has to get hurt, nobody has to get killed.'

'What about Joel Kennedy? And the child?'

'Joel killed himself. Cut his own wrists. Did you wonder why?'

'Who gave him the blades to do it?'

'That's kind of beside the point, isn't it? Why did he do it? That's the point.'

'Why?'

'Because he did kill the kid. Because he was dumb. He got it wrong and took too much blood. OK. I should have been monitoring more closely, I accept that, but in the end it was Joel, not doing his job right.'

'His job?'

'Joel was a nurse. Almost qualified. He was supposed to know what he was doing, but marijuana,' he looked pointedly at Stevie, 'isn't the best performance enhancer. There's a strong argument for saying whoever sold Joel the pot bears responsibility for the death of the kid. Joel got a lot of things wrong; times, dates, amounts. I'm surprised he only killed one. And the worst thing for him is that he had a soft spot for the kid, and the mother. Always a bad idea. Unprofessional. And then that fucking cremation ceremony! Jesus, talk about melodrama! He sent the whole thing up in flames, deliberately I guess. Anyhow, he was full of remorse, guilt, conscience. He was never going to recover from that. He chose the best course.'

'Why?' said Eamon. 'Why was he taking blood?' The question echoed in the vast room as Flieber watched his face.

'It has qualities, valuable qualities,' he said.

'You're selling it?' said Eamon with disgust. Flieber snorted.

'Is that what you think this is all about? Money? You think I'm like Pyotr? A drug merchant? A businessman? You got it wrong. I'm a scientist. Please, have some respect! Pyotr's selling the remains of what was once cocaine, manufactured by child labour in the Colombian jungle and cut what, ten times? Before it gets stuffed up the noses of freaks like your man Stevie here, to get his dick hard and make his pot addled brain tick over a bit faster, so he can think he's famous for a couple of hours. Do you know how many people die at the hands of drug lords every year?' He stood up. 'Fuck that shit! I'm a scientist. I completed my first degree when I was twenty years old. I was half-way into my doctorate, at the best university in the world, a doctorate that would have shaken the world, when it was fucked! Fucked by a bunch of fucking drug dealers! Jesus. I should be a professor by now!'

'What did the drug dealers do?'

'They killed...' he began, but stopped himself. 'Uh uh. Anyway, I'm not here to apportion blame. It's all done now. Let's cut all the bullshit and get to the point. I want you to stop them draining the dam.'

'What?'

'You heard me, you can do it. Pick up the phone to your lawyer. Get him to call SSE. It's your dam. It's your money.'

'Why?'

'Because...they're going to discover problems. Big problems. Let's just say it wasn't built to specification. And when they finish draining it, it's going to attract a lot of attention. Inspectors of all sorts, publicity, maybe even the cops, and I don't want that. You don't want that. Stop them, and it buys us time. I need another two days without cops crawling all over the place. Two days and we'll be gone, all of us, me, Sigurson, the women and kids, and you can have Rona back! Two days!'

'Sigurson,' said Eamon. 'Who's Sigurson?'

'Sigurson is what the world revolves around at this particular moment. Sigurson is the be-all and end-all, the alpha and the omega. And there is only one of him. Sigurson, as far as you're concerned, is Jesus Christ himself!'

'Sigurson has Rona?'

'I didn't say that! But yes, he does. He has Rona, and he has a knife, among other things, and he has no aversion to using it. He has a history. So make the call!' Flieber picked up the phone from its table and threw it at Eamon. 'Put it on speaker.'

'How easy do you think this is?'

'It's easy. You want an independent survey carried out, a consultancy brought in. You're losing thousands. You're outraged! It doesn't need to work, it only needs to make them pause, turn off the taps.' Eamon dialled the number of Richard Blackwell. Richard, as usual, was ebullient, cheerful, intrigued, and doubtful as to the possibility of success. Eamon got up and paced from the couch to the fireplace as he spoke. Kirsty emerged from the shadows with a tray of coffee and biscuits. Flieber poured for himself.

'This is important Richard,' said Eamon. 'I want you to understand what I'm looking for here, very clearly. I need you to make the same sort of effort you made when we had the Reid problem, do you remember?'

'Yeees,' said Richard.

'Pull out all the stops, deal with this. I'm counting on your special talents; the ones you keep in reserve for emergencies.'

'You mean...'

'Got to go Richard. People here.' He put down the phone and turned to Flieber. 'Satisfied?'

'What is the Reid problem?'

'Property case we had a while ago. Basically someone trying to steal land from the estate. That was the last time I think Richard had his abilities put to the test. He's very well connected. He'll get it done.'

'He'd better,' said Flieber. He wrote on a piece of paper. 'And you're gonna call me when you hear back from him. In the meantime, *Adios*.' He left by the front door. Eamon and Stevie sat in silence. They both jumped when the phone rang.

'Eamon!' It was Richard Blackwell. 'A little clarification if you please.'

'I mean I want you to do absolutely nothing, but to make it look as if you're trying.'

'Why?'

'I can explain later. I want you to do something else, immediately. Call Edgar and tell him, as a friend, in confidence, that you think I've gone a little mad.'

'Uhu.'

'Tell him... that I've got it into my head that he's involved in dealing drugs, something to do with Loch Houn and the Latvians building the dam. Say that I'm raving mad and I'm about to go to the police. Tell him that I'm here, at Duncul. And you're on your way, and you need his help to stop me.'

'Most exciting Eamon, what's this all about?'

'All in good time, Richard. It's worth a baron of beef and the '29 port.'

'Done deal my boy! Done deal!' Eamon put down the phone.

'There's something under the dam.'

'Obviously,' said Stevie, munching on a biscuit. 'What's the Reid problem?'

'You're the Reid problem. The problem that Richard did nothing about.'

'And when Flieber finds out?'

'That's the point. He won't. It's something they've drowned. We need to look at the papers.' Stevie followed him upstairs to the study. Joshua was sitting in front of the fire, staring into the flames. 'Look at the dam stuff, that folder there.' He spread out one of Joel's maps on the floor. The stone circles on the hill and the one in the centre of the dam loch were marked. 'They drowned a stone circle, according to Joel.'

'So what?' said Stevie. 'Is that all they're trying to hide?'

'And he was really pissed off about it, by the looks of things.' Eamon traced his finger around the urgent circles that tore into the map. He strained to read the spidery writing on the margins. '"*Need Solstice*",' he says here. 'Solstice is the twenty-first of December. That's two days from now. Is that a coincidence? That's what Flieber wants, two days from now. Joel had the same day marked on the calendar in the hut.'

'These stone circles are all about marking the solstice, apparently. The sun aligns certain stones on the shortest and longest days.'

'He was pissed off because they covered over the circle. It says here, *"the end of ancient knowledge."*'

'So he was an archaeology freak, among other things. What does that tell us?'

'He was, and they weren't. There's a whole folder here of letters about this sort of thing. They weren't allowing the proper surveys and the council was objecting.' He thumbed through the papers. 'It looks like they just bulldozed their way through all the requirements.'

'So what?' said Stevie. 'I doubt they're particularly concerned about the council finding out they covered some standing stones.' Eamon put the papers down and moved to the window to look over the trees towards the village, the gulag and the camera on the light pole. His eye was caught by a mark on the window and he raised a finger to rub. It did not rub off. A permanent marker lay on the window sill. The mark was an upside down V. He noticed another. He felt a gentle touch on his shoulder and turned to see Joshua's serious face. Joshua pulled at his arm and gestured to an armchair a few paces behind him. The drawing of the Stone of Duncul lay on the seat of the chair, and Joshua lifted it, pushed Eamon into the chair, and placed the drawing on his lap. He pushed Eamon's head up against the back of the chair and pointed to the window. Eamon looked puzzled. Joshua pointed again, and went to the window and placed his finger on the mark. Then moved his finger to another mark, a V the right way up.

'What's he trying to say, Stevie?' Stevie came over. Joshua came back to the chair and put a finger on Eamon's eyelid, then moved it slowly over to the mark on the window. Eamon saw it then. The mark was superimposed on the top of Ben Dui that lay ten miles beyond the village, a snow covered peak against dark clouds. Joshua pointed to the V. It was super-imposed on a cleft between two hills. Eamon chuckled.

'He's deciphering a two-thousand-year-old mystery.' Joshua pointed to the V on the window and the V on the drawing.

'This is a peak, and this is a glen, or where two hills meet,' said Eamon. He pointed to the mark that consisted of three vertical lines. Joshua went to one of the piles of drawings on the floor and picked up one of Joel's sketches of a ring of standing stones. He handed it to Eamon. Eamon pointed to the single line on the drawing. Joshua pointed at the other mark on the window. It lined up with a large boulder on the hill beyond the village. Eamon pointed to one of the small circles on the drawing. Joshua looked around the room and crossed to the cabinet where the whisky and a bottle of water stood. He poured some water into his hand.

'It's a loch,' said Stevie. 'Loch, boulder, peak, glen, standing stones. It's a map. What's the Spanish for map?'

'*Mapa,*' said Eamon.

'*Si, mapa,*' said Joshua.

'A map of what?' said Eamon, 'and what's this?' He pointed to the big circle in the middle of the drawing. Joshua looked at him steadily, and looked around the room. His eyes fell on the painting above the fireplace of Eamon's great-grandfather, Duncan Ansgar, in full Highland dress. He pointed to it, and pointed to another painting on the other side of the room, of some ancient aunt in a ball gown. Eamon frowned. Joshua frowned.

'People? A house?' Joshua shrugged.

'It's a tomb,' said Stevie. 'He's pointing at dead people, ancestors.'

'How can you be sure?'

'Watch.' Stevie picked up the rifle, pointed it to his head, and mimed pulling the trigger and dying. Eamon pointed to Stevie and then the centre of the design. Joshua nodded slowly.

'Dead people?' said Eamon. '*Muerta, muerto?*'

'*Muerto.*' Joshua nodded.

'And what's this?' Eamon pointed to a circle containing a cross. Joshua pointed to the window and the grey sky above the hills.

'Sky?' said Eamon.

'Sun, dummy. That'll be the sun,' said Stevie. Eamon looked from Stevie to Joshua and the three remained motionless, as if the air between them had become solid for a moment. Then they heard footsteps and Edgar Dupuy burst through the door.

'Ah, Edgar, I've been expecting you,' said Eamon. Edgar looked wildly at Stevie and Joshua and at the papers littering the floor.

'Eamon I...'

'Don't bother, Edgar. Don't disturb my guests. You and I have private matters to discuss. Come.' He led the way to the tower door.

Edgar began jabbering nervously as soon as the door had closed behind them and Eamon said nothing as he led the way down through the darkness and bare light bulbs.

'You've got it all wrong, Eamon. It's nothing to do with me. I mean it is, but not the drugs. I didn't know anything about the drugs until very recently. Nothing, I swear. Then I found out, but by then it was too late. You can't go to the police, Eamon. You'll ruin us both. You can't. I can speak to *Enerpro*. I can make them go away. Eamon, where are we going?'

'Got something to show you old pal. Follow me.' He led him into the basement and switched on the light and picked up a torch. Edgar followed him through the piles of junk to the low door to the stone room. 'After you.' He held the door open for Edgar. He closed the door behind them and shone the torch onto the stone. 'Have you seen this before?'

'No. What has this got to do with anything?'

'Apparently a lot. I still don't know what. It's not really the point of us being here though.'

'What is the point?' said Edgar. Eamon shone the torch in his face, watching the frown and the tense, half-grin flicker.

'The point is no-one can hear you scream.' Edgar raised a hand to keep the light out of his eyes.

CHAPTER NINETEEN

Vanneck awoke to the sound of his wife retching. Beyond this he could hear a low moan that seemed to be passing through the boat, and from outside a whistling and sighing above the clatter of rain on the black windows. The boat rolled and tipped. He tasted vomit at the back of his throat and whisky on his lips, which were open against the carpet. The pain in his right eye was intense, as if a knife was twisting in the socket. He tried to say his wife's name but his swollen tongue pronounced 'uli'. He pushed himself upright. She was on the floor next to the bed, hunched over and heaving. She emitted an animal, visceral sound, so unlike her that he looked to see if there was someone else in the room. Lockers above the bed and the wardrobe had burst open and clothes and shoes littered the floor. He crawled to her and put his arm over her shoulder. She collapsed face down to the floor, shivering, frail as a bird. At the same moment the boat gave a tremendous shudder. He tried to pull her upright but she resisted. He pulled a duvet over her and made his way to the bridge.

The light over the foredeck had gone out and the windows stared into a blackness only broken by the constant coursing of water over the glass. Vanneck switched on the wipers and peered out. He could see nothing. He looked at the satnav screen. They had changed course and were north of the northernmost Hebrides, heading east towards the mainland. The boat shuddered and plunged forward, foam pounding the screens. There was nothing he could do. He opened a locker and drank from a bottle of water. Nothing to be done but hang on. They were on course. He descended the stairs.

Lily was lying on the filthy floor, her limbs tangled in her nightdress, only moving as the boat moved. As he put his arms beneath her to lift he noticed her fingers twitching. He put her back onto the bed and poured water into her mouth. She swallowed but in the same moment vomited across the bedclothes.

'Jesus,' said Vanneck. She vomited again, from an empty stomach. The medicine cabinet above her dressing table was open, and bottles and vials had rolled into the corners of the room where they moved against the walls as the boat moved. He scrabbled around on his knees searching for the nausea pills, but when he found the bottle and put them in her mouth she vomited again.

'You've got to try and keep these down,' he said, but she only looked at him with sunken eyes and uttered a little moan. He looked at his watch and cursed. He had been asleep on the floor for more than six hours and she had been vomiting all that time. She was dehydrated. He had to get fluid into her. He left the room and went aft towards the medical bay, and in the corridor he slipped on the wet floor and fell heavily. In a panic he looked for the source of the water, and found it spilling from beneath the door to the galley. He cursed as he opened the door and a stream flowed out, a foot deep over his shoes. Spray and howling wind filled the room. A window had worn loose. No. He remembered he had left it open himself, when he had been cooking the other night, and he cursed as he slammed it shut. The pain behind his eye was getting worse, as if someone was trying to take it out with a spoon. He felt vomit rising in his throat. In the medical bay he tore open drawers and lockers until he found what he was looking for; a pack of saline drip, a cannula and a line. He tore open a pack of paracetamol, swallowed three, and returned to the bedroom.

He had to find a vein, a vein in the arm. He had seen it done; he had had it done. 'Shit shit shit! Fuck Fuck Fuck! FUCK!' He fumbled with the needle as he ripped open the pack, and dropped it on the floor. It was no longer sterile. Shit. He took a deep breath, went back to the bridge and thumbed the satellite phone.

'Flieber?'

'Sigma, how ya doin'? Where are you?'

'She's not well, Flieber. She's been vomiting for hours. She's passed out now.'

'Who?'

'Lillian! My wife!'

'What's wrong with her?'

'Seasickness. Colitis. Celiac. Arthritis. Heart condition. Old fucking age!' Flieber was silent. 'I need to get fluid into her. She can't drink, so I've got a drip. Saline solution.' Silence from Flieber. 'I need to know how to do this. I've never done it before. Have you?'

'No.'

'What was your first degree in? Didn't you do pre-med?'

'Only the bio-chem courses. No practical stuff. Intravenous. It goes into a vein.'

'I know that!' The pain in his eye was like a bee sting and his stomach was lurching with each movement of the boat. 'I need the practical part; you need to get a doctor to the phone.' Again, silence. 'You hear me Flieber?'

'It's not that complicated. You need a cannula, put it into the vein. Hold up the bag above her head.'

'It is that complicated! I need help dammit! How much do you put in? What flow rate?'

'I can google that.'

'I don't need google! I need a doctor!' There was a long pause.

'I can't do that, Sam.'

'Flieber you little shit! She's sick! She could die! Another day of this, another hour and she could die!'

'Sam, calm down. You are a very intelligent guy. I am a very intelligent guy. I'm sure we can work out how to put a saline drip into an arm. I'll google some stuff and you insert the needle and call me back.' Vanneck vomited onto the floor and groaned.

'This is an order, Flieber! Get a doctor on the phone!' Flieber did not reply. 'Flieber?'

'Half an hour, I'll call you back.' He hung up. Vanneck threw down the handset and left the bridge.

In the bedroom he fumbled with her arm. It was translucent white. He could see the vein beneath the skin, like a blue worm. The boat shuddered and plunged and he sprayed the contents of his stomach onto the floor. The vein. The needle. Put it in! He jabbed and blood flowed from the cut but she did not flinch. Her sunken eyes were closed now. He jabbed again. How do you know when it's in? The irony struck him; here was the man who ran the most important medical research facility on the planet, and he didn't know how to put in a cannula. He went back to the bridge, pausing to vomit on the stairway.

He sat in the captain's chair for a long time, drinking from the water bottle and trying to calm himself. He could put out a call to the coastguard. Yes. That was it. A Mayday. On the phone. Not the phone; the phone would only call Flieber. The radio. There was a handset on the console. He picked it up and listened to the buzzing sound. There was a dial with some numbers next to the handset, and the numbers changed when he turned the dial. Were these the channels? He needed instructions. There were lockers behind the captain's chair. He pulled out a flare gun, fire extinguishers and life-jackets. A packet of Solpadine fell out and he tore it open and swallowed two. There were no books, no manuals, nothing about the radio.

'God,' he said. 'Fuck you God!' He went back down to the bedroom. Her breath and pulse were both like distant echoes, already like memories. 'Fuck you Jesus Christ. You shit, you cunt!' He jabbed again at the blue worm. How do you know it's in? Turn the tap and see if the blood flows. Blood oozed from around the needle but there was no flow to the plastic tube. 'You shit!' He took it out and put it in, again and again. She made no sign that she felt the pain. The boat lurched and he was sick again, this time on the bed. The pain in his head was incredible, like a flame now. 'Jesus you shit! You motherfucking cunt!' He stabbed again and again at the crook of his wife's elbow, deep into the flesh, feeling the tip of the needle bump against bone. He tore open a bag of fluid and poured it into her mouth and over her face. She did not move. He threw the empty bag across the room and followed it to the dressing table, ripped off the mirror, and threw it to shatter on the opposite wall. 'Fuck you!' he shouted. 'Kill her then! Kill her! You kill her and see if I fucking care! You kill her! If she dies, it's you! You cunt!' He ran from the bedroom through the salon and opened the door to the balcony against the wind and rain. An alarm went off and a light began flashing. He screamed a long drawn out howl at the black sky that was finished by a cascade of sea that threw him to the deck against the railings. He picked himself up in a frenzy of strength and screamed again at the sky, holding tight against the rail as the wind, rain and waves tore at him. 'Fuck you!'

Back inside, he used a towel to bandage the wound in her arm. Then he pulled off the vomit-soaked cover and lay next to her, feeling the faint breath on his cheek. The pain in his eye was going, moving away from the eye and out into the room. The painkillers were killing it. He closed his eyes and held her and the boat shifted, slid, shook and churned the black waves, moving inexorably towards Loch Houn.

Rona's eyes were open when she heard the bolt rattle on the door of the container, but she closed them before he came in. She lay without moving beneath the blanket and felt the draught of damp air on her face, and heard the hissing of his clothes as he walked towards her. He paused. She could smell deodorant and it struck her as incongruous. You were a criminal, kidnapping women and children; you were a murderer perhaps, and you cared that you might smell? She squeezed the handle of the blade in her pocket as she listened to his breathing, then she smelt something else. Spice? Curry? She opened her eyes to see his face close to hers. He was holding a tray carrying pots of instant noodles, and without speaking he put one down. He crossed to where the women were sitting by the mattress. Rona swung her legs down from the bench and as her feet touched the floor she felt a pulse of anger go through her, like electricity. In one fluid movement she stood and followed him, and as he crouched she took the knife out of her pocket and raised it, watching the blue of a vein in the patch of neck between jacket and hat. But she could not stop the cry that emerged from her throat as she swung, and he turned and raised an arm. Her blade sliced into the back of his hand and blood streamed. She watched in shock as the dark red splashed onto the white floor. He stared at the hand and the flow of blood, and his mouth opened wide, then his eyes met hers and he screamed a strangled, nasal scream and tried to stop the blood with his other hand. Rona dropped the knife and ran.

Running from the brightness of the container into the dark she stumbled and stopped. She found herself in a strange, half-lit space; a vast, dome-like room, the ceiling supported in the centre by a thick concrete pillar. There were piles of storage boxes on the rough, stone floor; piles of cement bags, building equipment, a motorbike and a quad, and before her, bizarrely, a couch, a wardrobe, a coffee table and a landline phone, lit by a standard lamp. And there were arched entrances to tunnels in the sloping walls. She ran to one of them and into pitch black.

She put out a hand to the damp stone and felt her way, trying to slow her breathing. The roar of the blonde man echoed in the tunnel behind her. 'Rona!' She moved forward. The tunnel descended, then rose, and the wall she followed with her hand gave way to an empty space. She inched forward on hands and knees, found another wall, stood up, and followed the surface. The noises seemed to come from very far away; a faint clang, the sound of the container door shutting. 'Rona!', but the voice was hardly discernible. She found another opening, narrow and low, and crept into it. It was a crack in the rock that became a cave, the surface irregular and split, untouched by tool or hand. She crept into the earth and lay still, feeling the world spin around her.

'Grigor! Grigor!' The voice was coming from somewhere above him, above the earth, somewhere in the light, and he began to raise a hand. It took an enormous effort, as if his hand was attached to a dumbbell; forty, fifty kilograms. 'Grigor!' He was in a metal box, locked beneath the floor of the forest and the dark dripping pines. 'Grigor!' He opened his eyes and felt the saliva-soaked blanket over his face. Someone pulled it away and he looked into the face of Pyotr.

'Uncle!' He sat up, naked, on the edge of the bunk and placed his arms around Pyotr's waist, sobbing and groaning. 'Uncle, they tried to kill me!'

'Who tried to kill you?'

'I don't know, someone.'

'You're sick Grigor. You swam out to the boat, you got hypothermia.'

'I had to be clean. The bed and breakfast, it was dirty.'

'You've been sick. Shh now.' Pyotr handed him a bundle of clothes and Grigor got dressed and followed his uncle up onto the deck of the *Eloise*.

It was night. Lev and the other men from the camp were moving methodically, stowing boxes, loading bags of cement from the launch into the hold, making things ready to sail. Grigor sat on a hatch, nodding in greeting to the others, glad for some human contact. At first he felt agitated and weak. But the loch was calm, like the night he had swam through it, and the sky above the lights of the boat sparkled with stars. He began to feel better, as if the cool air and vastness of the sky were leaching out the poisons of the metal room and the fluorescent light. Pyotr, wearing a long black coat, stood on the bridge directing the stowing of boxes of papers and the pieces of equipment coming off the tender. A cardboard box thumped down on the deck in front of Grigor; he opened the flaps and saw reams of paper, files, and a pistol in a holster. Grigor stood up unsteadily and approached Pyotr.

'Uncle, what was in the box?'

'What box?'

'The box in the woods. The box I had to dig up with Sigurson.'

'What are you talking about?'

'I'm talking about the box, the metal box buried in the forest. Was it guns?'

'Grigor, maybe you should go below. Go get something to eat.' He took his nephew's arm and ushered him towards a doorway. 'We're busy here now. You take it easy.'

'There was no box?'

'No. I don't know what you are talking about.'

'Then why was I digging a hole in the forest?'

'I don't know.'

'Sigurson. Where is Sigurson?'

'Sigurson is left behind. I am finished with Sigurson,' said Pyotr, permitting himself a faint smile.

Eamon was in the kitchen and washing his hands in the sink when Stevie came in.

'So?'

'So what?' Eamon did not look up. He rubbed his stinging knuckles.

'So what did Edgar say?'

'He said she'll be under the camp. There's a sort of chamber. A tomb.'

'The tomb on the map? On the stone?'

'When they first started on Tarvin Lodge they got into trouble straight away, because of the archaeology and the ecological studies. They went charging in with diggers and bulldozers and they got into big trouble. They were threatened with fines and so on, and then Edgar had to negotiate some sort of settlement, and access for the archaeologists. But they had already found this tomb, this cavern. They had knocked in the roof with a digger, and Edgar panicked. Their solution was to build the camp right on top of it. The camp was supposed to be right up at the dam, but they put it there, on the road from the loch, to conceal the tomb, or whatever it is. They concreted over the roof and they use it as a store. That's where she'll be. He says there's a secret entrance from the camp but he doesn't know exactly where it is.'

'I said she'd be in the camp,' said Stevie. 'You wouldn't have had to waterboard him if you'd just listened to me.'

'I didn't waterboard him.'

'Whatever.'

'I just…'

'I don't need to know,' said Stevie. Eamon dried his hands. 'So you're just going to leave him in there?'

'For the time being. I don't trust him. If I let him out he could call Flieber or this guy Sigurson. I can't trust him further than I could spit. He'll be fine.'

'And now?'

'Now we go.'

Eamon sent Kirsty to get Mike Mack who was working in the gardens.

'It's important, Mike. You need to tell the Kennedys and tell your brother, tell the whole village. Whatever comes out, whatever the police say, Joel didn't kill the child. It wasn't a murder; it was a cremation. The child was already dead.'

When they were alone again he led Stevie to the gun room on the ground floor. Eamon had not used a gun in years. He took a shotgun from the rack and pulled open drawers and cupboards until they found a box of cartridges.

Samuel Vanneck dreamt that he was awake, lying on the bed and looking up at the ceiling. Lillian was in the ceiling, in the plastic or carbon-fibre or whatever it was. She was wearing her nightdress, and she was caught, as if the ceiling had been built around her. She could not move. He knew it was a dream and was aware of some other, awful knowledge; a memory of some undefined fact, a crime he had turned his back on, and he awoke to discover his wife's cold body in his arms and the storm abated, the boat moving easily on a light swell under a bright sky. For a long time he lay still, looking at her face, inches from his own. Her mouth was open but her eyes closed, and death had had a tightening effect on the skin, smoothing the wrinkles. The old, strange woman had departed with death, leaving behind the body of a woman two decades younger. But the lips had lost all trace of the blood within, and he knew that if he opened the eyelids the eyes would be dull. A cold hand was resting on his chest, and his own arm lay beneath her head and shoulder and was in pain. He moved it, and as she fell back on the pillow a sigh escaped her mouth. 'Ach,' he said, 'Lily,' which was both a scold and a word of comfort, and he felt a tear move to the lip of his eye, like a word in a strange language. Then he stood up and tidied the room. He pulled the vomit stained sheets from the bed, threw the bottles of pills and lotions that littered the floor into the sheets, and threw the bundle into the sea. He undressed and redressed her waxy limbs in a clean nightgown, and remade the bed. He laid her head on a clean pillow slip, and her arms by her side beneath a clean duvet. Then he went onto the bridge and called Flieber.

'We should be there by tomorrow.'

'How's Lillian?' said Flieber.

'What do you care?' Vanneck waited for Flieber to explain why he had not called back, but he didn't.

'I don't have a boat to meet you,' said Flieber. 'You're going to have to take *Rage III* down Loch Houn on your own; take it off autopilot. Are you OK with that?'

'Sure.'

'The loch is sheltered. Even if the weather is bad it's pretty calm. We'll wait until dark. I'll be on the end of the pier in a vehicle. You'll see the lights. I don't know about coming in to the pier. It depends on the tides, so you'll have to anchor and use the launch, 'cos there's no boat here now.'

'I'll work it out. How many are coming?'

'Three women, two children, Sigurson, me, but one of the women is in pretty bad shape. We might have to leave her behind.'

'What's wrong with her?'

'Tried to kill herself; cut her wrists.'

'Christ Flieber. You bring her, OK? For once do as your told. You get her on board. You got that?'

'I'll do my best,' said Flieber. Vanneck, staring out at the calm sea beneath a blue sky squeezed his eyes shut to clear them of tears.

'You got a plan?' said Stevie.

'We wait until dark. Then go out of the tower door, into the woods, cross by the Ash Bridge and walk over the hill.'

'And then?'

'As you say, we go into the camp, bang bang if we have to, find the tomb.'

'Sounds straightforward.'

'What choice do we have?'

They laid out the guns in the study along with heavy-duty torches, a crow bar and a ten-pound hammer, cable ties ('for tying folk up,' said Stevie), a first aid kit, chocolate bars and cans of coke. Eamon and Stevie dressed in the best camouflage they could find; tweed jackets and plus fours. Joshua looked at the guns with a mixture of trepidation and longing.

'What about him?' said Stevie, checking the action of the rifle, loading a shell and unloading it.

'I doubt there's much chance of getting him to stay behind,' said Eamon, 'better give him some clothes.'

They were packing up the bags when Kirsty came in, closely followed by the two detectives, Boyd and Maclean, and two uniformed officers.

Maclean surveyed the scene, the piles of notes and drawings, the guns propped against a chair and the boxes of ammunition, the backpacks and walking boots. 'Mr Ansgar,' he said. 'I was hoping for a little talk, but it looks like you're planning an expedition. A bit of shooting is it?' Eamon could not think of a reply. Joshua calmly carried on dressing, ignoring the police. Maclean took out a folded paper. 'The last time I was here we asked if we could look around.'

'I remember.'

'And you were reluctant to let us look around and asked if it was necessary, and I said if it was necessary, I would obtain a warrant.' He placed the piece of paper on a table. 'It is necessary.' He picked up a large drawing of the Stone of Duncul. 'William,' he said. 'You take Peter and Jane downstairs, start at the bottom and work your way up. Do you have a cellar, Mr Ansgar?'

'Yes,' said Eamon, picturing Edgar, bruised and bloodied, cowering on a blanket in the stone room.

'Do we need keys?' Eamon took the keys out of the desk drawer and handed them over.

'Start in the cellar, William,' said Maclean. He began walking around the room, picking up pieces of paper and looking at them. 'This is Joel Kennedys work isn't it? I recognise the handwriting. What is all this about Eamon?'

'I'm trying to work that out myself.'

'Where did you get all this?' Eamon did not reply. 'Why are the remains of your car at the top of the road to Loch Houn? What is your relationship with Clarice Wright? We have her in custody. She is not talking, yet, but we found your number on her phone. The best thing to do is tell us the truth, Eamon.' He sat down in an armchair. For a full minute the four men remained silent, Maclean's eyes moving from Joshua, to Stevie, to Eamon; then his phone buzzed in his pocket and he answered it, and his eyes widened in shock. 'They've found someone in the cellar...' he said. But as he spoke Eamon, Stevie and Joshua ran towards the corner of the room.

CHAPTER TWENTY

Eamon pushed the book and the bookshelf swung open and they slipped into the gloom of the tower stair. He pulled the door behind them and locked it, and they ran down the stairs to the sound of thumps and kicks. They twisted through the darkness, down to the tower door and out across the lawn into the trees. The voice of one of the uniformed officers barked after them, 'Stop right there!' He had come out of the front door and was rounding the corner of the castle. The three men ran and soon heard the sound of the Ash ahead. They reached the bank of the swollen river and stopped. Behind them, from the trees, they heard the policeman's voice repeat the command.

'Shit,' said Stevie.

'Jump,' said Eamon. 'Together, stay together, come on!' They jumped into the swirling brown water. It was ice cold and thunderous, and the current whipped them away from the bank into the centre of the river in a few seconds. They were ten yards apart with Eamon ahead. He shouted out that they should swim towards the opposite bank, then he turned his head and swam.

He saw the Ash Bridge fly above his head, and the trees signalling at the sky shifting above him. Freezing water invaded his mouth and nostrils. If he was to the south of the centre as he rounded the bend, he knew, he would be swung out by the current into the flooded field at the bottom of Burnum farm. Otherwise, if the river carried him on, there was a long straight stretch where it was flowing fast and relentless towards Loch Oich; it would be miles until they could get out. But at Burnum he felt the ground beneath his feet, and pulled himself from branch to branch out of the stream. He looked back to see Stevie coughing and spluttering, and then the head of Joshua, bobbing with each steady stroke, flying past, further out, near the centre of the current. But the head stopped downstream, where a fence descended into the flood, and Joshua pulled himself out along the wire. The three met in the field and Eamon led them at a jog up the track to the farmhouse. He looked behind them for flashing blue lights. They could drive as far as the Ash Bridge, he reasoned, but after that there was no access to the river bank by car, not for several miles downstream. If the police were determined to look for them, they would call out a helicopter, but it would be an hour at least before it arrived from Inverness.

Rona's quad was parked at the open back door. The three trooped into the kitchen and undressed, draping soaked tweeds, socks and shirts over the stove and on the pulley above. Stevie found a tumble dryer and they began feeding in the clothes. Eamon searched upstairs in the unfamiliar house, and stripped quilts and blankets from the beds. Then the three sat around the stove. Joshua made tea. They kept the lights off and spoke in whispers, listening for the sound of tyres on the track that led through the fields to the road.

'If they come here we're fucked,' said Stevie. Eamon went upstairs to a bedroom that overlooked the track to keep watch. It was her room. He sat on the edge of the single bed. There was a guitar in the corner, watercolours of ponies on the walls, a poster of a Native American with a line about money not being edible, and a poster of Bob Marley. The remnants of girlhood. There was an untidy pile of her clothes on a chair, a bra hanging on the back. He looked at the books on the shelf above a small desk; Jane Austen, Dostoevsky, Henry James; not exactly light reading, and he could not resist a smile. He could smell her scent. He put his hand on the pillow, and let himself desire her. He felt her presence filling him and her absence revealing a void. 'I'm coming to get you,' he said. Then he moved the chair covered in her clothes from his line of sight, and stared out of the window at the track and fields beneath the low sky.

It was dark before the clothes were dry. They found a backpack and a torch. They searched the house for a weapon but found only a locked gun safe. They were considering how to open this, when Eamon held up his hand for silence and they heard a helicopter in the distance.

'They'll have infra-red,' said Stevie.

'They don't know where to look,' said Eamon. 'Once we're on the hill, in the dark, we're out of sight. I say we go now.'

'What about this?' Joshua stood poised with a mash hammer above the gun safe.

'Leave it,' said Eamon, 'I know where there's guns.'

They moved fast and silent through the band of oak at the bottom of the hill, and then up the path towards the full moon chased by the clouds.

Rona pushed herself into the rocks, willing that they swallow her, wishing that she could ossify herself. His voice was closer, but still far off. But if he knew these tunnels, these caves, whatever they were, he would find her eventually. She wondered why she had thrown the blade to the ground, and felt ashamed as well as horrified. She had drawn blood. In spite of all he had done, he had not done that. She had drawn first blood. She had led the way through a door through which he could now enter. And she had seen, in his wide blue eyes as he looked from his hand to her face, that the next blood would be hers. But she also thought with satisfaction of the scar she had made, across the back of his right hand; it was a vicious mark that he would always bear.

Whether an hour passed or several she could not tell. Time stood still; time stretched to encompass an eternity beyond the age of the rocks that surrounded her. The voice in the distance grew quiet, and was replaced by her heart and the ringing of blood in her ears. She was surprised by the flicker of the torch, and a muffled thumping and scratching; the hiss of his clothing against the rock, and his heavy breathing. The torch shone directly into her eyes from his forehead, and his breath flared out beneath it. She could not stop herself from crying out.

'Shh,' he said, gently. She felt his hand around her ankle and she drew the leg back and kicked but the hand did not let go. He was too strong, and he pulled. She kicked with the other leg and he grasped that ankle too. She screamed and he pulled. She tried to hold onto the rocks around her, but she felt skin shred from fingertips and nails crack. Her jacket slid up, exposing her waist to the cold stone. He pulled her out and she saw what she had felt her way through in the dark; a low round chamber with a ceiling made of great slabs of stone. He turned her over and she groaned as a knee pressed into her chest. 'Shh!' he said more urgently. 'Stop.' And she stopped moving as she saw the long blade glint in the torchlight and felt it, ice-cold, against her throat. 'Good,' he said, and she obeyed him, turning over and putting her hands behind her back and letting him tie them together again. 'You understand now, don't you?' he said in a soft voice. He made her stand and made her cry in pain as he pushed her hands up towards her shoulders, and pushed her from the chamber into the tunnel. 'Boys are stronger than girls.'

Eamon opened his eyes and looked across the room at the figure of Duncan Fraser in his oilskin trousers. He was making tea, and Joshua was sitting on the crate next to the stove, warming his hands. A dull light was filtering in through the rain-spattered glass. Stevie was still asleep, stretched out on the couch.

'Hello yourself,' said Duncan, warming the pot. Eamon pulled himself upright. A copy of the Stone of Duncul was propped on one of the armchairs. Scrawled beneath the drawing were the words, *'Understanding precedes Knowledge'*. 'I found one you missed,' said Duncan. Eamon picked up the drawing. He shook Stevie awake.

'We need to borrow your guns,' said Eamon, when they were seated around the stove, breakfasting on tea and porridge. Duncan was happy to hand out ammunition and guidance; 'This one,' he said, opening the bolt on a heavy looking rifle, 'has a bit of a bulge on the barrel, but she still shoots true, you just have to give her a bit of elevation. I have another two like it but worse. This one,' he broke a shotgun open, 'is fine with the buck-shot, but no good with the balls. They take on a life of their own. Is it deer or birds you'll be shooting?' Silence invaded the room, crowding around the hissing of the kettle and the sound of Joshua cleaning his porridge bowl.

'People,' said Eamon, inspecting the rifle.

'Uhu,' said Duncan, looking gravely at them both. 'Well if that is the case Duncul you'll maybe be wanting a grenade.' He rose and took it from the bottom of the gun case. Eamon felt the weight of it in his hand and asked if it worked. 'You won't know that until you try, but there was two others and one worked and the other did not,' said Duncan.

'We need to use that too.' Eamon pointed to the telescope in a leather case that hung on a nail.

In the now heavy rain the four of them climbed to the face of the hill above the forest, and Eamon used the telescope to look down the glen. The long, winding dam loch had been replaced by a long, winding band of mud and shingle, with a narrow stream shining down its centre. The dam was crawling with policemen in yellow jackets or white overalls, men in suits, police cars and vans. A helicopter perched on a piece of flat ground at one end. A long white tent lay over a section of the base of the dam. Eamon looked further along the glen to the camp. There were two police cars there, and men moving about. He handed the telescope to Stevie.

'That's a crime scene tent,' said Stevie, when he had adjusted the eyepiece. 'Same as the one they put up in Tarr Bow. They've got half the police in the Highlands down there; something pretty bad must have happened. And it looks like Pyotr's done a runner; the *Eloise* has gone.'

'But Sigurson is under the camp,' said Eamon, 'according to Edgar.' He took out the drawing of the Stone of Duncul. Raindrops wet the paper. 'According to this map.' He looked at Stevie's smile. 'What's so funny?' Stevie pointed to the writing beneath the drawing, '*Understanding precedes Knowledge.*'

'Joel,' he said. 'Joel is funny.'

'What does it mean?'

'It means what it says. It's not a map. That's why he could never work it out. That's why it drove him crazy. But at the same time he knew it

fitted with his ideas about knowledge and God and understanding, that
he used to talk about when he was stoned. Intuition, that's what that is.'

'I don't follow.'

'Think about it; you know where the tomb is, so it makes sense, but
no-one could ever find the tomb by using this drawing. It's all about your
perspective. You have to be in it, or on it, to see these marks; the hill
tops, the glens and the lochs, making sense. They only line up *from* the
tomb. It's not a map for people that don't know, it's a map for people who
already know.'

'What's the point of that?'

'I don't know what the practical point is, that's for archaeologists to
think about. But Joel's point was metaphysical, about life, the universe
and everything. You can't know anything that you don't already know.
Understanding precedes Knowledge, man!'

'All I want to know is whether it can help us to get into the tomb.'

'It might, but we won't know until we're right there.'

They took turns watching the dam. Vans arrived and set up floodlights
along the top and along the base. The helicopter took off and hovered
above, flew off and circled above the loch, then returned to the dam.
'They're pretty excited about whatever they've found,' said Stevie,
handing the telescope to Eamon. 'They've brought in a man in a funny
hat.' Eamon looked and saw a chief inspector or commissioner in
wellingtons walk across the mud at the base of the dam, into the white
tent. 'We're just getting wet here,' said Stevie. Eamon ignored him.

'We can't get anywhere near the camp with all those police around,'
he said. Stevie suggested going around, over the heather and boulder
field behind the camp, under cover of darkness. Eamon shook his head.
'They're up and down the road, every five minutes; they're going to
search the camp. If we get caught, we're wanted remember, and we've
got guns. They won't listen to us. If they find an entrance to the tomb,
and go blundering in, Rona and the women and children could all be
killed. We have to get rid of them.'

'How?' They sat in silence.

'What you need is a diversionary tactic,' said Duncan.

'Yes, but what? It has to be big,' said Eamon. Duncan pointed with a calloused finger to the hillside opposite. Eamon raised the telescope and looked at the five white tanks in their metal cages, sitting next to the road that led to the wind-turbine sites. 'What's that?'

'Petrol,' said Duncan, pronouncing it 'peteral'.

'Why is it there?'

'Poison,' said Duncan.

'What?'

'I've no doubt, Duncul, you'll have heard about the lampreys?'

'Yes.' Eamon half remembered something that Edgar had said.

'Apparently peteral is the thing to get rid of the lampreys.'

'So they can build the turbines?' Duncan gave a grave nod.

'Now a man with five tonnes of peteral and a grenade can surely make a diversion.'

'And if the grenade doesn't work?' In reply Duncan took out a lighter and lit his pipe.

The four retreated to the cabin to dry off and eat. They waited for the descent of darkness. Eamon took the shotgun and Stevie the rifle. Joshua refused the offer of another. 'He's wise,' said Duncan. 'This one is not particular about where the shells go. I'll keep her for myself.' Eamon handed him the grenade and wished him good luck. 'No,' said Duncan. 'You take the luck for yourself Duncul, I think you'll be needing it.' Eamon, Stevie and Joshua stepped out into the rain and set off down the path towards the dam. An hour later, as they crouched in the heather at the northern end, they saw the flash of the explosion and then, seconds after, heard the boom echo across the glen.

They looked up to see a fireball launch towards the sky and mushroom outwards, orange and yellow laced with black. On the dam, lights went on and engines started. They were close enough to hear the voices talking into radios and phones. But there was no panic or fuss. Two cars left the dam and drove up the road in the direction of the explosion, which had now become a fire on the hillside. Eamon cursed himself. Of course it was not enough. He should have seen that. He thought about what Stevie had suggested, working their way around from the south of the camp, but now that the explosion had gone off they had made that impossible. The police would be all over that hillside. He considered going down towards the loch, and coming back over the rough ground and hillocks. He was thinking about how long this would take when he heard the whiz of a bullet in the air to his right, then the crack and echo of a rifle from the hill opposite; whizz, crack, crack, whizz, crack, crack, in rapid succession. Duncan was firing on the dam, over the heads of the police, and the shells were landing a few yards from where the three sat in the heather.

'Shit,' said Stevie. Whizz, ping, whine as a bullet hit a rock next to them. Joshua lay face down on the ground.

'We should move,' said Eamon.

'Wait,' said Stevie. 'Look.' There was chaos on the dam, men running back and forth, diving for cover. A floodlight exploded, showering glass. The headlights of the two cars that had gone up towards the explosion were coming back, at full speed. The helicopter engine began to whine and the blades began to move, but the pilots jumped out and ran to a car. The rest of the floodlights went off as the generator died, then the firing stopped and the engines started and cars raced out along the top of the dam and down the road towards the loch. The two cars in the camp raced out. In five minutes the only sounds were the rain and the distant engines, as the line of tail lights twisted towards Loch Houn. 'Well, that worked,' said Stevie.

'How long until they come back though?'

'They won't come back in the dark. But in the morning they're going to bring helicopters and guns, lots of them, and they'll probably shoot us on sight.' When all the lights had reached the pier and turned and disappeared up the Glencul road, the three men moved at a run, weapons at the ready, along the dam top. When they were midway Eamon paused. Beneath them at the base of the dam the rain drummed on the roof of the white tent. An aluminium ladder had been lashed to the railings.

'We should look,' said Eamon. 'It might be important.' He led the way down and entered the tent with a torch. Duck-boards had been laid over the mud. Lights on tripods were aimed at the concrete face of the dam, but they were switched off. Eamon shone his torch. For a moment he thought it was a painting, a graffiti; the grotesque effort of some deranged street artist. There were arms, legs, hands, heads, and here and there a face, in low relief, pressing against the surface of the concrete; and here and there the surface of the concrete had erupted, revealing cavities containing white bone. It was a portrait of hell, or a macabre last judgement; the dead rising from the grave; the dead embracing each other in despair. They were in the concrete and coming out of the concrete, bodies; ten, twenty, thirty bodies; it was a grave. In Afghanistan he had seen this number of bodies together, laid out in the square of a village that he had called to be bombed. He had seen it before, there, then. But this was here, now, at Glenfashie, at home. He held up his hand to the wall and to the face of a child.

'God,' said Stevie from behind him. Joshua stared and stood still, as still as the figures in the wall, as if he too were impregnated with stone. 'What happened here?'

'I don't know,' said Eamon. 'They weren't just dealing drugs.' He moved the beam of his torch over the wall. They had been thrown in, he reasoned, while the concrete was being poured. Three years ago; he tried to think. They had been buried, disappeared; but they had decomposed and, being close to the surface, the rotting had burst through the concrete. No-one would have ever known if the dam had not been drained. But then a glimmering fragment of something caught in the torchlight, high up, above his head. He moved to it and reached up with his light. It was a fishing lure; a mep. And his mind leapt across a decade and a half, and he was fishing with Joel Kennedy in sunlight on the bank of the Ash, Joel with his child's rod and his lucky mep; the one he never lost; the battered brass plate and red ringed body, and the triple hook. The lure he would wade into the Ash for; the lure he would dive into Loch Cul to retrieve. He had left it here. He had said goodbye to all of his childhood here, one sunny day on this dam, when he had dived into hell. Glencul's dam; my dam, filled with this. *Everything leads to Duncul.*

'We should get on,' said Stevie, and somehow this broke something in Eamon, some resistance that he had reserved against horror. 'We should get on,' from this rain-drenched tent over this pile of bodies, on towards the next pile of bodies. A tomb awaited; the madman that had taken Rona, the women from the bothies, and the children. They climbed the ladder, up into the soaking rain and darkness.

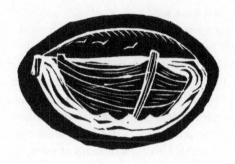

CHAPTER TWENTY-ONE

'You cut down smoking boss, I notice,' said Lev. They were drinking vodka on the bridge of the *Eloise* as she dipped and rolled through the night. The vodka was good; someone had brought it from Poland, and the two of them were drinking it neat. Pyotr was relaxed. For better or worse they were out of it all. They were going home. She would be waiting for him.

'I have no choice. I can't smoke three packs a day until we reach Riga, or I'll have to give up completely. We could be two weeks on this boat.'

'Why not put in at Lerwick?' said Lev. 'We could do with more of everything.'

'No, we will not put in. Even if we have to starve a little. We will go ashore where we know people, where we know the police. I will go down to forty a day, then thirty, twenty and ten by the time we reach Riga. I'm thinking of the health benefits. And you could lose a little weight.' He patted Lev's stomach. Lev refilled the glasses.

'You think they're going to find the bodies?' he said. Pyotr's face darkened.

'Yes. I do.'

'But it's concrete boss, solid as rock.'

'One or two is normally fine, but that was seventy-six bodies. He came up the loch with seventy-six bodies, that Spanish asshole.'

'What happened to him? He disappeared. Did you shoot him?'

'You know, I pointed a gun at his head, I cocked it. I was pulling the trigger, what stopped me I don't know. Perhaps I'm getting old. Perhaps I've seen too much blood. Perhaps seventy-seven bodies to deal with by morning would have pushed me too far. I told him and his friend to fuck off back to Spain, and if I ever saw or heard of them again I would do far worse than shoot them. Believe me, he got the message.' He drank back the vodka. 'When we get to Riga I'm retiring. I'm old. That little shit Flieber kept telling me how old I am. Well, he's right. They'll find the bodies and perhaps that's my fault. I should have thought. I panicked. "Get rid of them before morning," he kept saying. I could have dug a hole in the peat.'

'The concrete was the best. Every time you dug a hole in the peat, even to put in a fence post, someone from the government would come and complain about the little insects and the animals and the ancient houses of the Picts. You had no choice.'

'Yes. You're right. Fucking Picts! Fucking newts, fucking lampreys, fucking dragonflies! Fucking Flieber! I hope the little fucker gets caught!'

'He will talk, all about you,' said Lev.

'I don't care. They won't find me once I am back in Latvia. Take some advice, Lev. Don't spend your whole life chasing money. Don't be an idiot. Find a woman, settle down.' Pyotr drank and refilled the glasses. His hand was raised in a toast when the sound of shouts came from below them, then a shot and glass breaking. The door to the wheelhouse flew open and Grigor stood in the doorway, breathless, with blood on his face, holding a pistol.

'Uncle,' he said, his voice quivering. 'He made me dig a grave.'

'Who? What?' said Pyotr, almost smiling.

'Sigurson! He made me dig my own grave!'

'Grigor, why are you pointing that gun at me? Put it down.'

'Because we are going back! Stop the engines, turn around!'

'Don't be ridiculous my boy. What are you talking about?'

'You gave him the order! You told him to dig up the box, uncle! What was in the box? Tell me! What was in the box?'

'I don't know.'

'No, you don't! Because there was nothing in the box; no box, no guns, just a hole in the ground. A grave! For me! For Grigor Semyonovitch! To be buried in Scotland, in the forest! Why you want me dead?'

'Sigurson doesn't work for me. You were on loan. He asked for a favour.' A man was creeping up behind Grigor, on the other side of the wheelhouse door. Pyotr kept talking. 'He asked for help, for a bodyguard, you were the best we had. Then something happened, you hit someone, what did you do?'

'I pushed him in the river.'

'You pushed Eamon Ansgar in the river, and Sigurson said you should lay low for a while, and I agreed. He sent you to a bed and breakfast to stay out of the way.' The man pushed the door open gently, and lunged at Grigor from behind. The gun went off and Grigor pulled the man over his shoulder onto the floor, and brought a heel down on his nose. The man groaned and writhed, blood spilling from his mouth. Grigor steadied the pistol at Lev, then at Pyotr, but Pyotr had fallen forward onto the table, face into the ashtray. A hole the size of a fist pulsed blood from the back of his skull. Lev stood up and put out a hand to hold over the wound, but could not bring himself to touch the blood. He turned to Grigor with a look of disgust and took a step towards him, but Grigor brandished the pistol and gave a long formless yell. Lev stopped and raised his hands.

'Grigor,' he said.

'Take the wheel,' said Grigor, 'I am captain now.'

The gates to the camp were open. There were no lights and only the beam of Eamon's torch shone through the rain. They moved from cabin to cabin, Stevie holding the rifle at the ready, suspecting in each dancing shadow the figure of Sigurson or another; suspecting in every trickle and splash the sound of a footstep, the cocking of a gun or drawing of a blade. Exhausted, they took shelter in the cabin that had been the camp office, with the desk before the window, the map of the dam on the wall, and the smell of stale cigarette smoke. Eamon searched the filing cabinet, hoping for a map of the camp, but the files had been cleared. He sank to the floor with the others.

'What did Edgar say exactly?' said Stevie. Eamon tried to remember, and remembered Edgar's bruised face and bleeding lip in torchlight, and the Stone of Duncul looming above his head. The problem with torture, 'enhanced interrogation,' was not that it did not work; it worked too well. The subject would tell you anything you wanted to hear if you hurt him enough. Edgar had said 'under the camp'. Had he said there was an entrance in the camp? Eamon was soaked and exhausted and his mind flickering with images; the burning boy, Edgar's face, Rona hurt and tied up, and the faces emerging from the wall of the dam. They had until morning to get Rona and the others out. The police would be back; an army of them, and they would be armed this time. He searched in his pocket for the drawing of the stone.

'Maybe this can be used now, now we're here,' he said to Stevie. Stevie sniffed.

'Not in the dark it can't.'

'They'll be back as soon as it's light. Edgar will talk. He'll tell them where we've gone.' Joshua and Stevie watched him pace. He brandished the drawing. 'Doesn't this tell us anything?'

'We have to wait until morning,' said Stevie, stretching out on the floor and making a pillow of his backpack. Eamon remained sitting, shotgun at the ready. Joshua sat on the floor with his knees pulled up under his chin. Eamon thought of Duncan and wondered what his plan was now. Perhaps he would sit tight in his cabin, and bluff it out when the police arrived. After all they were not looking for an eccentric old fencer; they were after gangsters of some sort, gangsters that Eamon Ansgar was involved with, somehow.

'You don't know who I am, do you?' said the blonde man. He had tied her to the pillar in the centre of the room, arms behind her back, body and mouth wrapped with duct tape. The fleece that had pulled up as she was dragged from the cave remained pulled up, exposing her. He held his long curved blade against her belly. 'The name's Sigurson,' he said.

'James Sigurson.' He smiled, pushing his face close to hers and taking a deep breath through his nose. 'I've never done this before. I couldn't. But since you cut me,' he held up his bandaged hand, 'I can do it now. I'm scared it won't be good. I'm worried once it's over, it'll be like sex; the empty feeling afterwards, you know? Maybe you don't. I'm in the zone now, I don't want it to end. I like the feeling now, right now.' He breathed deeply and closed his eyes. 'I want to open you up, here.' He pushed the blade against her, and she tensed and drew back. 'But I'm not supposed to. Apparently there's a plan.' He put the knife in a sheaf in a pocket, and sat down on a crate a few feet away, leaning forward to rest his elbows on his knees.

'I could have done it before. I was supposed to do it before, but it's like virginity. You want the first time to be special. The first kill has to be pure, you know, kosher. It has to be done right; no fight, no mess. It has to be artful. That's why I didn't do it. I let them go. Do you believe in destiny? I do.'

'I was a driver, for Pyotr. Driving drugs down to Glasgow from here. I was living in a flat in Maryhill. My name wasn't James Sigurson. It was James Peery. A woman turned up one day. Flieber was with her, but it was the woman I noticed. She was amazing. She was wearing a sort of mini-skirt business suit. I was wearing boxer shorts, and I was stoned and hungover. The flat was a mess, pot noodles and beer cans. It stank. I thought I was dreaming. She smelt like summer, in the middle of winter, in Glasgow. She had long straight brown hair, all shiny. She did all the talking. Flieber just sat there nodding, holding a briefcase. You've got to imagine it. This woman comes in, and she starts talking about my ancestors and my mum and dad. My dad was a bastard, and my mum's a mental case in a home. Anyway, I didn't really take it all in, I just watched her, thinking, "this is a dream". Then she asks for my blood. You've got to understand I'd been smoking skunk. Surreal doesn't even begin to describe it. Flieber opens the briefcase and they've got a syringe and all that stuff. I went along with it. That was the beginning of my destiny. It turned out I had a major destiny. In a way, I'm everyone's destiny. I'm definitely your destiny. We've got to wait a while now. You should maybe get some sleep.' He turned his back on her and went over to where the armchair, the wardrobe and the standard lamp stood under the low, sloping ceiling. He sat, and picked up a games console from the coffee table and began to play.

The three in the camp office were awoken by a helicopter overhead. The noise passed up the glen towards the forest, and was replaced by the softer thudding of the rain. Eamon, holding the drawing, went to the window. The view was of the boulder strewn hillocks leading down to the loch, and the loch winding away to the west, meeting the sky between the shoulders of two hills. Something about the light from the sky struck him as odd, and he looked at his watch. 'It's two o'clock.' he said.

'Shit,' said Stevie. Eamon led Joshua outside.

'Look, *mapa, mapa.*' He stabbed the paper with a finger and pointed at the surrounding hills. 'Isabel Mtetu,' he said, jabbing the circle in the centre. Seeing a ladder lying against the shed he propped it against the cabin, and the two of them climbed onto the roof. Eamon looked around at the already darkening landscape, and at the drawing. Upside down V's were mountaintops. V's the juncture of two hills. Vertical lines something else. Circles were water. He tried to see the features through the gloom, but he could only half remember the code. Joshua took the paper from him and looked to the south, to the east, to the north. Eamon watched the road towards the pier and listened for the helicopter. It was there, barely audible, to the east, up Glenfashie. Joshua sat down, cross- legged, looking at the drawing and at the hills. Eamon paced and smoked. He tried to speak, but Joshua held up a hand to stop him. Eamon climbed down the ladder and went into the office.

'We need to search the camp again,' he said to Stevie. Together they went through every cabin and under every cabin, jumping on floors, pulling up carpets, looking behind every tub and barrel lying around the fence. They looked under the pickups and diggers in the workshop, even moving a pile of cement bags to look beneath, all the time listening for the sound of a car or the helicopter, which ranged back and forth in the distance. Eamon felt panic rising as they took cover in the office.

'Edgar could have been lying,' said Stevie. 'Maybe there's nothing here.'

'You're right. And there's no boat on the loch. They could be gone, already, by road or by boat. This is a goose chase.'

'If they are still here, somewhere in the glen, and they're going out by boat, they're going to go down to the pier. They have to. So we wait for them there.' Eamon nodded at the logic.

'Where though? It's all open, there's no cover.'

'The old boathouse; we can watch from there.' Outside there was a fierce glimmer from the low sun breaking the clouds.

'We'll do that,' said Eamon. He went out and climbed the ladder to the roof to call Joshua, but the African was not there. The drawing lay on the roof weighted down by a stone, soaking up rainwater. The rain had stopped, and beams of sunlight coming from low in the west lit their faces with an orange light.

Eamon called for Joshua, and Stevie climbed the ladder. 'He's gone. He was here a minute ago. Joshua!'

'Look,' said Stevie. Behind, to the east, the helicopter blades were scything the air towards them. 'Look,' he pointed towards the sun. Eamon shielded his eyes. The disc of the sun had become visible as it descended from orange to a fiery pink, and lay now between the mountains at the far end of Loch Houn, like a ball nestling in a cupped hand, and the light flowing from it along the surface of the loch was like a stream of fire. 'Look,' said Stevie. Eamon looked. Beyond the perimeter fence the boulders were casting jet-black shadows on the heather stretching towards them, and the figure of a man moved, jet-black, his shadow a hundred yards long. He was moving towards the light, towards two huge boulders, and his figure was narrowed by the light, so that he glowed and disappeared and reappeared as he walked.

'Where's he going?' said Eamon.

'He's following the Stone of Duncul,' said Stevie, crouching to look at the drawing. Eamon stretched out his hand.

'No, don't touch, It's aligned.' The symbol for the sun, the symbol for a glen, the symbol for water and two parallel vertical lines pointed in the direction of Joshua.

'He's found it,' said Stevie, but as he spoke the sun disappeared beneath the sea, and the figure of Joshua vanished into the twilight.

'Get your gun,' said Eamon.

Rona moaned softly and raised her head. James Sigurson was listening to the handset of the phone that lay on the coffee table. He nodded, smiled, nodded and put it down. He looked up directly at her, and she closed her eyes and bowed her head. In a moment she felt his presence close by; the smell of the deodorant, the sound of the clothes. She felt his breath on her face. It smelt of instant noodles. 'Do you know what he says?' said Sigurson. 'You won't believe what he says. He says that there are police everywhere, helicopters, cars. Don't worry, it's not because of your boyfriend. It's because they've found the bodies. He says, "If I can't get to you, you have to kill them. If I can't get to you, *take their blood*." Can you believe that? That's cynical, you know? Besides, I'm not a doctor, and I've only got wee syringes.' He left her and opened the container doors.

He led out the two children and ordered the two women to support the one with the bandaged arms. He brought a chair for her. He was strangely solicitous, speaking gently and helping her to sit down, then wrapping a blanket around her shoulders. The other two women huddled with their children on the floor. Their faces were downcast and blank, surrendered to whatever strange whim the smiling blonde man would think of next. Rona strained to watch them, but then ahead of her a shadow appeared in one of the tunnel mouths leading from the cavern. It was almost shapeless in the dark, but it moved out into the light, and became a dark skinned, tall, thin man who walked soundlessly, without hurry towards the women and children. When they saw him there was a collective indrawing of breath, and the woman with the bandaged arms, who until that point had been slumped listlessly on the chair, stood up.

I told you to trust me. You are mine. You are my child. When you are cast down, it is I who casts you. When you are raised, it is I who raises you. When you were taken from the forest of your birth I was with you. When you sailed into the endless ocean I was with you. When they took the Singa from you, and cast you onto the streets to eat rubbish like a dog, I was with you. When you swam into the English sea to drown I was with you. I raised you into the light, and I will cast you down, but I am always with you. I am with you now, as you breathe in her breath, as her heart beats next to yours and her arms encircle you. You are mine, now, and until the end of time.

Eamon and Stevie crouched at the entrance to the cavern, watching as Joshua embraced Isabel Mtetu. Eamon could see her face, and in his memory there would always be a smile there, a faint smile that wiped the age from her brow and frightened eyes. For a few seconds the cavern was wrapped in the silence of their embrace, as if the world had stopped. Then Sigurson appeared in the bright doorway of the container to their left, and moved smoothly with the long knife in his hand. He put one hand on Isabel's shoulder, and with the other slid the blade into Joshua's back, up to the hilt. Joshua made no sound and did not loosen his embrace. Isabel, eyes closed, kept her faint smile as the knife slid out followed by a trickle of blood, and slid in again, three times, while Joshua did not move. Stevie raised the rifle and cocked it, but at the click of the bolt Sigurson saw the two men, and in a second he was standing behind the pillar, holding the blood soaked knife to Rona's throat. Joshua collapsed to his knees, still held by Isabel.

'Drop it!' shouted Sigurson. 'Come out, with your hands up.' Eamon and Stevie obeyed. 'Over there, move!' He gestured to the container. 'Move! You want to see her bleed?' He pressed the blade against the flesh of her belly. Eamon and Stevie moved. 'To the end,' said Sigurson. 'Sit on the bench!' He turned to the women. 'Close it!' he said, and when neither of them moved he bellowed; 'Door!' The women scrambled to the doors of the container and slammed them shut.

He slit the tape holding her to the pillar and Rona fell forwards to the floor. He stood over her with the knife, his breath coming fast and saliva wetting his lips. Then the phone on the table rang, and he kept his eyes on her as he answered. Rona felt no urge to fight nor run. She understood them now, the tamed women. She felt mute inside. She rested her head on the floor, and looked up at the face of the woman with the bandaged arms, as the bandages soaked up the blood of the man dying next to her, a few feet away. The woman was pushing a blanket against the wound in his back. She was moving frantically, a half-dead woman brought alive by panic, fear and love. The blood pooled in the hollows of the stone floor. Sigurson affirmed something into the phone; 'Right. We're moving now.'

He came back and pulled Rona to her feet.

'Pity,' he said into her ear. 'You were supposed to be first. But it was good. Much better than I thought. Now I want more, so you're going to walk.' He turned to the women and shouted at them to move towards the tunnel Eamon and Stevie had come out of. The two stood with their children and obeyed, but the bandaged one, kneeling in a pool of her lover's blood, screamed at him;

'No!' The sound echoed around the chamber, taking Sigurson by surprise. But he recovered himself.

'That solves that problem,' he said, and pushed Rona to her knees again. He walked to the woman and raised the knife, but as he moved it towards her and she uttered a final, resolute 'no!', he turned his hand so that the handle struck the side of her head, and she fell, stunned, over the body of Joshua. He hit her head again and again. When he turned to face Rona there were flecks of blood across his smiling face. 'Stand up.' Rona felt herself pulled, pushed, kicked and cursed into darkness. Ahead of her the two women draped in blankets held their children's hands, and stumbled along the passage. Soon she felt soft ground beneath her and rain and wind on her face.

A steady wind was blowing from Loch Houn, and tall clouds were tearing across the full moon. Sigurson pointed his torch and urged the women on, down, towards the track where a lightless van was parked.

Inside the container Eamon ran and kicked at the door. 'It's held with a steel bolt,' said Stevie. 'An inch thick.'

'The bench,' said Eamon, 'we can use it as a ram.' He knelt on the floor and used a knife to undo the screws that held it. Stevie helped him pull it from the wall. They swung it back, and charged at the door. It shuddered as they hit. They swung again and again, but nothing moved. They sat down panting and sweating. In a frenzy Eamon turned and began hacking at the steel of the door with his knife. Stevie put his hand over the knife.

'Stop,' he said.

'We've got to try!'

'No. Stop. Listen.' There was the sound of steel moving on steel.

'The bolt.' said Eamon.

'Shh.' There was silence, then a creak, silence, then a creak. 'Don't push.' They took their weight off the door. There was a snapping sound as the bolt was released. The rubber seal opened, and the cold air from the cavern blew in their faces. Eamon pushed the door and it opened an inch but stopped. He pushed, and together he and Stevie heaved. They heard the movement of something heavy across the rough floor and saw blood. It was Joshua. Eamon knelt and strapped a makeshift bandage across the wound in his back. Stevie crossed to the body of Isabel and felt for a pulse. 'She's alive,' he said.

'Where did they go?' said Eamon. Joshua pointed to the tunnel mouth. 'We can't take him,' he said to Stevie. Stevie shook his head, but pointed to a box against the wall.

'Flares,' he said. 'If we light them at the entrance, that will bring the police here.' He picked up the box and the rifle and ran. Eamon followed.

The van bore the logo of the electricity company, and the man with long curly hair who opened the back doors wore a fleece with the same logo, but his accent was out of place.

'The yacht's here,' said Flieber. 'Where's Isabel?'

'She didn't make it,' said Sigurson, pushing Rona onto the floor of the van.

'We don't need this one.'

'We need her until we're out at sea.' They got into the front seats. 'I'm impressed. How did you get past the cops?'

'The cops are all up past Tarvin Lodge, shooting at somebody.' Rona lay on the metal floor that smelt of oil and mud with her face against the thigh of one of the women. One of the boys lay on her other side, and she could feel his breath against her cheek. The van bumped and rolled. The women and children were not tied, but they lay with their hands by their sides, staring up at the roof of the van, as if this was normal.

Eamon and Stevie ran as fast as the twisting passage would allow, to the entrance between the two boulders. As they came out the clouds moved, and the moon lit up the loch twisting towards the shadows of the mountains. Stevie pointed out the sleek shape of a boat far out in the deep channel. The van was on the road to the pier, moving without lights. Stevie lit three flares and tossed them into the heather. 'Run,' said Eamon.

The tyres hummed on the tarmac. When the van stopped Rona could hear the lapping of the waves against the pier and she could smell the sea. The front doors slammed, but the men did not come to get the women. For what seemed like a long time they lay in darkness, broken only by flashes of moonlight as the clouds moved. Then she heard the sound of an engine on the water, and the doors were pulled open. She was pulled by the feet out of the van and made to stand, and then pushed and cursed at in torchlight, then moonlight as bright as the torches, towards the end of the pier and down the steps to the waiting launch. A thin man with a white beard stood at the wheel. Rona was struck by the look on his face; alert and careful but at the same time frozen in shock.

Eamon and Stevie reached the stretch of tarmac before the pier just as the boat pulled away with its the wake glowing in a burst of moonlight. Stevie knelt to steady his aim. With his chest heaving from the run, Eamon put his hand on the barrel. 'It's a cannon. You don't know what you're going to hit. Come on, there's a boat.' They ran down onto the shore.

The rusty chain succumbed to the butt of the rifle, and they wrenched open the doors. The 'Mirabelle' lay upturned. They threw off the ropes, nets and sheets of corrugated steel, and pulled her over. She was a heavy, plank-built dinghy, ancient but still sound. They threw in two sets of oars and heaved her out of the mess of the boat house towards the loch, down the rough, broken slipway, over rubble and seaweed, until she floated.

'Row!' shouted Eamon, ready to throw up, his lungs burning. He looked behind him across the water but the moon had been covered, and neither the yacht nor the launch showed a light. He heaved at the oars, getting into time with Stevie, and the boat began to speed up. He pulled and felt Stevie catch the rhythm, and felt the strength of his brother in his own arms as they slid over the dark sea. Again he looked over his shoulder, and this time saw a light, but it was further to the west than where the yacht had been, seawards, and moving fast. Eamon pulled, and looked over his shoulder, pulled and looked. It was another boat, a big one; he could hear the thudding of its engine. A powerful searchlight was shining from the roof of the bridge. Then the moon came out from behind the cloud and both men forgot to row.

CHAPTER TWENTY-TWO

The sleek, vicious shape of the yacht crouched at anchor ahead of them, and the launch had tied alongside at the foot of a chrome ladder. The women and children, Rona with her hands bound, an old man, and Flieber, and forward along the deck, Sigurson, stood transfixed by the searchlight from the *Eloise*. Sigurson shielded his eyes as the light bore down on him, and with it, a torrent of noise; the drumbeat of engines, the rushing of the bow wave, a wail from one of the women, and a scream drawn out to the limits of breath, 'Sigursaaaaaan!' The yacht seemed to cower into the water as the *Eloise* hit and did not recoil. There was a hideous sound that grated to Eamon's marrow; tearing, snapping, screeching; the sound of taught metal in agony and carbon-fibre exploding into splinters and dust. The hull of the *Eloise* obscured the figures standing aft on the yacht, and only Sigurson was visible, thrown backwards to the deck. But the yacht's anchor held, she spun on its axis and the *Eloise* turned with her, while the sea churned around them and a wave was launched from the impact to roll out across the loch. And as the ships turned in each other's embrace, a figure jumped from the wheelhouse of the *Eloise* and vaulted over the handrails to the lower deck. It was a man in a bomber jacket with a shaved head who moved with the control of a trained athlete; a man that Eamon had last seen looking down upon him from the Ash bridge, wearing a sardonic grin. He paused at the guard rail at the prow of the *Eloise* that now hung above the stricken yacht, and looked down on the figure of Sigurson struggling to his feet. Then in one movement that was flowing and poised, like a gymnast launching from the bar, he swung himself with right foot forwards into the air. He caught Sigurson square in the chest, and landed on his feet. Sigurson drew his blade.

'Row!' shouted Eamon.

Samson Vanneck felt the *Rage III* tip and hunker into the water. He had become used to storms, but even the worst waves did not do this. This time the boat did not attempt to right itself. There was a moan from the Singa woman next to him, but it was not a cry for help nor even an expression of fear. He reached out and held his hand against her face. But the boat gave another lurch, casting him away from her across what had become a deck of windows, and he picked himself up and made his way to the bedroom where his wife's body lay.

In the last two days the skin had taken on a waxy sheen. He had spent those days in a frenzy of learning how to stop and steer the boat, operate the engines and lower the anchor and launch. He had mastered all this, but had not been able to work out how to turn down the internal heating, and his wife's room had been kept warm. The stench of decaying flesh had filled the room, mingling with the scents from the bottles and tubs that had been scattered and broken by the last storm. He had knelt by the bed, and held her hand, willing warmth to return. He had gazed at her appalling face, the lips drawing thinner and tighter over the teeth as each hour passed. He had groaned in agony, feeling as if some other being had entered somewhere between his liver and lungs and was crying to get out. He had cried and dribbled on to the sheets. He had cursed God and angels and saints that emerged from long buried memories. He had paced and spat and broken everything to hand, torn skin from his knuckles on the walls of the cabin, and split his forehead on the unbreakable windows.

And he had moved about the yacht, calm and methodical, learning how to control her. But he had been unable to stay away from the dim, fetid room and the corpse. In that room lay all that had softened him and taken him out of himself, away from ambition and vanity. And when he was not in the room she hovered before him; her dead face on the windscreen before the rippling sea; her hand in his when he turned a cold steel crank or pushed the throttle; her voice in his head with each bump and rattle of the boat, each stroke of the wind, each slap of a wave and every fall of his foot on the deck. He had kept returning to the room, and in the end had began talking to her.

'Sorry,' he had said to the corpse, stroking its hair and squeezing its bony hand. 'Sorry,' breathing in its filthy stench. 'Sorry,' he had said, and had gagged and had to leave for air.

The boat tipped and she slid from the bed. He knelt and held her, and then lay with his back against the wall and his arms around her thighs. They felt stiff, hard and slick. Her head was thrown back, so that he could not see her face, only the sharp bone of her upturned chin, the skull beneath the skin. He felt the water creep, ice cold, around his legs, but his face remained impassive as he looked up to the circling moon. Feet thumped over the windows that were now the roof. He heard urgent cries, and the groaning and cracking of the boat, as if it were splitting open, giving birth, he thought. And the thing that had made its home between his liver and lungs, the small beast that had nestled there, relented and left, and he felt empty as he welcomed the water of the loch, willing it to fill him up, and to take him down.

The engine of the *Eloise* churned the water white at her stern, forcing her amidships of the *Rage III*, but the anchor chain of the yacht that led from the bow held fast; the two boats pirouetted, as the yacht, lying on her side and broken open, sank lower. Eamon and Stevie rowed while Sigurson and Grigor fought cross the upturned windows and railings of the forward half, Sigurson with his knife and Grigor with his hands and feet. Sigurson slashed and Grigor kicked; Sigurson stabbed and Grigor punched. Grigor hit, once, twice to the face and kicked to the stomach. Sigurson reeled, staggered and advanced. The yacht lurched and rocked.

Both men fell. Both men recovered. The boats turned and they were out of sight to Eamon and Stevie. The brothers pulled through the waves that slapped at the bows of the *Mirabelle*. The yacht and *Eloise* turned, and Grigor and Sigurson reappeared. They were closer now, and Eamon could see that Grigor was wounded. There was a deep gash on his cheek, and blood was streaming and dripping over his arms and legs. But he was grinning, and attacking; his arms and legs flailing; turning kicks, right-left combinations, straight kicks to the chest, straight kicks to the kneecaps of Sigurson, but missing, kicking and punching air, while Sigurson stepped back and forward, and on each forward movement flicking his blade and slicing at arms and legs. Openings appeared in the satin of the bomber jacket. Grigor jumped and kicked for the face, still grinning, and landed nimbly, throwing punches, and Sigurson leaned into the flailing arms, almost slowly, letting them glance off the side of his head as he slipped the knife into Grigor's jacket. The jerking limbs of Grigor folded in on themselves, all at once, like the legs of a touched spider. Sigurson withdrew the knife and found himself standing above a crouching man with a shaven head, bowed forward and exposing the white neck to the glare of the *Eloise's* searchlight, and the moon spinning on the axis of the world. He clasped the handle of the knife with two bloody hands and brought it down into the base of Grigor's skull, raised it up and brought it down. The boats turned and Eamon could see no more. The rear of the yacht swung towards the rowing boat. Stevie grasped a handrail, pulling them against the hull.

Eamon ran forwards and up along the tilted windows. Ahead the figures of the two women and two children lay face down, clinging to the side of the boat. 'Get them to the dinghy,' said Eamon. Stevie put down the rifle and took one of the women by the arm and a child by the hand. Eamon clambered ahead, around the hole where the *Eloise* had hit. Lights had appeared on the pier and a powerful beam was swinging from side to side across the loch. Another beam shone from the helicopter overhead. Sigurson was limping ahead of him, towards the bow of the yacht. In one hand he held the long bloody knife, and with the other he held Rona by her hair. She tripped and stumbled as he pulled her.

'Sigurson!' shouted Eamon. 'You've got nowhere to go. Leave her.'

Sigurson turned and grinned, standing on the bowsprit. There was blood on his mouth and between his teeth. He held Eamon's gaze and tipped Rona's head back, so that her throat was uppermost and brightened by the moonlight. Then in a swift movement he raised the blade up, high above his shoulder.

The explosion came from behind Eamon, to his left, and he felt it like a blow to the side of his head. The knife fell clattering to the deck. Sigurson staggered, and looked down at the gaping hole in his groin. He fell backwards, still holding her hair and taking her with him into the loch. Eamon turned to see the woman wearing a woollen hat and a ball gown standing with the smoking rifle. Then he ran to the bowsprit. Sigurson was lying on his back, kept afloat by his padded jacket and trousers. Eamon dove.

He swam down, blind in the black water and deaf with the ringing in his ears. His lungs forced him up to the moonlight again and he saw the figure of Stevie leaning out from the bowsprit, his mouth open in a shout. He swam down, deeper and deeper, feeling the pressure grip around his head and limbs. His lungs screamed for air, but he would not return to the surface, to light, death and blood; to the suffocating air, to cruelty, avarice, revenge, the gyrating boat and the moon twisting above, the lights approaching from the shore, the police with their guns, the questions, the dark castle, the shuffling servants; to a life gone irrevocably wrong. He would not return; he swam down, pulling through water that grew more solid with each stroke, searching for the bottom, for weeds and rocks he could clasp himself to, and wait for his lungs to open and his mind to stop. He pulled himself towards death and towards nothingness, and felt the first weeds, tender and silky, welcoming his hand. He grasped, pulled and reached with his other and felt her face, the little nose and full lips clasped tight against the pressure of her breath. How often by the firelight, or while they stood and smoked on the roof, or as he was saying goodbye beneath the light at the front door, he had wanted to reach out and touch her face. He kicked and pulled towards the surface, towards the moon and twisting metal, towards the deafening sound of the helicopter, towards bodies and cries and the beams of searchlights, towards police and questions and his brother. On the surface she breathed and he cut the tie from her wrists as he held to the side of the yacht, and she turned to him, clasped his face, and kissed, crying and gasping for air even as she kissed, and placing a hand behind her head, he leant forward and kissed in return. Then they pushed out, away from the maelstrom and into the calm of the dark loch, as the *Rage III* turned and groaned and sank lower.

Epilogue

Two days after Christmas, Detective John Maclean sat back in an armchair while Kirsty put the tea tray between him and Eamon. Rona stood by the bay window, looking out over the beech trees which glowed in the evening light. They were silent until Kirsty had left the room.

'No Detective Boyd this time?' said Eamon.

'This is personal, not official,' said Maclean. 'I've been looking at your service record Eamon. Apparently you were some sort of policeman in Afghanistan.'

'Not really,' said Eamon. 'I interviewed suspects. The evidence gathering wasn't my job.'

'But you have experience of getting the truth out of people?'

'Yes.'

'Then you'll understand how important instinct is. Knowing when something doesn't make sense.'

'Yes.'

'There are some gaps in your statement. Holes. I hesitate to use the word "lies".'

'I don't know everything. I don't understand everything. Perhaps when you raise the wreck of the yacht, you'll discover the whole truth.'

'You say that you spent a whole day and a night in the heather, waiting above the dam, and coincidentally someone blew up five tonnes of petrol on the hillside and began shooting at the dam, giving you the chance to enter the camp.'

Eamon said nothing. 'You entered the camp in order to rescue Miss McColl, without weapons of any kind. And on the yacht, as it was sinking, a shot was fired, from a large calibre rifle, hitting James Sigurson in the groin and causing his death, and you did not see who fired.' Eamon looked at his tea.

'Sometimes you only need to find the motive, and it all makes sense,' he said. 'I presume you have spoken to the Singa women, through an interpreter.'

'Yes.'

'And?'

'As you said, they were drugged and raped by Sigurson. Repeatedly. The children are his. You're saying one of the women shot Sigurson? How? With what?'

'I didn't say that,' said Eamon. 'Perhaps one of the men on the *Eloise*? You said you found the body of Pyotr Tiranasov. Killed how?'

'A pistol. We have it, and it's not the same weapon that killed Sigurson.' Eamon shrugged. 'The weapon that killed Sigurson was the same calibre that shot out the lights on the dam the night before, a .303 rifle. Second World War type of thing. It was fired from the hill above the explosion. Look. I have heard your story. I believe your story. We have Gurt Flieber. We've got the contents of his caravan, his laboratory, where he was processing the blood, his hard-drive with the recordings from the camera in the gulag. We've got him talking. We have Clarice Wright. We know how the child in the gulag died. We found a quarter of a tonne of cocaine on the *Eloise*. We know how the bodies came to be in the dam. We know how Pyotr Tiranasov died. We know how Grigor Semyonovitch died. We know how Sigurson died, though we don't know who killed him. But you know what my boss wants, above all else? He wants to know who fired at the police.'

'And when you went up the glen in the helicopter, you found what?'

'No-one. We found no-one except a seventy-year-old man, living on his own in a shed.'

'With weapons?'

'One small bore shotgun for which he has a licence.'

'Motive?'

'None that I can imagine.'

'So your conclusion?'

'My conclusion is that it was you. It all points to you. You had a motive. You used the same unregistered weapon to shoot Sigurson, and you threw it in the loch.'

'Very well,' said Eamon. 'It was me. What now?' A thin smile spread on Maclean's thin lips.

'Eamon, you have no intention of leaving Duncul, have you?'

'None.'

'Your family has been here for eight hundred years. Am I right?'

'Yes.'

'And I believe you are taking on an immigration case, six cases of illegal immigration, that you intend to fight to your dying breath.'

'My lawyers are at work on it as we speak.'

'So it is likely that we will meet again. And give Duncan my regards when you see him next.' Detective Maclean rose and made his way to the door.

'He knows,' said Rona, when he had gone. 'He knows everything now.'

'Yes,' said Eamon, 'but I think he also understands.' She crossed the room and stood before him, close enough to touch, and he took her in his arms.

'I should go,' she said. 'Mother is coming home tonight.'

'Well I should go to,' said Eamon. 'We'll welcome her home together.' He took her hand and they left by the tower door.